Enrollment Form

☐ **Yes!** I WANT TO BE A *PRIVILEGED WOMAN*.
Enclosed is one *PAGES & PRIVILEGES*™ Proof of
Purchase from any Harlequin or Silhouette book currently for
sale in stores (Proofs of Purchase are found on the back pages
of books) and the store cash register receipt. Please enroll me
in *PAGES & PRIVILEGES*™. Send my Welcome Kit and FREE
Gifts -- and activate my FREE benefits -- immediately.

More great gifts and benefits to come.

NAME (please print)

ADDRESS   APT. NO

CITY   STATE   ZIP/POSTAL CODE

PROOF OF PURCHASE ONLY

**NO CLUB!
NO COMMITMENT!**
*Just one purchase brings
you great Free Gifts and
Benefits!*

Please allow 6-8 weeks for delivery. Quantities are limited. We reserve the right to
substitute items. Enroll before October 31, 1995 and receive one full year of benefits.

Name of store where this book was purchased_____

Date of purchase_____

Type of store:

☐ Bookstore   ☐ Supermarket   ☐ Drugstore
☐ Dept. or discount store (e.g. K-Mart or Walmart)
☐ Other (specify)_____

Which Harlequin or Silhouette series do you usually read?

_____

Complete and mail with one Proof of Purchase and store receipt to:
U.S.: *PAGES & PRIVILEGES*™, P.O. Box 1960, Danbury, CT 06813-1960
Canada: *PAGES & PRIVILEGES*™, 49-6A The Donway West, P.O. 813,
North York, ON M3C 2E8

SIM-PP5B

▼ DETACH HERE AND MAIL TODAY! ▼

"You can't keep me here,"

Courtney said, her voice tight.

The look that flickered in J.D.'s eyes made her doubt the wisdom of arguing with him, but he said only, "We're in the middle of the Montana wilderness. There are no roads. I have no radio. It's spring, and it's muddy as hell out there. The nearest trail is a two-day hike on a good day. This isn't a good day."

"Tell me about it," Courtney muttered. "Look, just point the way and I'll get out of your hair."

He raked his hands through his shaggy mane. "Maybe it's the concussion."

"What?"

"You don't seem to understand English," he said tightly. "You're not going anywhere. Not today. Not tomorrow. And maybe not the day after. Not until *I* know more about what the hell is going on."

Dear Reader,

We've got six more exciting books for you this month, so I won't waste any time before telling you all about them. First off, we've got *Caitlin's Guardian Angel*. This book represents a real milestone; it's the *fiftieth* Silhouette title by one of your favorite authors: Marie Ferrarella. It's also our Heartbreaker title for the month, and hero Graham Redhawk certainly lives up to his billing. You'll find yourself rooting for him in his custody battle for the adopted son he adores—and in his love for Caitlin Cassidy, the one woman he's never forgotten.

By now you know that our Spellbound titles are always a little bit different, and Lee Karr's *A Twist in Time* is no exception. Join forces with the hero and heroine as they journey into the past to investigate a murder whose solution is the only way to guarantee their own future. Laura Parker begins a new miniseries, Rogues' Gallery, with *Tiger in the Rain*. Years ago, Michaela Bellegarde brought Guy Matherson the best luck of his life. Now he's forced to turn to her once again—but this time, danger is on his trail. Leann Harris returns with *Trouble in Texas*, the story of a woman doctor "stranded" in a small Texas town. Love with the local sheriff is definitely the cure for what ails her, but, as so often happens, the road to recovery is not an easy one. Historical author Jessica Douglass makes her contemporary debut with *Montana Rogue*, a story of kidnapping, rescue—and romance. Don't miss it! Finally, welcome new author Amelia Autin. In *Gideon's Bride* she tells the story of a mail-order marriage threatened by the bride's deep, dark secret.

So sit back and enjoy all six of this month's Intimate Moments titles, then come back next month, when we bring you six more compellingly romantic books by some of the best writers in the business.

Yours,

Leslie Wainger
Senior Editor and Editorial Coordinator

Please address questions and book requests to:
Silhouette Reader Service
U.S.: 3010 Walden Ave., P.O. Box 1325, Buffalo, NY 14269
Canadian: P.O. Box 609, Fort Erie, Ont. L2A 5X3

MONTANA
ROGUE

JESSICA
DOUGLASS

Published by Silhouette Books

America's Publisher of Contemporary Romance

SILHOUETTE BOOKS

ISBN 0-373-07665-7

MONTANA ROGUE

JESSICA DOUGLASS

is thrilled to be writing her first contemporary after many historical romances. She's always been fascinated by dark, brooding, vulnerable heroes and is delighted that her readers feel the same!

Jessica lives in Illinois with her husband, son and pets—including two cats and a dog.

To Barbara Schenck and Paula Jolley,
two friends to ride the river with.
(That's "cowboy" for pretty darned terrific.)
Thanks for being there. Thanks for staying.

Chapter 1

Darkness swirled all around her. Deadly. Dangerous. Courtney Hamilton struggled against the black void, knowing even in her befuddled state that her life depended on her becoming awake, aware. Alert.

But her confusion persisted. Where was she? What was happening? Why couldn't she wake up? Think clearly?

In the midst of the darkness was a cacophony of sound. An engine—thunderous, deafening. Voices—muffled, indistinct. And something else. Static. Short, staccato bursts of radio static.

What kind of hallucinatory nightmare was this?

Courtney shook her head in a vain attempt to clear it. She tried to open her eyes and failed.

Enough of this nonsense, she reasoned groggily. She was in her bed in her father's ultramodern log house retreat in Elk Park just outside of Butte, Montana, and she was having a bad dream. That was all. Heaven knew, considering her life of late, she was more than entitled to one.

She could put an end to this madness in an instant. All she had to do was toss back her blankets and pad over to her bedroom window. From there she could look out onto the stunning beauty of the pine-bristled ridge that formed the backdrop of the secluded twenty-acre property. Her father had had the house built ten years ago, when Courtney was only nineteen. She'd loved it instantly, and still considered it home, though she'd spent precious little time there over the years. In fact, this was her first trip back to Butte in four years. And that only with great reluctance, because of her father's heart attack three weeks ago.

So do it, her mind thrummed. *Get out of bed and walk to the window.*

I will, she vowed muzzily. *Just as soon as my head stops spinning.* But first she would find out what was making that racket.

Again she tried to open her eyes. Again she failed. Her heart fluttered nervously. This was certainly the oddest dream. . . .

Courtney raised a hand toward her face. And froze. Her hands were bound together at the wrists! Merciful God. What?—

In a single blinding instant it all came roaring back to her. The phone call. The urgent voice. The terrible words: *Your father's had a relapse. Hurry!* The dash to her car. The mad fumble with her keys, the lock.

And then . . .

And then . . .

Hands. Hands grabbing at her from behind. Hands slamming her against her car. Hands forcing a sickly, sweet-smelling cloth against her nose, her mouth.

She remembered voices—harsh, threatening—remembered her knees buckling...

Then she remembered nothing else.

Until now.

Courtney sat very still, forcing her throbbing head to clear. She couldn't see, but she could hear, she could feel. The noise, the sensation of flight. She was in a helicopter.

Bound. Blindfolded.

Kidnapped!

The realization sent a jolt of pure terror ripping through her. She started to struggle, her fingers tearing frantically, futilely, at the ropes that manacled her wrists.

"Hold still!" a hard voice snarled against her right ear.

Instinctively she tried to shrink away from the voice, but pressure at her shoulders and hips held her fast. A safety harness? Courtney settled for huddling lower in her seat.

Ahead of her she sensed yet another presence. The pilot?

"Who are you?" she demanded shakily. "What do you want?"

Something cold and hard pressed against her neck. "I want you to shut up," the voice beside her demanded.

Courtney shuddered.

A gun.

She fought back tears of panic. *Get hold of yourself,* she ordered. Panic was an option she couldn't afford. Four years of working in a Philadelphia battered women's shelter had taught her that much. Panic got people killed.

But her thoughts were still so muddled. She felt weak, exhausted. Whatever drug they'd used on her seemed to have sapped her strength, as well. She needed time to regain her senses. "Please," she began. "Don't do this. My father is ill. He—"

"Your father's holding his own," the pilot's voice cut in from the seat ahead of her.

"You don't understand," she insisted. "He's had a heart attack. And now a relapse."

"The relapse is a lie," the man said. "My friend in the back seat made the call to your father's office."

Courtney stilled, absorbing this new bit of information. "Thank you," she heard herself say. The pilot hadn't had to tell her about their ruse.

"You're a real piece of work, fly-boy," the man with the gun snarled. "Pretty little blondes get to you, do they?" The gunman chuckled. It was not a pleasant sound. "She is pretty, ain't she? Big green eyes, if I remember what's under that blindfold. And long legs...."

Courtney trembled, envisioning him licking his lips. She couldn't make out the pilot's terse reply, but it was obvious he said something the other one didn't like, because the gunman's response was both agitated and defensive. "What the boss don't know, won't hurt us," he snapped, running his hand suggestively along Courtney's arm. The bulky-knit sweater she wore did little to prevent her flesh from crawling.

Calm, she ordered herself. *Whatever happens, stay calm.*

"Besides, fly-boy," the gunman went on, "this ain't your call. You wasn't supposed to pilot this bird. If Al hadn't gotten sick..."

"Shut up!" the pilot snapped. "She's blindfolded, not deaf!"

But Courtney was already filing away the gunman's slip. A name. Al. It wasn't much. But it was something. If they could make one mistake, they could make others.

"Ol' fly-boy thinks he's pretty smart, don't he?" the gunman gritted against her ear. "But it's me who's going to be doing the talking once we get to the cabin. Fly-boy came in late on this one. He don't know the half of what the boss has in mind for you."

Courtney's heart thudded in her breast. Cabin? The very word conjured images of remoteness and isolation. Montana had more than its share of both.

If they were even still in Montana.

Fly-boy...don't know the half of what the boss has in mind for you. God above, what did that mean? Were they planning to kill her? Or worse?

Enough! The last thing she needed to do was to start imagining scenarios of what these bastards might do to her. She needed to concentrate, think. The police would want details.

She trembled. If she lived to see the police. "Whatever you're being paid," she said, hating the tremor in her voice, "my father will double it. Triple it. If you just take me home."

Neither man said a word. Courtney took it to mean they were at least listening. "Call my father's office," she urged. "Talk to his partner, Fletcher Winthrop. He'll get you any amount of money you want. No questions asked."

"Maybe we should think about it, fly-boy," the gunman said. "We're the ones takin' all the chances."

Instead of answering him, the pilot addressed her. "You're in enough trouble, princess," he said. "I'd think twice about putting ideas into my partner's head. You want my advice? Just sit back and enjoy the ride."

Courtney dug her fingernails into her palms. What arrogance! She'd like to tell him what he could do with his advice. But she forced herself to be silent.

"How much farther?" the gunman asked. "Them rocks and trees down there all look alike to me."

"Maybe half an hour," the pilot replied.

"Hear that, sweet thing?" the gunman said, sidling close again, so close that Courtney guessed he couldn't possibly be wearing his seat belt. "Half an hour, and you and me can get real cozy. Real cozy."

Courtney swallowed the bile that rose in her throat. *Calm,* she repeated inwardly. *Calm.* They were just trying to scare her. Her father's partner would pay whatever ransom these men eventually demanded. Then they would let her go. They had to let her go. Coming back to Butte had taken every ounce of courage she possessed. Surely the Fates couldn't be so cruel as to have brought her home to die. Especially when her sole purpose for returning had been to dare make one final effort to make peace with her father.

Oh, God, Daddy, she thought miserably, *it can't end like this. It can't.*

Four years ago Quentin Hamilton had all but crushed the life out of what spirit she'd had left, when her marriage to Roger Winthrop, Fletcher's son, had ended in divorce. Even knowing how much her father had doted on Roger, she never would have believed

Quentin would take Roger's side over his own daughter's. But he had. The cold, judgmental words he'd used against her that last, ugly day still had the power to cut deep. Courtney had fled Butte, fled her father and Roger, not knowing if she could ever pull together the shattered pieces of her life.

But somehow with the help of some of the loyal, supportive friends she'd made back East during her college days, she'd done just that. At least she'd thought so, until Fletcher Winthrop's call had come through to her office at Angels' Wings, the battered women's shelter for which she served as assistant director.

"You'd best hurry, Courtney," Fletcher had told her. "The doctors aren't sure he's going to make it."

Courtney had gripped the phone so hard, her knuckles went chalk white. Part of her was terrified for her father, but there was another terror, as well. Four years she had stayed away from Butte, stayed away from a mountain of brutal memories.

"I know what you're thinking," Fletcher said, his voice surprisingly gentle. "But you don't have to worry about Roger. I've got him running our corporate offices in Rio."

"I'm sorry, Fletch. This must be difficult for you, too." This was her first conversation in four years with a man she'd once considered closer to her than her own father.

"Your marriage to Roger didn't work out, Courtney," he said matter-of-factly, and she could almost picture him shrugging his bear-size shoulders. To her, Fletcher had always looked more like a defensive lineman than the cofounder of a multinational conglomerate. "My son was a jerk. You were right to divorce him. You know I don't harbor any ill will toward you."

"I appreciate that." Her voice cracked as she thought of her father's very different verdict on the collapse of her marriage. "More than you know."

"Quentin's been my partner for forty years. Please, Courtney, he needs you. You can make things right. I know it."

Courtney had known all along what her decision would be. "I'll take the next flight out."

And so she had come home. Come home despite the feeling of dread that had all but overwhelmed her as soon as the words were out of her mouth. Come home despite memories she still feared had the power to destroy her.

Her father needed her. That was the reality she focused on. Not on memories of her brief, but ill-fated marriage to Roger Winthrop.

The moment her plane had touched down in Butte, she'd rushed to the hospital, only to find that her father had lapsed into a deep coma. In the three weeks since, he had not regained consciousness.

The peace she had hoped for between them had had to wait.

And now...now...

Beneath her blindfold, tears threatened, spilled over.

"Awww," the voice mocked beside her, "the little lady is crying. She's scared."

"Leave her be," the pilot growled.

"You know," the gunman muttered in Courtney's ear, "I'm gettin' pretty damned tired of him tellin' me what to do. He ain't the boss of this here gig." As if to prove his point, he eased Courtney's skirt up her leg.

"Don't touch me, you pig!"

"Now, is that friendly?" Without warning he slid his hand beneath her sweater. When it closed around her breast, reason vanished.

Courtney screamed. Wild, unthinking, she fought against her bonds, striking out blindly with her manacled wrists. A lucky blow connected solidly with the side of her attacker's head. He cursed and fell forward, one of his flailing feet catching her in the side. In the next instant the helicopter lurched violently. A tearing, grinding noise sounded above the roar of the chopper's engine.

The pilot swore viciously. "The rudder control's gone! I have to try to set it down."

"Here?" the other man shrieked. "There's no clearing. Where the hell?—"

"Brace yourselves!"

The chopper whipped about like some maniacal, out-of-control amusement-park ride. Courtney's mind reeled, even as time itself seemed to slow down, compress. Beside her she could hear the gunman sobbing, grappling frantically with his seat belt. Ahead of her the pilot continued to swear softly.

She was going to die, she thought with a curious mix of wonder and detachment. The reconciliation with her father would never take place. Would he ever know that she had at least tried? Would he care?

Images of her life began to flood through her—a kaleidoscopic display that was somehow both instantaneous and meticulously detailed. Wistful scenes of a mother who died much too young, of a workaholic father who never made time for his lonely little girl. Interposed throughout came flashes of Roger, his benevolent features contorting into a monstrous caricature.

Courtney fumed, furious. She was not about to die thinking of Roger Winthrop!

And just that quickly Roger was gone, vanished, though in the next heartbeat she could almost have wished him back. A single memory rose up to haunt her then, sear her to her very soul. For the first time in years she allowed herself to think of another man— to see *his* face, hear *his* voice.

Dark, tousled hair, to-die-for blue eyes and a smile to melt a Montana glacier. A man who'd been a part of her life for scarcely a week ten years ago. But, oh, what a part he had played.

Jack Sullivan.

The single biggest mistake of her life.

Not because she'd spent one night with him. But because of all the nights since that she'd spent without him.

If only she hadn't been such a coward that day....
If only she'd had the courage to tell him the truth....
If only...

The impact with the ground drove the air from her lungs. She felt an instant of excruciating pain, then nothing, nothing at all.

Courtney was dimly aware of the bonds at her wrists being cut away, aware of the blindfold being removed, but she couldn't summon the strength to open her eyes. She wasn't even sure she could, if she wanted to. Her head throbbed; her whole body was one big ache.

And she was cold, mind-numbingly cold and soaking wet. Her fingers shifted and she felt a layering of icy wetness beneath her. She shivered convulsively. She was lying in a snowbank.

Her head still spinning, she raised a hand to her face and winced. Blood. No wonder she couldn't open her eyes. Her whole face seemed caked with dried blood. Heart thudding, Courtney tried feebly to push herself into a sitting position. A pair of strong hands prevented her.

"Don't move," came a deep, masculine voice.

Courtney shrank back, stifling a scream. "Don't touch me. Don't—"

"It's all right," came the voice, gentle now, reassuring. "You don't have to be afraid of me. I'm not going to hurt you."

"Liar! You've already—"

"It's all right," he repeated firmly. "It's not what you think. Those men who did this to you—they're dead. Both of them. I heard the crash, found you here."

Her outburst had drained what strength she had left. Courtney sagged back, struggling even to comprehend what the voice was saying. Her thoughts were so jumbled. Her head throbbed, and she was still so afraid. Dead? Is that what he'd said? Her kidnappers were both dead? She tried to center on her benefactor's voice, but found she could key in on nothing familiar. But then the helicopter engine had been so very loud....

If her rescuer was not one of her kidnappers, then—

"Who are you?" she managed. "Where—?"

"Easy now. You need to save your strength. I need to get you someplace warm and safe. You're already borderline hypothermic, and it's going to be dark soon."

"My eyes..."

"Don't try to open them. You've got a bad cut on your forehead. I'll get it cleaned up as soon as I get you to my place."

My place? Courtney recalled the gunman mentioning trees, rocks and wilderness. *My place?* "Please . . . take me home."

"Can't risk it in the dark."

"Who are you?" she asked again.

"I guess for now you can consider me your guardian angel."

Courtney was not reassured. This is crazy, she thought. He's one of the kidnappers. He has to be. She should fight, run. But she found she hadn't the strength or the will to do either. Unconsciousness hovered close, threatened to envelop her yet again.

Those same strong hands now trailed over her arms, her legs, her middle. Knowing hands, gentle hands. Matter-of-fact, efficient, there was nothing at all improper in their exploration, and yet there was a tenderness about them that made her almost want to weep.

Then his voice came again. Different somehow, more strained. A memory stirred, and she did weep.

Jack. Ten years fell away as nothing. He was here and he was holding her, whispering sweet, sweet words to her of longing and regret. She wasn't sure, but she thought she might have said his name. And just that quickly the comforting presence beside her was gone.

"You're going to be fine," he said, his voice still kind, but not the same.

More tears fell. It had been her imagination. Jack wasn't there at all. Nor, if she was thinking straight, would she even wish him to be. God above, it had been Jack Sullivan's rejection that had sent her fleeing into

Roger Winthrop's arms, plunging her into all the misery that followed. No, the last thing she ever needed in her life was to cross paths with Jack Sullivan again.

"Please," she whispered, hating the pleading tone in her voice. "Don't hurt me." Every skill, every defense she'd ever learned in how to handle a crisis seemed to have deserted her. Not in years had she felt so defenseless, so lost. She was completely at this man's mercy.

"Nothing seems to be broken," he told her. "You're going to be all right. You're one lucky lady."

"Yeah, lucky," she murmured.

And then she was being lifted, carried, cradled in powerful arms. "You'll be okay, I promise. Those two bastards who did this to you will never hurt you again."

It was the oddest thing, but Courtney could have sworn her guardian angel's voice held a sudden threading of pain.

"Sleep now," he told her softly. "Sleep."

Courtney slept.

She came awake slowly. Eyes still closed, thoughts muzzy, she became aware first of the pillow beneath her head, the softness of the blankets that covered her. A shudder of indescribable relief flooded through her. *Thank God.* It had all been a horrible dream after all.

She was in bed.

She was home.

She was safe.

Courtney Hamilton opened her eyes—and screamed.

Chapter 2

Arms flailing, Courtney battled the beast that hovered above her. A black bear? A grizzly? Had she lived through the crash of the helicopter only to be dragged into the lair of some ravenous forest creature?

A grip of iron manacled her wrists.

"Be still!" a voice commanded. "You're going to hurt yourself."

Courtney fought harder, her senses still reeling, her vision cloudy. The beast leaned closer, and she could just make out a mane of shaggy dark hair. She screamed again, trying futilely to twist away.

"Please," the voice said. "I don't want to have to tie you to the bed." Oddly, the chilling words were spoken soothingly, even desperately. "You're safe now. No one is going to hurt you. I promise." Even more incredibly, the words were coming from the beast itself.

Courtney stilled, though her heart hammered in her chest. Gulping for air, she stared at the hairy, shadowy figure that loomed over her. She was hallucinating. She had to be. How else could this creature be talking to her?

"It's all right," the voice went on. "You have a little cut on your head that scared me for a while, but it bled worse than it looked. You were lucky to get out of that chopper alive."

Lucky? Where had she heard that before?

Courtney forced herself to take in several steadying lungfuls of air. She hadn't panicked in the helicopter. At least not until that horrid man . . .

Unbidden tears sprang to her eyes.

"What is it?" the beast asked, a sudden alarm threading his voice. "Are you in pain? Is there something I missed?"

The concern in that deep, husky voice got through to her at last. The concern both in his voice and in a pair of warm brown eyes. Bears didn't have warm, brown eyes, did they? Brown yes, but warm? Nor did they dress in red flannel shirts and blue jeans.

"If you don't intend to hurt me," she managed shakily, "then take your hands off me."

His hands fell away at once, but not before she saw the barest trace of hurt in those remarkable eyes. "I didn't mean to scare you," he said.

Courtney frowned. Now he sounded annoyed. "Who are you?" she asked, though the question that sprang more readily to her lips was "What are you?"

He didn't answer. Instead, he stood and backed away from the bed several steps, regarding her so intently that Courtney had to fight down a new unease. *No one is going to hurt you.* He'd said that, hadn't he?

she tried to reassure herself. But while his words might have been soothing, his appearance was anything but. She stared at him. She couldn't help it.

Dark hair shot through with gray spilled down to broad shoulders. A lush beard all but obscured his mouth. Between the beard and the hair that tumbled across his forehead, all she could see of his face was a hawklike nose and those brown eyes. Teddy-bear eyes, she thought, then grimaced. This was hardly the time for sentimentality. This man may have rescued her from a wrecked helicopter, but she took no solace in the presence of her disheveled knight errant.

In fact, the phrase *out of the frying pan, into the fire* seemed suddenly determined to take root in her brain.

"You said..." She swallowed hard. "I did hear you say that those men on the helicopter...that they were...that..."

"They're dead," he said simply.

Courtney closed her eyes, ashamed of the relief that rippled through her.

"Don't shed any tears over 'em," her dark-haired host put in, uncannily seeming to read her mind. "From the way they had you hog-tied, they weren't planning to hold any parties in your honor. At least none you would've wanted to attend."

Courtney shivered. "Thank you."

"No thanks necessary. I didn't do anything."

"You brought me here." She glanced around, taking note of her surroundings for the first time. Wherever *here* was. The walls of the tiny room were fashioned of chinked logs, the fireplace—fire blazing—had been built with ragged-edged fieldstone, the furniture—what there was of it—would have embarrassed a Neanderthal. "Where are we?" she ventured, not certain she wanted to hear the answer.

"My cabin. That is," he amended, "it's mine now. It used to belong to a friend of mine. He died."

There was an undertone to his words that spoke of more than sorrow at the death of his friend. But Courtney took no time to puzzle it out. She had her own more immediate problems to deal with. "Those men . . . they said they were taking me to a cabin."

His eyes narrowed. "So?"

"So I never saw what either one of them looked like. Maybe—" She stopped. What was she doing? If this man was one of her kidnappers, it was hardly prudent to let on that she thought so. "I mean . . ." She fumbled. "I didn't mean—"

"If I was one of them," he interrupted, with more than a little irritation, "would I have bothered to cut your ropes, take off your blindfold?"

"I . . ." She hesitated. She supposed it didn't make any sense. "I'm sorry."

He said nothing.

Unconsciously, Courtney reached toward her throat, tugging nervously at the tiny charm that hung suspended there on a sterling silver chain. She'd forgotten she had it on. Ten years ago she'd found the exquisitely wrought-silver wolf in a Butte jewelry store. She'd bought it because it reminded her of Jack, and at the time she'd still harbored the faint hope that he would come back to her, that he hadn't meant the ugly words that had ended their one and only night together.

Later, when it became painfully obvious that she had just been another Jack Sullivan one-night stand after all, she'd come close to throwing it away. But by then the wolf had become a kind of talisman, a symbol unto itself. She couldn't part with it, no matter how much it hurt to look at it. So instead, she'd tucked it into a dresser drawer in her bedroom. Two days ago she'd found it again. For reasons she had yet to fathom, she'd put it on. Discovering that it had survived the crash gave her a measure of peace she couldn't have explained in words.

"Not many folks in Montana would appreciate someone with an affection for wolves."

She blinked, startled from her reverie. "People who don't like wolves, don't know them," she said defensively. "They're strong, loyal, loving..."

"Whoa!" He held up a hand. "You're preaching to the converted. I'm kind of partial to 'em myself."

Courtney bit the inside of her lip, strangely reassured by this serendipitous bond between herself and her unpredictable companion. She began to massage her wrists, wincing at the pain where the rope had chafed them. Then suddenly she stilled, noting for the first time that not only were her wrists bare, but her arms, as well. A new horror streaked through her. Heart thudding, she lifted the coverlets and gasped. Beneath the blankets she was stark naked.

"How could you?" she cried, shooting her benefactor an accusing glare.

He rolled his eyes. "What would you have had me do? You were lying in three inches of snow. Your clothes were soaking wet. I couldn't very well put you to bed with wet clothes on, could I?" When she didn't answer, he prompted again, "Could I?"

"I suppose not," she conceded.

"I swear to you, I compromised your modesty as little as possible."

Courtney was not reassured. Beneath the blankets she trembled. It wasn't her modesty that concerned her, so much as the utter defenselessness she felt at being naked in the same room with this thoroughly intimidating stranger. If he made any threatening moves, she could hardly go careering off into the snow in her birthday suit. "Where are my clothes?" she demanded.

He inclined his head toward the fireplace.

Propped against the wall beside the hearth was a stripped tree branch that apparently served as the man's clothes rack. Draped haphazardly across the branch were what was left of her bulky knit sweater and wool blend print skirt. Tossed atop the skirt were her equally wretched-looking bra and panties. Each garment appeared stiff with dried mud.

"There's a creek about five hundred yards from here," he told her. "I was going to wash them out, but—" he shrugged "—I figured I should tend to you first. I didn't want you waking up in a strange place all alone."

"How long have I been here?"

"Since last night."

The notion that she had been in this man's company—unconscious—for several hours did nothing to assuage her unease. But then, she reasoned, if he truly meant to harm her, wouldn't he already have done his worst?

Out of the frying pan...

No! She couldn't afford to think that way. She recalled the crash, remembering vaguely the gentle hands that had cut her bonds away, the kind voice that had whispered words of comfort and encouragement. For the space of a heartbeat she had even fancied that the voice behind those words belonged to Jack Sullivan, a notion made all the more ridiculous as she cast a covert glance at the uncivilized-looking brute standing in front of her.

The man might have briefly *sounded* like Jack. But he certainly didn't *look* like Jack, not unless Jack had fallen on some seriously sorry times, a notion that, she was ashamed to admit, didn't exactly displease her. They were of a similar height, that much she would grant. But Jack's shoulders hadn't been quite so rounded, nor his face quite so haggard, as though life had dealt him one too many blows. And, of course, Jack's eyes had been blue. Montana sky-blue. A blue filled with a fiery passion he'd once claimed burned only for her.

Her heart twisted. Just one of many velvet-tongued lies.

"How did you find me?" she blurted quickly, too quickly, as memories crowded close.

This time, if her host noticed her distress, he chose to ignore it. "I was hunting. I heard the copter go down."

She frowned. "It's April. Hunting season's in the fall."

He snorted. "You'd rather I hadn't been there?"

Courtney decided it was in her own best interest not to answer that one. "Where are we? I mean, are we still in Montana?"

"Yep."

When he didn't elaborate, she grimaced. It seemed he was content to do this one syllable at a time. "You say you were hunting. So you're what? On vacation?" she offered hopefully.

"I live here."

Courtney resisted the temptation to roll her eyes. Why had she already known that? Aside from the fact that the man looked like Grizzly Adams on a bad hair day. What had he said earlier, about her being lucky? She was lucky all right. Lucky enough to be kidnapped by armed thugs, and then "rescued" by some wacko survivalist living in the middle of nowhere. If her luck held, she'd soon discover that he was stockpiling weapons for Armageddon and on the prowl for the perfect Mrs. Bigfoot.

To avoid a bout of hysteria, Courtney pressed her fingers to her aching temples.

"Are you in pain?"

She was surprised at the sudden solicitousness in his voice.

"My head hurts," she admitted. "I feel a little punchy, like I had too much to drink. Those men used something to knock me out."

"Chloroform most likely."

Courtney nodded. She'd smelled the sickly sweet anesthetic once during a biology experiment in high school. "But the effects of the chloroform should've worn off by now, don't you think?" How could she be having a rational conversation with a man that under ordinary circumstances would have sent her screaming in the opposite direction?

"Could be a mild concussion."

She raised her eyebrows. "You're a doctor?"

"A survivor."

Courtney almost laughed. Well, at least he hadn't said surviv*alist*. "I appreciate all you've done, Mr....ah, I'm sorry, you haven't told me your name."

He glanced away from her, not answering.

"If it's Conan," she mused aloud, "maybe it's better that I don't know."

He shot her a dark look. "Just call me J.D."

"Now that wasn't so hard. You're J.D., and I'm—"

"I'm well aware of who you are, Miss Hamilton."

Her heart jumped. "How could you?—"

J.D. walked over to a small wooden table beneath a curtainless window. On the table Courtney spied the oversize canvas carryall that had passed for her purse for the past two years. Without so much as a by-your-leave he opened the bag, retrieved her wallet and flipped it open to her driver's license. "Courtney Anne Hamilton," he read aloud. "Philadelphia, Pennsylvania. Blonde hair. Green eyes. Five foot six. Your weight—"

"Thank you," she cut in testily. "Thank you very much. Did you rummage through the rest of my bag, as well?"

He upended the tote bag's contents onto the table-top. "Credit cards, three hundred fourteen dollars in cash, an odd amount of change, makeup, a pair of diamond stud earrings, an address book, lipstick, a preliminary draft of this year's prospectus for Winthrop-Hamilton Industries, a computer disk, a couple of tampons and—" he held up two foil-wrapped packets "—your hope chest?"

Her cheeks burned. "If you'd be so kind as to put those back where you found them...."

"Yes, ma'am." She could hear the smirk in his voice. What kind of Good Samaritan was this? When she'd been all but unconscious, the man had been tender, compassionate and kind. Now that she was awake, he was nothing short of a boorish oaf. Why?

"Look, Mr. ah..."

"J.D.," he repeated evenly. "Just J.D."

Her lips thinned. "If I've done something to offend you—"

"You have."

She could feel herself flinch. "What?"

He began shoving her things back into her purse. "You're here. I don't like company."

"It's hardly my fault that I was in a helicopter that crashed in your backyard." She looked past him out the window at the rolling expanse of lodgepole pine and rock beyond. "Especially considering the size of your backyard. Where are we anyway?"

"The Sapphires," he said, not looking at her.

She blinked, surprised. "You're kidding? Maybe I do have a little luck left, after all." The Sapphires were a heavily forested ridge of mountains in the Deer Lodge National Forest, scarcely thirty miles from Butte. Back in her teenage forest-ranger-wannabe days, she had even hiked some of the range's more accessible trails. Apparently she hadn't been unconscious in the helicopter for as long as she'd thought. "Well, we can take care of both of our dilemmas at once, can't we?"

"Excuse me?"

"You can get me out of your private domain by taking me home."

"Can't be done."

"I beg your pardon?"

"You heard me."

"I'll pay you. Whatever you want. Keep the cash from my purse. I'll add to it—"

"I don't want your money."

"But you can't keep me here."

The look that flickered in his eyes made her wonder if that thought hadn't indeed crossed his mind, but he said only, "The roads are out. It's spring and it's muddy as hell out there. The nearest trail's end is a two-day hike on a good day. This isn't a good day."

"Tell me about it," Courtney muttered under her breath.

"What?"

"Nothing. Listen, I've done some hiking. Just get me my clothes and you won't even have to leave your little house in the big woods. I'll get myself home."

He raked his hands through the shaggy mane of his hair. "Maybe I can blame it on the concussion."

"What?"

"The fact that you don't seem to understand English," he said tightly. "You're not going anywhere, Miss Hamilton. Not today. Not tomorrow. And maybe not the next day, either. You don't know it yet, but you've got a badly sprained left ankle. Be sides—" he paused for emphasis "—there are two dead bodies less than a mile from here. I don't think I want to go anywhere with you until I know more about what the hell is going on."

Inside, Courtney recoiled at the reminder of the dead kidnappers, but to J.D. she merely chucked her chin up a notch and snapped, "I was being kidnapped. What more is there for you to know?"

"Where were they taking you? Do they have confederates waiting in the woods somewhere? How much of a ransom were they after?"

She glared at him. "You may find this difficult to believe, but they didn't take me into their confidence." The last thing she needed to think about were accomplices roaming the countryside.

"Then what did they say?"

"I don't remember," she said. "What business is it of yours anyway?"

"It could be important. Think."

Courtney closed her eyes, and for one horrible moment it was as if she were back in that helicopter, hearing the gunman's threats, feeling his hands on her. "I can't think about it. Please don't ask me."

"You have to."

"Why? What does it matter to you?"

"It doesn't matter a damn to me, babe. But anything you can think of might help the police later."

Her anger waned a little. "You're right, of course. I'm sorry." She forced herself to think, to remember. "They did say one thing. They mentioned a boss."

"Any names?"

"No. I mean, there was one name. A slip of the tongue, I think. The pilot was supposed to be a man named Al. But someone else had to step in for him when Al took sick. Is that anything?"

"Not really."

"Well, it's the best I can do!" she shot at him, shoving herself into a sitting position. It was a move she instantly regretted. Her head spun, the blankets covering her slipping nearly beneath her breasts. She didn't miss the sudden fire that blazed in her reluctant host's eyes, a fire swiftly subdued, crushed. She recalled his claim to have spared her modesty as much as possible. What if he had not? What if...?

She forced the thought away. If she didn't, she would quickly lose what minimal composure she had left.

"You don't understand," she told him, despising the desperation that had crept into her voice. "My father is very ill. I need to get home. My disappearance could cause a setback in his recovery." She wasn't about to tell J.D. that her father was in a coma, and that even if he weren't he might not have the slightest interest in seeing his only child.

"I'm sure Quentin Hamilton will survive."

Her brows furrowed. "How do you know my father's name? That's not in my purse."

"Oh, it probably is," J.D. said blandly, "on that little line where you write in who to notify in case of an accident. But even if it isn't, it doesn't take an Einstein to put your name and that prospectus together with Winthrop-Hamilton Industries. So, you're what? The CEO of the Philadelphia branch? In charge of oil slicks on the Monongahela?"

Courtney curled her fingers into her palms. "The Monongahela runs through Pittsburgh," she said stiffly. "I handle spilling toxic waste into the Delaware."

He surprised her by grinning slightly, as though impressed by her sarcasm.

"Correct me if I'm wrong, J.D., but that tone of yours suggests that whatever grudge you've got against Winthrop-Hamilton is personal. Is it?"

"That's not your business."

"Maybe it is, since I'm the daughter of the real CEO of Winthrop-Hamilton. And I've been kidnapped."

"So we're back to that again, are we?"

"Maybe we never left it."

"Think what you like. I couldn't possibly care less."

Courtney took a deep breath. "Look," she said slowly, "fate seems to have been ill-mannered enough to throw us together, so let's try and make the best of it, shall we?"

"Are you patronizing me, Miss Hamilton?"

"On the contrary, mister, I'm trying very hard not to hate you."

"Don't do me any favors, okay?"

"Then help me get to my father."

He waved a hand at the room's accoutrements. "What can I say? Beam me up, Scotty? What we lack in the latest communications satellite, we make up for in rustic charm."

"I'm thrilled that you find all of this so amusing," she grated. "But I must get word to my father and my father's partner. I need them to know that I'm all right." She eyed him with a sudden wariness. "That is, if I am all right."

J.D. let out a disgusted breath. "Get it through your head. If I meant to harm you, you'd already be harmed."

"Maybe," she allowed, "but . . . do you mean to let me go?"

"Why in God's name would I want to keep you here any longer than?—" He stopped, his eyes going wide, as though he'd suddenly come up with the answer to his own question. "Don't tell me. You think you're going to be Jane to my Tarzan, right?" He snorted derisively. "Don't flatter yourself, sweetheart. My taste in the fairer sex doesn't run to spoiled rich bi— ah, women."

Courtney flushed, unaccountably stung by his attitude. How dare he judge her by her last name and his own best guess of her net worth? She supposed it would come as quite a shock to Mr. Holier-Than-Thou if she told him her true bank account balance. And what she had been doing for a living up until her father's heart attack three weeks ago.

But none of that was any of this conceited bastard's business. "You must have some way to contact family, friends," she pressed.

"Don't have any," he said.

"Why doesn't that surprise me?"

He scowled.

"Do you think you could at least find me something to wear? I don't like feeling so...so..."

"Naked?" he supplied.

"Vulnerable," she corrected.

His eyes darkened with an emotion she couldn't name. She was certain he had another flippant remark in mind, but for once he kept it to himself.

Instead, he stalked over to a battered dresser and pulled out a clean flannel shirt and a pair of jeans. "You're welcome to these." He tossed the clothes onto the bed.

When he continued to stand there, Courtney crossed her arms in front of her. "You expect me to dress in front of you?"

"Why not? You haven't got any secrets from me, remember?"

She felt her cheeks heat.

He seemed to catch himself, and for an instant Courtney could have sworn he actually looked ashamed, then just that quickly the look was gone. "Tell you what," he said. "You can have all the privacy you want. I've got a little business to attend to."

"Business? We're in the middle of nowhere."

He eyed her steadily. "I've got a couple of bodies to bury. Much as I'd like to, it doesn't seem right to leave 'em to the animals."

Courtney flinched. "You're right, of course," she said in a small voice. "I hadn't thought..."

But J.D. was already crossing the wood-planked floor and catching up the rifle that hung above the mantel.

"Why do you need a gun to dig a grave?" she heard herself ask.

Those coolly assessing eyes were on her again. "You never know what kind of varmints you might run into in the woods, Miss Hamilton."

She didn't miss the double meaning of his words. Unconsciously, she gripped the blankets tighter against her breasts. J.D.'s mouth twitched slightly at the gesture, whether in annoyance or amusement she couldn't have said.

"How long will you be gone?" she asked.

"Miss me already?" he mocked.

Her lips thinned. "I'd just like to know, all right?" As unpleasant as J.D.'s company was proving to be, having him around seemed preferable to being alone in the middle of nowhere with a badly sprained ankle and who knows what or whom out there in the woods looking for her.

"No one's going to find you here, Miss Hamilton," J.D. said, his voice gentling slightly, as though he sensed her fear and had at least a modicum of sympathy for her. "I wouldn't leave you if I thought you were in any immediate danger."

She stared at her hands. "Thank you."

"I won't be gone long," he assured her. "An hour or two at most. Help yourself to whatever you need around the place." He added with gruff politeness, "Anything I can get you before I head out?"

"I...I'm a little hungry." Actually she was famished.

J.D. tromped over to several shelves lined with canned goods along the far wall. "What's your pleasure? Peaches? Pears? Spinach? Sauerkraut?"

"Peaches. Please." Her stomach rumbled, and she blushed.

He brought a can over to her, along with a small bowl, spoon and a can opener. "Anything else?"

"I . . . No, no thank you." Her body was telling her that she needed to make a call of nature soon. But no way was she going to tell J.D. that.

He strode to the fireplace, hunkering down to arrange a couple of extra big chunks of wood on the fire. One of the logs slipped and jammed into his left arm. J.D. cursed with more fervor than Courtney felt the incident called for, but she said nothing. Then he stood and crossed to an ancient ladder-back chair, where he snatched up the well-used sheepskin coat draped over the back of it. Shrugging into the coat, he flinched noticeably when its left sleeve slid over his left arm.

Courtney's eyes went wide. "Are you hurt?" she demanded.

"It's nothing. Snagged some skin on your helicopter, getting you out yesterday."

"Let me take a look," she offered, feeling responsible for his injury. "It might need more tending than whatever you managed one handed."

"I said it was nothing," he repeated tightly.

Settling the rifle under one arm, he used his free hand to grab up a spade that had been propped against the wall near the door. Without so much as a backward glance he stalked from the cabin.

For long minutes Courtney sat in the bed, unable to move, her thoughts as scattered as her emotions. The man's mood swings were enough to give her whiplash. The notion that her life could rest on such temperamental shoulders was not exactly a comfort in her overstressed state.

Kidnapped. She still couldn't believe it.

Had it only been yesterday morning that she'd been seated at her father's desk in his office suite? She'd just ejected a computer disk she'd been unable to make heads or tails of, when his private line had rung.

Your father's had a relapse! Hurry!

In a heartbeat she'd been headed for the elevator. She remembered taking time only to grab her purse, and . . .

And, Courtney realized slowly, to tell Sarah Carpenter what had happened!

Sarah Carpenter. Her father's secretary for nearly two decades. Within minutes, dear, loyal Sarah had probably placed a half-dozen phone calls of her own, making inquiries about Quentin's health. How quickly would Sarah have discovered the lie? And once she had, what would she have thought, done?

Called Fletcher Winthrop, of course! Courtney's spirits rose a little. It was just possible Fletcher would have suspected foul play even before the kidnappers had made known their demands. Maybe there weren't just bad guys out there looking for her. Maybe there were a few good guys, as well.

Courtney managed a shaky smile. Now, if only she knew for certain which one J.D. might be. . . .

Tugging on the man's oversize blue flannel shirt, her gaze tracked unwillingly to the window. The tree-bristled slopes of the Sapphire Mountains had once been a haven for an emotionally bereft teenager. Now the towering trees and impervious granite seemed only

to taunt her, threaten her. She clutched the tiny silver
wolf at her throat. Out there somewhere, a dark-haired
and unpredictable stranger was digging two graves. It
occurred to her that he could just as easily be digging
a third.

Chapter 3

Jack Sullivan sank back on his haunches and surveyed the mound of freshly piled stones in front of him. He dragged in a deep lungful of air and winced. His chest ached from hours of exertion in the thin mountain air. He doubted the temperature had nudged much above thirty-five degrees all afternoon. Ground frost had quickly convinced him to give up the notion of digging two separate graves. He'd turned instead to the ubiquitous rocks scattered along the pine-studded slope. Two makeshift wooden crosses jammed into the earth at the head of the mound provided what he hoped was the appropriate final touch to his interment activities.

Taking a disinterested swipe at the sweat on his face, Jack pushed wearily to his feet. The ragged gash on his left forearm throbbed dully. From the looks of his sleeve, it had begun bleeding again. He grimaced, more in annoyance than pain. The damned thing

needed stitches. He settled for wrapping the redden-
ing gauze with a clean bandanna, then knotting it with
his teeth. It would do. It would have to do. No way
could he let Courtney tend the wound. Yanking his
bloodstained shirtsleeve back into place, he grumbled
a sour curse. Kidnapped heiresses, mangled helicop-
ters, grave digging—it had been one helluva twenty-
four hours.

Giving his head a bemused shake, Jack cast a glance
skyward. "Calling in markers, God?" he muttered,
wondering what other explanation there could be for
how his life had managed to cross paths with one Miss
Courtney Anne Hamilton.

Again.

Jack Sullivan would be the first to admit his life had
not always traversed the straight and narrow. But he
must have strayed farther from the path than he'd
thought for the Almighty to torment him yet again
with Courtney.

His gut clenched, a shaft of guilt rippling through
him. How much further could he stray than what he'd
done to Courtney one hot, stormy night ten years ago?
The pain and betrayal in her green eyes had haunted
him for months afterward. Haunted him, but done
nothing to change his mind. He'd done what he had to
do. To this day, he was convinced of that. Maybe his
methods had been a bit crude, but the results had been
what mattered. He'd put an end to Courtney's starry-
eyed fantasies about Jack Sullivan once and for all.
Surely that had to be a plus in the Almighty's record
book.

"You wish, Sullivan," he gritted aloud. Big, noble
sacrifice? Was that his rewrite on that night? Like hell.
He'd done what needed doing, but there'd been noth-

ing at all noble about it. Nobility required honesty, guts. Instead, he'd opted for the coward's way out. Just as he'd done three hours ago at the cabin. He'd looked Courtney straight in the eye and didn't even have the guts to admit who he was.

She doesn't need to know, he argued inwardly.

Yeah, right, his conscience countered. *For her sake? Or your own?*

Jack swore, annoyed by his sparring thoughts. It wasn't his fault Courtney had gotten mixed-up in this mess, a mess far beyond anything she yet suspected. Soon enough her kidnapping would be the least of her worries. But he would deal with that bit of unpleasantness later. One disaster at a time was all he could handle.

If only she'd stayed the hell away from Butte. Two more weeks. That's all he'd needed. Two more weeks and everything he had set in motion three months ago would have been set to pay off. Instead, everything was in danger of collapsing. All because of one unforeseen wild card.

Courtney.

Jack raked his right hand through his tousled, shoulder-length dark hair. He was being a damned fool. How could there even be any debate? He should be on his knees with gratitude that she hadn't recognized him. With luck he might still be able to pull everything together, gain the full measure of justice that was his due. No, not justice—revenge. If Courtney had seen through his disguise, and then guessed the true scope of that revenge . . .

Jack closed his eyes. For his sake—and Courtney's—it was best that he remain anonymous. For now.

The hair, the beard, the slightly slumped posture—all had been carefully thought out, as had the barest trace of a rasp he'd added to his voice. The brown contacts had been a stroke of genius, if he did say so himself, though at times they irritated the hell out of his baby blues. Not that he was complaining. The disguise had worked to perfection. Not one person had recognized him since his return home.

Home.

Jack cursed feelingly.

Did he even consider Montana home anymore?

The wind picked up, soughing mournfully through the needles of the lodgepole. Overhead, an osprey called to its mate. Jack let out a soul-weary sigh. The easier question might be—could he ever *not* think of Montana as home?

Especially here. So close to the cabin. Pete's cabin. Jack's gut twisted.

Pete Wilson. His mentor, his friend.

Pete Wilson. Dead. Murdered.

Jack's hands balled into fists at his sides. It had been Pete, the Butte street cop, who had been there to pick up the pieces for a rebellious, grieving teenage boy after Jack's father had died. It had been Pete who offered his cabin to the man Jack had become when Jack's life had gone straight to hell one Los Angeles night eight months ago.

No. He couldn't afford to think too much about Pete. Didn't dare. Thinking about Pete could make him reckless, careless.

He shook his head, scarcely believing the twists and turns his life had taken these past ten years, twists and turns that had taken him far away from the pristine blue skies of Montana to the smog-ridden grit of L.A.

and back again. Back and face-to-face with Courtney Hamilton.

If only he didn't remember how vulnerable she'd looked ten years ago. How damned innocent, how lost. Hell, if only he'd never met her at all.

But he had. And there was nothing he could do to change it. Instead, he would just have to factor in this unforeseen bit of bad luck and make the best of it.

Taking her down the mountain would be a major risk—in more ways than one. God only knew who they might run into. And whose side they'd be on.

Keeping her at the cabin was a whole different can of worms, one he didn't even want to think about opening.

Take me home. Her voice had trembled with a fear he could tell she'd been trying valiantly to keep under tight control.

His response? He'd turned her down flat. And scared the hell out of her. A realization that continued to gnaw at his gut. But he'd had no choice. Still didn't. He gave her credit, though. She'd stood up to his J.D. guise with more moxie than he would've predicted for a woman of her pampered upbringing. In fact, she'd come through the whole ordeal of a kidnapping and helicopter crash in remarkably feisty spirits. The Courtney he'd known ten years ago would not have fared as well.

But she'd been all of nineteen back then. An innocent in more ways than one.

This Courtney was stronger, tougher. And yet, underneath the gutsy exterior, he'd sensed some of the same fragility and vulnerability that had so attracted him to her ten years ago.

Muttering an oath, Jack kicked at a stray stone, sending it tumbling toward the silent hulk of the wrecked helicopter. Enough about Courtney. They'd had a one-night mistake ten years ago. And it had ended the only way it could for a wealthy young socialite and a Black Irish laborer from the wrong side of anybody's tracks. If he was real lucky, he'd be back in L.A. before she even remembered she'd ever met a man named Jack Sullivan. Though for just an instant, when he'd knelt beside her at the crash site, he could've sworn she'd said his name. But between his own adrenaline and her semiconscious state, he decided he must have been hearing things.

Tromping away from the mounded stones, he headed toward what was left of the helicopter. His thick-tread hiking boots crunched through the ankle-deep snow still lying along the uneven turf in stubborn, shadowed patches.

When he reached the wreckage, he made a three-sixty around it, hunkering down here and there to inspect what was left of the landing skids, the jumbled cockpit, the smashed tail assembly. He let out a low, admiring whistle. He had expected worse. The craft would never fly again, but neither had it been demolished.

For that, he supposed, he could credit the pilot. He'd been good, damned good.

But there were more important things to consider now than the vagaries of fate. Overhead, clouds were settling in. He sniffed the air and frowned. Snow. He intended to be back at the cabin before it hit. Quickly he retrieved a small ax from the belt at his waist, then set about chopping away at a stand of young pine, his movements made slow and awkward because of the still-bleeding gash on his left arm. From a distance at least, the branches would obscure the chopper from prying eyes.

He would assure Courtney, should she ask, that he'd hidden the wreck to protect her from any unsavory types who might be looking for a downed helicopter with a kidnapped heiress aboard.

He grimaced. Maybe someday he'd even tell her the truth.

An hour passed before he'd piled up enough branches to satisfy him. But before he tossed them over the copter, he approached the wreck one more time and peered through the spider veins of smashed Plexiglas that had been the cockpit bubble. Maybe there was still something salvageable inside. Raising his right boot, he took dead aim on the center of the ruined panel and gave it a hard kick.

The damaged Plexiglas split, cleaved in two. Ignoring his protesting back, he jerked the bigger of the two sections free and tossed it aside, then leaned into the mangled opening. The sharp stench of spilled fuel assaulted his nostrils and an involuntary shudder rippled through him. It had been a flat-out miracle that the copter hadn't exploded in a ball of flames. He thought of Courtney being in the copter when it hit and shuddered again.

Jaw tight, Jack forced the thought away. Mindful of the jagged metal protruding nearly everywhere, he began to rummage through the copter's ruined interior, hoping to find something worth salvaging.

He spied a first-aid kit jammed beneath a rear passenger seat. With considerable effort he pried it loose, wishing he had thought to look for it yesterday.

Luckily he'd had enough emergency supplies at the cabin to care for Courtney's injuries.

The rest of his search proved fruitless. Back aching, arm hurting, Jack eased himself out of the wreck and straightened. He'd put it off long enough. He needed to get back to the cabin. In her current state, Courtney wouldn't appreciate being left alone for too long. If he timed it right, she might even be glad to see him. Glad to see J.D., he corrected.

Working quickly, Jack layered the pine branches over the wreckage. When he finished, he shrugged into his coat, gathered up his shovel and rifle and started down the slope. Four steps later he came to an abrupt halt. Out of the corner of one eye, he'd seen it. Lying in the snow some dozen yards from where he stood. A dark, lethal-looking object.

He walked over to it, bent down to retrieve it, then turned the .38 caliber Smith & Wesson over in his palm. White heat flooded through him at the notion of it having been used to threaten Courtney.

He shut away the image. In its place another image, every bit as disturbing, rose up to haunt him— Courtney lying on his bed at the cabin, shivering, unconscious, naked. It was an image he had been battling vainly to suppress all day.

Damn, she was beautiful. Even more beautiful than he'd remembered. It had been impossible not to look. He'd assured himself it was because he'd needed to check her for injuries.

But the memories seared him. Memories of ivory-white legs and coral-tipped breasts.

Quickly he'd covered her, but she'd continued to shiver violently. He'd had no choice but to massage her legs, her arms, knead warmth back into her cold flesh. She'd moaned softly, instinctively shifting toward the warmth of his body sitting next to hers.

Warmth, hell! His body had been on fire.

Furious, Jack jammed back the thoughts, but not before he felt an unwelcome stirring in his loins. Lust, pure and simple, he told himself. It had been nearly two years since he'd been with a woman. Not since Wendy. Even then, his marriage had been over and done with long before they'd both admitted defeat and gone to see a lawyer. Such a prolonged abstinence made his response to Courtney perfectly natural, he assured himself. And had nothing at all to do with memories of a hot, storm-edged summer night spent naked with her tangled in the sheets of his bed, his body craving hers the way an addict craves narcotics.

His hand shaking, Jack checked the safety on the Smith & Wesson, then tucked the weapon into the waistband of his jeans. Memories like that he could do without. It was imperative that he remain detached, impersonal. About Courtney. About everything. If he didn't, he could damn well get them both killed.

He glanced again at the wreck, a sudden thought occurring to him. The damned chopper had a radio. Had it survived the crash? There was only one way to find out.

Ten minutes later Jack Sullivan headed down the forested slope toward the cabin and Courtney.

Courtney pushed herself to a sitting position in J.D.'s bed and cast an anxious glance toward the door. Blast it all, where was he? He'd promised to be back in an hour or two. From the lengthening shadows beyond the cabin's curtainless windows, her best guess put his absence at closer to five hours and counting.

Five hours seemed more than enough time to bury a couple of bodies, didn't it? She shuddered. How on earth would she know how long it took to bury a body?

"Come on, J.D.," she murmured. "Get back here." Even J.D.'s company was preferable to none at all.

At least she'd managed to sleep away most of the five hours, the only exception being the twenty-minute ordeal she'd gone through when her bodily needs had finally coerced her into hobbling outdoors. That twenty minutes had convinced her, as J.D. could not, to abandon any notion she might have had of hiking out of these woods anytime soon. Alone anyway.

Between the chill mountain air and her aching left ankle, she'd had to concede that she would never make it. Not without help. Like it or not—and she most certainly did not—for the time being she was dependent on her enigmatic host. A reality that hardly boosted her flagging spirits.

Again she stared at the door, willing it to open. But it remained stubbornly closed. How far from the cabin had J.D. said the copter had gone down? Less than a mile? Could she find him if she tried limping after him? She closed her eyes. In which direction?

Her memories of the crash and its aftermath were fuzzy at best. The only indelible impression she had was of her rescuer's tenderness and caring. The man had cradled her against him, allowed the warmth of his own body to seep into hers as he'd carried her to the cabin. And he'd done it with an injured left arm.

Courtney sighed, undone by the ambiguity of her emotions where her benefactor was concerned. On the one hand, he scared her to death. On the other... She trailed her fingers through the tousled mane of her blond hair. On the other, there was something about him that niggled at her. Something almost familiar. Which was, of course, absurd. If she'd encountered a talking grizzly bear anywhere in her past, she would have remembered.

Again her gaze tracked to the door. "Some guardian angel," she grumbled. If J.D. stayed away much longer, he was going to have to turn in his wings.

Courtney frowned. Guardian angel? Now where had that come from? How could she think of J.D. as anything even remotely celestial?

And then she remembered. In her semiconscious state after the crash she had demanded to know who was lifting her away from the wreckage.

I guess for now, a husky voice had murmured, *you can consider me your guardian angel.*

She stared out the nearest window. Could guardian angels be harmed? What if hers had met with some disaster? A fall. A real bear. Or worse.

What if her kidnappers had managed to get off some sort of distress signal before the copter crashed? Even if they hadn't, when the appointed time for a rendezvous had come and gone, would their boss have had a backup plan ready to set in motion? J.D. had mentioned the possibility of confederates roaming the hillsides searching for them. What if they'd found J.D.? Would he lead them here? Would he—?

A board creaked and Courtney nearly leapt from the bed. It was only the settling noises of the log house, but it might as well have been a bomb. Her whole body shook.

Annoyed by her increasing agitation, Courtney flung back her bedcovers and eased her legs out over the side of the bed. She needed to distract herself. Her

imagination was fast becoming her worst enemy. She
would be back in Butte soon enough, she assured herself. Even now, Fletcher Winthrop was likely mar-
shaling forces to find her. But she needed to be
pragmatic, as well. The good guys didn't know where
to look. Her first line of defense, therefore, would be
up to her. She drew in a steadying breath. Up to her,
even though what she wanted most in the world to do
was to crawl back into bed and pull the covers over her
head.

She'd spent a lot of time these past four years
learning how not to be a victim. But she knew only too
well how easy it was to fall back into old patterns. Especially under times of stress. She would have to be on
her guard in more ways than one.

Gingerly, Courtney tested her bad ankle on the
planked wood flooring. Her earlier venture outdoors
had only served to aggravate the injury. She'd used a
fire poker as a makeshift crutch then, and took it up
again now. Half hobbling, half hopping, she made her
way to the fireplace. First things first. The cabin was
freezing. The fire J.D. had built up had long since died
back to glowing embers. Lying in bed, Courtney
hadn't found the chill as noticeable, but if she intended to reconnoiter the cabin, she would have to re-
build the fire.

Balancing on her good foot, she struggled for several minutes to get the flames crackling again. Sweating, exhausted, she leaned against the mantel and
drank in the revitalizing warmth of the fire. Eyes
closed, for a moment she could almost believe that she
was home.

As a child, she had often sneaked into her father's
study and nestled herself in his massive red leather

chair in front of the faux marble fireplace. She would sit there for hours and imagine the arms of the chair to be her father's arms, and that he really hadn't abandoned her to yet another business trip after all. To her child's heart, she would've traded every fancy present he'd ever brought home to her, just to have had more of his time.

Courtney let out a shaky sigh, wondering how her father was getting along. Had he made any progress at all? Regained consciousness? Or had he—?

Enough! she ordered herself sharply. She didn't dare let her thoughts grow morbid. She needed to stay focused on the situation at hand. Determined, Courtney gripped her makeshift crutch and began her painful trek about the cabin. No longer elevated, her swollen ankle now throbbed to every beat of her heart. But she didn't stop. She needed to familiarize herself with every square inch of the place, even if to do so tweaked her conscience. She was, after all, violating J.D.'s privacy, wasn't she?

Courtney stifled a humorless laugh. Privacy? The man had certainly afforded her none when he'd stripped her of her clothes. Not that he'd had much choice, she admitted. Still, the idea of those big hands of his gliding across her naked flesh, even on so noble a quest as seeking broken bones, did little to quell the odd heat that suddenly sifted through her.

She told herself it was from embarrassment.

Annoyed at her unsettling thoughts, Courtney concentrated on her search. In a dilapidated dresser she found more clothes—more faded jeans, flannel shirts and underwear. She shook her head. She supposed she should give the man credit. He certainly seemed immune to Madison Avenue's dress-for-success hype.

The rest of her quest turned up an assortment of hiking equipment, enough dehydrated food and bottled water to make it through Armageddon I and II, a ten-inch hunting knife and a locked steel box. Courtney ignored everything but the knife. Carefully she withdrew the wicked-looking blade from its hand-tooled leather sheath. The tempered steel glinted ominously in the fiery orange glow of the fire. She didn't even hesitate. Resheathing the knife, she immediately carried it over to J.D.'s bed and tucked it under her pillow. The full ramifications of such an act she would consider later. Right now she would take any illusion of safety she could get. Especially since there was still no sign of J.D.

Stutter-stepping her way to the closest window, she peered out into the heavily shadowed forest. What if he really had been hurt? Shouldn't she at least try to find him? As though to mock her, a light snow began to fall. A heavy ground mist obscured all but the closest trees. Courtney's shoulders slumped. If J.D. was hurt, he would have to get back to the cabin on his own. She wouldn't have the first idea where to look.

Another thought, equally unpleasant, came to her. What if the man had just plain deserted her? Decided she wasn't worth the hassle? Hadn't he been more than a little blunt about his feelings toward uninvited guests? And what if there was more to it than that? Perhaps he didn't cherish solitude, so much as require it. Courtney's heart skipped a beat. Maybe she should've paid more attention those nights she flipped past "America's Most Wanted."

For a weary moment her gaze shifted longingly toward the bed. Her ankle now ached abominably, and she had to fight the seductive urge to lose herself to the oblivion of sleep. If she slept long enough, maybe J.D. would come back and she could stop worrying about him. And about herself.

All the more reason that she didn't dare lie down, not yet.

Leaning more heavily on the fire poker than ever, Courtney made her way to a door in the cabin's back wall. She had assumed it opened to the outside just as the front door did, but she wanted to be certain. She was astonished to find instead a small workroom. A canvas drop cloth covered the wide knotty pine table that took up most of the space in the room. A series of mysterious lumps and bumps suggested a number of objects underneath the cloth. Sliding onto a hip-high stool beside the table, Courtney lifted the cloth and gasped. Before her were a dozen or more of the most exquisite wood carvings she had ever seen, all of them focused on a single subject—wolves. A pack of wolves on the hunt, a pair of wolf pups tumbling at play. Each piece remarkable in its precision, its minute detail.

She found herself drawn to one piece in particular. A work in progress. A lone wolf with its right front foreleg caught in a trap. The agony on the animal's face was stunning, overwhelming. She could *feel* its suffering. *Feel* its terror, its fury at being caught in the cruel jaws of the trap.

Courtney fingered the charm at her throat, fighting a sudden impulse to yank the canvas back over the carvings. She knew where her thoughts were headed, and she didn't want to go there. She'd been fighting her memories since the instant that helicopter had spun out of control.

But she was so tried, exhausted. And every muscle in her body ached. More than that, her defenses were down. They had been ever since that call from Fletcher about her father's heart attack. And then the kidnapping... She just didn't have the strength to stave off the memories any longer.

Jack Sullivan would win this one. Just as he had won ten years ago....

It had been her nineteenth birthday. Courtney had spent the day packing personal possessions in preparation for the move she and her father would soon make to their new log house retreat in Elk Park. The log house was now habitable, and in fact she intended to spend the night there. But it was still hard to leave the stately old Victorian mansion on Granite Street, where she'd grown up. In a lot of ways it was Courtney's last connection to memories of her mother, who had died in a car accident when Courtney was barely seven years old.

Most of the family possessions had already been moved to the new house. But Courtney was taking her time with the last few items, like her mother's elegantly wrought silver hairbrush. Courtney sat on the floor of her nearly empty bedroom and caressed the soft bristles, feeling an unexpected rush of emotion. Birthdays it seemed, even after twelve years, could still be hard to get through without a mother.

Her mood was scarcely boosted by the fact that she'd spent the day alone. Her father was on another one of his business trips, this one to Japan. He wouldn't be back for two weeks. Courtney let out a melancholy sigh. A phone call would have been nice, but at least he'd remembered to send flowers. Or rather, Courtney thought morosely, his secretary, Sarah Carpenter, had remembered to send flowers.

You could be in Hawaii, she reminded herself. Lolling on a beach in a sexy bikini, getting an eyeful of brawny surfer types wearing their own brand of skimpy attire. Last summer she'd done just that. Two of her best girlfriends had gone back this year for more sun and surf. But Courtney had declined to join them.

She grinned sheepishly, tucking the silver hairbrush into a nearby box. Not that she was missing out on her quota of ogling. The construction crew doing the work out on the Elk Park property had more than its share of pinup candidates. In fact, there was one carpenter in particular that she found almost too intriguing. Tousled dark hair, muscled biceps and taut buttocks encased in worn denim jeans had had her spending entirely too much time peeking out of the newly hung windows of the first-floor family room. Outrageous behavior, Courtney had chided inwardly, considering that she was practically an engaged woman. But then, it didn't hurt to look, did it? Besides, she assured herself, she was just curious about the man's eyes. He was forever wearing safety glasses, and she just wanted to know what color his eyes were. His eyes. That was all.

Courtney's mouth twisted. She'd like to hear herself explain her sudden interest in ophthalmology to Roger.

Roger. A twinge of guilt rippled through her. Roger Winthrop was, after all, the real reason she'd decided against Hawaii. She'd just been so certain that her birthday would be the day that he'd finally pop the question.

And then he'd left for Chicago six days ago. On more Winthrop-Hamilton business.

Courtney smiled a little. But hope was not lost. Early that morning Roger had called and assured her that he would be back in Butte by late afternoon. He was interrupting his hectic schedule setting up a new W-H branch office just to be with her.

"I'm taking you to dinner," he'd announced on the phone. "And I won't accept any arguments to the contrary. In fact, if I'd have had any sense, I would've called yesterday, told you to hop a plane and meet me downtown here in the Windy City. There's a five-star restaurant in the Loop I would've loved to show you off in!"

"I don't care where we eat, Roger, just as long as you're there."

"Ah, Courtney, I've missed you, too. Be ready tonight, okay?" A buzzer sounded. "Gotta go. See you soon." He sent her a kiss through the phone, then hung up.

Courtney glanced at her watch and gasped. She hadn't realized how late it had gotten. Roger would be here any minute. Quickly she abandoned her packing chores and hurried to her closet. Very little of her wardrobe remained at the house. From what was left she chose a simple cotton print skirt and a peasant blouse, trusting that Roger would be pleased.

She really had missed him. Sometimes their courtship seemed to be happening so fast, too fast. Other times, when he was out of town, as he so often was, she would find herself wondering if their relationship really existed at all.

Even so, she'd been flattered six months ago when Roger had returned to Butte from two years of schooling abroad and, just like that, announced his intentions to court her, then marry her, claiming his absence had only made him realize how much he loved her. For herself, Courtney had long harbored a secret crush on Fletcher Winthrop's only offspring. Roger's new air of European sophistication had made him seem all the more alluring.

She'd just finished arranging her honey-blond hair in a halo of soft curls, when the doorbell rang. Courtney hurried down the stairs from her second-floor bedroom and threw the front door open wide. Roger stood on the porch, resplendent in his Armani suit, silk shirt and custom-made tie, his blond hair cut to *GQ* perfection, his classic good looks the cause of many a turned female head whenever they were out together. Courtney wanted nothing so much as to fling herself into his arms and enjoy the pleasure of a welcome-home kiss.

But the look in his green eyes stopped her.

"What on God's earth are you wearing?" he demanded.

Self-consciously, Courtney's hand flew to the exposed area above her bodice. There was nothing at all provocative about the blouse. It wasn't as if she'd snugged it down to display her cleavage or anything. "I...I..." she stammered, flustered and hurt. He hadn't even said happy birthday.

"Go back upstairs," he said, stepping into the entryway of the hundred-year-old Victorian mansion. "Change into something more suitable. I'll wait."

"But, Roger..." Her voice wavered a little.

His scowl dissipated. "Damn, Courtney, I'm sorry. Forgive me. It's been one hell of a long day." He pulled her close and kissed her lightly on the mouth. "Happy birthday, sweetheart."

The thrill Courtney had anticipated didn't materialize. She was still stung by his reproach. "The only other clothes I have are a pair of blue jeans and a couple of old sweatshirts. Most of my things are at the new place in Elk Park."

"Of course. How stupid of me. I've been under so much pressure in Chicago, I just . . . well, I guess I was just picturing how I know you would've looked if I'd taken you someplace spectacular back there. You look fine. Wonderful. My God, you could wear a gunnysack and make it look like Christian Dior."

Courtney relaxed a little. The man had just gotten off a plane. And he'd made the long trip especially to see her. He could've just settled for the phone call. "Shall we go?"

He took her arm and led her out to the curb, where he'd parked his new Jaguar.

"You're going to bring me back here, right?" she asked.

"Of course." He nuzzled her neck. "I've missed you. Very much."

As unobtrusively as she could manage, Courtney took a step away from him. She enjoyed his obvious affection, but she couldn't shake the letdown she was still feeling. "I'm going to need to take the Jeep out to the new house."

"You're staying there tonight?"

She nodded. "I've got a lot of unpacking to do before Daddy gets back in a couple of weeks. You know how he hates clutter."

"So I'll take you out there in the Jag."

"The roads aren't very good. Your car . . ."

"Will be fine. Get in."

After the unpleasantness about her clothes, Courtney wasn't about to risk another argument. With a sigh she climbed into the Jaguar. Thankfully, the drive to the restaurant proved uneventful. Roger relaxed, became his usual, more congenial self. By the time their dessert arrived at the restaurant, Courtney was having a thoroughly delightful time.

"And you should have seen the way I had the place jumping," Roger said. "That Chicago bunch really knows what they're doing. It's going to be a terrific boon to the company. Even my father will have to be pleased."

"I'm so glad for you, Roger," she said, and she was. Ever since Fletcher Winthrop had promoted Roger to an executive vice presidency some five months before, Roger had been under a tremendous amount of pressure to get things up and running in various cities throughout the world, Chicago being only the latest.

"I couldn't have done any of it, if I hadn't known you were always here waiting for me, darling."

She blushed, genuinely pleased.

The waiter returned to pour her a second glass of wine, and Courtney was about to raise it in a toast when Roger reached into the pocket of his suit coat and extracted a tiny, velvet jewelry box. "This is for you, dear heart. Happy birthday. And many, many more."

Courtney's heart turned over. Was Roger about to make an official proposal? And why, when just such an occurrence had been exactly what she had thought she wanted only hours earlier, did she feel herself suddenly riddled with doubt?

Because it was perfectly natural to feel that way, she assured herself. Every engaged woman who ever lived had moments of doubt. Didn't she?

Eagerly, Courtney opened the velvet box. Instead of a ring, she found herself staring at a pair of exquisitely made emerald-and-diamond earrings. Courtney dismissed the odd relief she felt. "Oh, Roger, they're beautiful."

He flashed her an adoring smile. "Not half as beautiful as you are, Courtney."

She blushed.

He reached across the table and caught both of her hands in his own. His skin was warm, and yet Courtney felt a sudden, strange chill. "I love you, Courtney," he said fervently. "And I think the time has finally come to ask—"

"Excuse me, Mr. Winthrop." The waiter stepped back up to their table. "I'm sorry to interrupt. But you have a phone call. The party says it's quite urgent." The waiter set the phone on the table and left.

"Excuse me, darling," Roger said, snatching up the receiver with obvious annoyance. "This had better be—" He stopped in midsentence, his face flushing. "Yes, Father. Yes. I've told you— Yes." His jaw tightened. "I'll do what I can, but— Father, please, I— Yes, Father." Roger replaced the receiver. For a long minute he didn't speak.

Finally the silence grew so awkward that Courtney felt compelled to say something. "What did Fletcher—?"

"He wanted the same thing he always wants," Roger snapped, cutting her off. "The moon, the sun, a couple of minor galaxies. Those damned idiots I've got working for me in Chicago have screwed everything up again. And somehow, as always, it's my fault. The Chicago office was supposed to be up and running in three weeks by my father's calculations. Unfortunately, it's going to be more like two months. He just won't listen. What does he expect when he hires incompetents . . . ?"

"But I thought—" She stopped and amended her thoughts to, "You'll show him, Roger. You always do."

He shook his head. "Sometimes being the son of the co-owner of Winthrop-Hamilton isn't the enviable position people think it is."

"Tell me about it. I'm the daughter of the other guy, remember?"

"But Quentin's not grooming you to take over the company."

Courtney sighed. She didn't want the company. Had never wanted it. And yet perversely, it would have been nice if her father had at least offered. Sometimes she wondered if she and Roger had been switched at birth. Her father adored Roger. And Fletcher Winthrop had always been like a doting uncle to her.

Roger ordered a Manhattan, a double.

"Don't you think the wine was enough?"

"Don't tell me what to do, Courtney." He finished off the drink in two swift gulps. "I get quite enough of that from dear old Papa."

"I'm sorry. I didn't mean to sound like I was ordering you about. That is, everything's been so wonderful, I— Thank you again for the earrings."

"You're welcome."

He stood and came around to help her with her chair. "Let's get out of here. Your new house doesn't have a phone yet, does it?"

"No. They're coming out early next week I think."

"Good."

Courtney wondered what that was supposed to mean, but decided against asking. Whether or not Fletcher could call out to Elk Park hardly mattered, since Roger wasn't going to be staying there. But Roger was just a little too drunk, a little too unpredictable right now. And she was suddenly very tired, even though it was barely nine o'clock. All she wanted to do was lie down in her own bed, which she now fervently wished wasn't a half hour's drive away at the new house.

Outside, it took Roger three times to get his key into the lock on the passenger door of the Jaguar. He opened it and gestured grandly for her to get inside.

"I think you'd better let me drive," she told him.

He stiffened, his generous mouth tightening in a stubborn line. "You're not driving my Jag."

"Then let me call someone, get us a ride. You've had too much to drink to be behind the wheel."

Grumbling, he handed her the keys. "All right, all right. You can drive. Just be careful."

"I'll take you to your apartment. Then I'll leave your car at my place while I take the Jeep out to—"

"Absolutely not. I always see my dates to their doorstep. It's a Winthrop policy. My father raised me to be a gentleman."

"And he did a fine job, but—"

"No buts." He looked at her, his green eyes suddenly pleading. "He'll be calling me all night, Courtney. All night. Just let me sleep in one of the guest rooms, okay? I'll be a good boy, I promise.''

He really did look boyishly endearing at that moment. ''All right,'' she said. ''But just for tonight.''

''No problem. Tomorrow I have to head back to Chicago. The king commands.'' They climbed into the car. ''Be careful.''

''The roads . . .''

''Just be careful. It'll be fine.''

A half hour later, Roger was cursing bitterly. No matter how slowly or how carefully Courtney drove, his low-slung car was taking a beating on the dirt road that led to the Hamilton Pine Ridge grounds in Elk Park.

Despite Roger's sour mood, Courtney couldn't help but smile as she approached the new home she and her father would share, at least when he wasn't out of town on business, and she wasn't off to Wellesley for college. Nestled in amongst a two-hundred-year-old stand of lodgepole and spruce, the house looked as though it had been carved out of the landscape itself. And in some places it had.

Both in the front, where a massive porch arced across the front and right side of the four-thousand-square-foot home and in the back where a huge deck opened onto much of the land's twenty acres, trees had been built around and accommodated, appearing to grow up right through the woodwork. In the atrium her father had planned for the center of the house, a half-dozen trees and a tiny rill would serve as their own private wilderness within a much larger one. If she and her father agreed about nothing else, it was their love for this land.

"What the hell is that man doing here?" Roger muttered, interrupting her musings, as they pulled to a stop in front of the house.

Courtney's heart skipped a beat. Of all the workman to still be here.... "There's, uh, still a lot of work to do," she stammered. "It appears that the man is a carpenter and he's...he's working on the porch rail."

"I can see what he's doing, for crying out loud. I meant what is he doing here? Now at nearly ten o'clock at night!"

"Daddy's paying top dollar as always. There's one or two crews here twenty-four hours a day. Daddy wants everything done by summer's end."

"Some crew. He's one guy."

Courtney watched the man straighten and tug a blue bandanna from his hip pocket. Always before, he had worn white T-shirts. Today he was wearing denim. Unbuttoned to the waist. And those blasted jeans clung to the well-defined muscle of his thighs like a second skin. As she watched—or was that stared?— the man wiped away the sweat that dripped from his face, then pocketed the kerchief and returned his attention to his work.

"Courtney?"

She jumped, looking guiltily back at Roger.

"Are you going to spend the night in the car?"

Quickly she climbed out. Together she and Roger headed toward the porch. Before they reached it, Courtney paused. Roger halted beside her. "Maybe this isn't such a good idea," she began.

"What?"

"Your staying here."

Why did it suddenly seem so important that the man on the porch not get the wrong idea about her? And why in heaven's name would it be the wrong idea? Why was she even thinking about what he might be thinking?

"I'm tired, Courtney," Roger said. "And you were right. I have had too much to drink. I should just sack out for a while. I don't think I could negotiate that road in the dark."

The sun had long since dropped below the horizon. And the lingering light, so common in this high altitude, was now beginning to fade. Courtney's shoulders sagged. He was right. She no longer had much choice in the matter. "I'll make up a guest room for you."

Again she started toward the house. She hadn't gone two steps, when Roger suddenly grabbed her by the arm and swung her around to face him. Then he pulled her close, so close, she could smell the liquor on his breath. "Maybe we can do better than that. Maybe it's time."

"What are you talking about?"

"A guest room won't be necessary." He threaded his fingers through her hair. "I think I should spend the night in your room."

Courtney's spirits sagged. "You know better than that, Roger. We've talked about this before. More than once. We agreed to wait. To make a real commitment."

"What more of a commitment do you want? I love you."

Courtney was painfully aware that the workman on the porch had paused in his task. "Can we... can we talk about this in the house?"

"I want to talk about it now. Your father's in Japan. I'm sure I can persuade Mr. Hammer and Nail to hit the road. It's your birthday. I've been planning this night for a long time. If my father hadn't—''

Courtney pulled free. "The guest room, Roger. That's the deal."

"Do you have any idea how hard it is for me to keep my hands off you? I want you, Courtney. I love you. And after what my father's been putting me through..."

"Roger, don't do this."

He laid his hand on her bare shoulder. "Haven't we played out the virgin act long enough? You want it, too. I know you do. That's why you wore this blouse." His hand slipped lower.

Courtney jerked back. "I wore this blouse because I thought you would like it. I... You can't expect me to be some kind of antidote to your father's bawling you out." She didn't dare cast a glance at the porch. She would die of humiliation if she did.

Roger's green eyes glittered. "You make it sound like I'm a naughty little boy."

"I didn't mean it that way. Roger, please, just go inside and lie down. Sleep it off."

"I'll show you how good it can be. Just let me—" He grabbed her arm, his fingers tightening.

"Roger, please!"

"Get your hands off the lady." The man's voice was silky soft, yet somehow lethal. "Or I'll take them off for you." He was standing directly behind her.

"I don't take orders from the hired help," Roger snapped. "And this isn't any of your business, mister."

"Maybe you'd best ask the lady's opinion."

Roger let go of her.

Courtney rubbed at the red marks his grip had left on her arm. There would be a bruise there in the morning. Roger stared at her, looking positively stricken. "My God, Courtney, I didn't mean..." He touched her cheek. "Please forgive me. I had no idea. I'm sorry. Please. I'm so sorry."

Courtney's senses were on overload. She was still in shock. She took a step back only to collide squarely with the bare, sweating chest of the carpenter. She yelped in surprise. Despite her emotional turmoil, it took no more than a heartbeat—a crazy, trip-hammer heartbeat—to realize that studying this man from a distance hadn't done him justice, hadn't done him justice at all. Dark hair covered a magnificent chest. Sweat trickled down that muscled plane to arrow into faded, beltless denim jeans. He'd crooked his thumbs into the waistband of those jeans, so seemingly nonchalant, and yet all Courtney could think of was a panther ready to spring. No, not a panther. A wolf. Just like the one he had tattooed on his left forearm. She had to remind herself to breathe.

"You all right, miss?"

She managed a weak nod.

He took off his safety glasses, and for the first time she could see clearly that his eyes were blue. Montana-sky blue. The most striking blue she had ever seen. Eyes that regarded her with a mingling of sympathy and concern that unfortunately only added to her abject embarrassment.

"You sure you're all right?" he repeated.

"Fine," she said. "Thank you, Mr.—?"

"Jack. Jack Sullivan."

She nodded. "Mr. Sullivan."

"Jack."

"Isn't it past quitting time, Sullivan?" Roger put in testily.

Jack ignored him. He looked at Courtney. "You know, it occurs to me that a lady like you deserves better than this sack of—" he paused "—silk suit."

Roger bristled, but made no move toward Sullivan.

"Please," she said weakly, "I'm fine. Really. Maybe Roger's right. Maybe you'd best go."

He seemed to consider the idea for a long moment, then shrugged. "Whatever you say, ma'am."

She let out a shaky breath. "Thank you."

"You're welcome." He turned to go.

"I, uh, I like your tattoo." She cringed. What a perfectly inane thing to say.

Jack chuckled. "Long story behind that," he said, his lopsided grin heart-stoppingly intimate all at once.

"I'd like to hear it."

"I'd like to tell it."

"Get the hell out of here!" Roger said. "Now."

"It's all right," Courtney said.

Jack paused a heartbeat longer, then headed for his truck.

"I didn't know muscle-bound types appealed to you," Roger muttered peevishly, well before Jack Sullivan would've been out of earshot. "I'll have to start working out more at the gym."

"I don't want to fight anymore, Roger. I..."

"Neither do I, darling," he assured her, his voice softening considerably. "Forgive me?" He caught her hand and pressed her fingers to his lips.

The gesture might once have made her shiver with delight, but now she extricated her hand as quickly as she could manage. "I'm going to bed, Roger. Alone."

"I am sorry, Courtney. Please believe that."

"I do." He was tired. Out of sorts. And a little drunk. She supposed she needed to make allowances. Besides, he really did look miserable. Like a lost puppy. She had to forgive him. After all, she loved him. Didn't she? And she would in all likelihood marry him someday.

Then why, her conscience prodded, had she spent the past several days surreptitiously ogling a carpenter named Jack Sullivan?

A lady like you deserves better...

The man was a stranger. A summer day fantasy. Yes, he'd been kind. Yes, he had incredible blue eyes. But she didn't even know him. He could be married. Have five kids.

She glanced toward his truck to find him watching her. Nothing intrusive, just watching. As though still afraid to leave her in Roger's company. "You do good work, Mr. Sullivan," she called. "Thank you again."

"My pleasure, ma'am. See you in the morning."

Morning. Yes, he would be back, wouldn't he? Her pulses quickened. Surely it wouldn't hurt to see him again.

Wouldn't hurt...

God in heaven, had anything ever hurt more?

As Courtney sat beside the worktable in J.D.'s mountain cabin, she let the tears fall. Nothing like a trip down memory lane to hearten the soul, cheer the mind. God, what a fool she was. What a fool she had been.

Jack Sullivan had indeed been a fantasy, a fantasy that had burned hot and bright, and just that quickly had burned itself out. But not before it had seared her heart to ashes in the process.

How had she ever imagined she could spend a night in Jack Sullivan's bed—then walk away. Forget.

Forget his hands, his mouth, his passion, his need...

"Enough!" She slammed her hand down so hard, it hurt. Enough. Exhausted, drained, Courtney pushed to her feet and took up her fire poker crutch. Hobbling back into the cabin's main room, she made her way to the bed. She'd just about made it, when the door to the cabin slammed open.

"What the hell do you think you're doing?" J.D. boomed.

Courtney gasped, startled. Her ankle rebelled, collapsed. She cried out, felt herself falling. In the space of a heartbeat, he was there, catching her up in his powerful arms.

"You all right?" he asked.

She could smell the musky, male scent of him, see flecks of snow clinging wetly to the ebony waves of his hair.

"I'm fine," she croaked. "Please put me down."

"I intend to."

He eased her into a sitting position on the bed, then started to straighten. He stilled, his gaze sliding past her, his brown eyes hooded, unreadable, but his mouth set stone hard. Courtney twisted her head to follow his gaze, already knowing what she was going to see. From under the corner of her pillow, as clearly visible as a bloodred flag in a snowbank was the hilt of the knife.

Chapter 4

Courtney sat on the bed and trembled. J.D. didn't move, didn't say a word. He just stood there, staring at the knife. Courtney bit her lip, heart pounding. What was he thinking? What was he going to do? She wished she could see his eyes. But they remained hooded, unreadable.

Did he think she'd hidden the knife to use as a weapon against him? "I can explain," she offered nervously.

J.D. straightened. "It's okay," he said. "I would've done the same thing."

"What?"

"If I were you, I'd have made damned sure I found a weapon."

"You...you aren't angry?"

"On the contrary, I admire a resourceful woman."

She studied his face—what she could see of it through all that hair—and decided she believed him.

She felt oddly warmed by the compliment. "Thank you. I think."

To her surprise he grinned. Courtney's heart turned over for just a second there— No. She was being absurd again. Perhaps she'd suffered more of a head injury in the crash than she'd realized. But when J.D. had smiled like that, she could have sworn... She took a long, slow breath. An afternoon of old and bitter memories, that's all it was.

As for J.D.... He seemed to catch himself and the smile vanished. He turned away from her, first replacing his rifle in the stocks above the mantel, then shrugging out of his sheepskin jacket. During both tasks Courtney noted that he still favored his left arm. She considered making another offer to tend it for him, but decided they had other things to settle first. Like where he'd been for nearly six hours. She was about to ask when he tugged a second weapon from the waistband of his jeans.

"Where did you get that?"

He laid the .38 on the table near the window. "It belonged to one of your friends."

"My fr—?" Her lips thinned, as she realized he meant the kidnappers. He must regret that smile more than she'd thought. "You buried them then?"

"As best as I could manage."

Courtney shivered. "That must've been awful for you."

He shot her a curious glance, but said nothing. Instead, he crossed to the cupboards on the opposite wall and began pulling out various foodstuffs, among them cans of kidney beans, tomato paste, sauce, even a bag of raw onions. He spread out his booty beneath the cupboards on what passed for a countertop. "You hungry?" he asked.

"Starving," she admitted.

He stalked toward the ancient wood-burning stove several feet to the left of the cupboards in the room's far corner. "I'll see what I can do about fixing us something to eat."

"I'd appreciate that." The brief connection she had felt with this man was gone or, more precisely, walled off by J.D. himself. Sighing, Courtney eased her swollen ankle into an elevated position on the bed, then settled back to watch her mysterious roommate move about their cramped quarters. Now that the initial shock of her kidnapping was wearing off, she found herself becoming more and more curious about this man. Sizing people up had long since become an occupational hazard. Her early assessment? Isolated wasn't just how he lived. It was who he was. Or what he had become.

"J.D.?"

He flicked a match into the wood-burning stove, then looked up at her, his expression strangely wary. "Yeah?"

"I, uh, I didn't put the knife under the pillow specifically with you in mind. I put it there because you said that the kidnappers could have accomplices roaming about. I just wanted you to know that...that it wasn't anything personal."

He snorted. "I'm touched."

Courtney folded her arms in front of her. "You don't have to be sarcastic about it."

"Actually, Miss Hamilton," he drawled, "I'm just trying to get a mental picture of you engaging in hand-to-hand combat with armed thugs."

"You'd be surprised," she said testily.

He cocked an eyebrow at her. "I probably would at that."

"I thought you admired resourceful women."

"Resourceful, yes. Nuts? That's another story."

She slapped a hand against the bed. "Maybe I wouldn't have had to hobble about this shack in search of weaponry if you'd been back in an hour or two as you'd promised."

"Missed me, huh?"

"I most certainly did not!" The man was insufferable. "I think I'm at least entitled to an explanation, don't you?"

"Not much to explain. I never tried to bury anybody before. Especially in frozen ground."

The stark simplicity of his words hit her harder than she would've predicted. After all, she knew why he'd gone out. But up until this moment she hadn't realized how much she'd been thinking of her kidnappers in the abstract, not as once-living, -breathing human beings, who might have had mothers who loved them. The whole kidnapping—but for this cabin and this bearded stranger—still seemed almost surreal, more hallucination than fact. "It's strange, isn't it?" she mused aloud. "Those two men died virtually sitting next to me. And I don't even know what they looked like."

J.D. tossed a chunk of wood into the stove. "They looked dead."

She winced.

"Sorry." He began opening various cans and dumping their contents into a pot he'd put on the stovetop. To it he added several chunks of dried meat. Courtney decided against inquiring about their species of origin. His concoctions now simmering, J.D. turned his attention to two raw onions and a clove of garlic. He picked up a paring knife and began chopping away, all the while keeping his back to Courtney.

She took his body language for what it was—a deliberate attempt to shut her out. But after hours of anxious waiting, she wasn't about to be denied the distraction of a conversation—even one with her inscrutable host. "Can I ask you a question?"

"You can ask," he said, his tone implying that that didn't mean he was going to answer.

"Do you think those men...?" She bit her lip. "Do you think they suffered?"

He snorted incredulously. "I hope to God they did."

"Don't say that!"

He turned to stare at her. "You mean that, don't you?"

"Of course. Why wouldn't I?"

"Why?" He snatched a towel from a peg on the wall to wipe his hands, then stepped toward the bed. "I can't think of too many people who'd give a damn if men like that died horrible deaths. I doubt their plans for you were anywhere near as benevolent."

"Maybe not," she allowed. "But that doesn't mean I want them dying in agony."

J.D. shook his head, clearly puzzled by her attitude. "No, I don't think they suffered," he said at last. "The one in the rear seat was thrown clear of the wreckage. His neck was broken. The pilot..." J.D. crossed to the hearth, hunkering down to add another log to the fire. "The pilot was still strapped in his seat. Internal injuries I suppose."

"I see." Courtney toyed with the charm at her throat. "It's all so strange, isn't it?"

J.D. jabbed at the blazing logs with the poker. "What's that?"

"Fate."

"How do you mean?"

"That both of those men should die, yet my injuries should be relatively minor. I guess my number wasn't up."

He angled a glance at her. "You a big believer in fate, Miss Hamilton?"

She didn't miss the curious undercurrent in his voice. "As a matter of fact, I am," she said. "I think things happen for a reason."

J.D. blew out a disgusted breath and rose to face her. "Don't tell me. There's some mysterious cosmic purpose behind your being kidnapped, right?"

"That isn't what I meant," she said slowly, annoyed at his mocking attitude. "But I don't think it hurts to be open-minded. Who's to say? Maybe there is a reason for me to be in this particular place at this particular time." If he could needle her, she could needle him right back. "Maybe it's both of our karmas, J.D. Maybe every bit of this has played out just to bring you and me together. What would you think about that?"

At the very least she expected a bark of laughter or a derisive curse. She got neither. Instead, for just an instant, she could have sworn his eyes looked haunted. And maybe just a little unnerved. Then he seemed to collect himself. "I'll tell you what I think, Miss Hamilton," he said, leaning the poker against the hearth. "I think the cosmic purpose behind your kidnapping is dollar signs. A whole galaxyload of dollar signs."

"I thought money was the motive myself at first," she conceded. "But now I'm not so sure. I can't seem to shake the feeling that if those men hadn't died, I'd be the one in a shallow grave somewhere."

J.D. stiffened ever so slightly. "That doesn't even make sense. They could hardly ransom a dead hostage."

"It's just that I keep remembering what one of them said—the one with the gun."

J.D. strode back to the stove and shifted the onions around in the skillet, then spooned them into the pot that held the other ingredients. To the casual eye he might have seemed unperturbed, almost disinterested. But Courtney wasn't watching him with a casual eye. She had seen him stiffen when she'd said she felt the kidnappers meant to kill her. What struck her about his reaction wasn't so much that he'd had it, but that he had tried so hard to conceal it. As though he didn't want her to know. Why should it matter to him that he show a little feeling at the notion that she might have been murdered?

"Don't you want to know what the man said?" she prodded, when he didn't ask.

He shrugged. "Does it matter? He's dead."

"Aren't you the one who told me to remember everything I could about the kidnapping? That it might help the police later?"

He turned slightly. "Okay. What did he say?"

"He said . . ." Courtney shivered. She'd been determined to deliver the man's threat matter-of-factly. Instead, she remembered too well the man's vile tone. "He said that I didn't know the half of what the boss had in mind for me."

The knuckles on J.D.'s hands went chalk white, but his voice betrayed no particular emotion. "He was probably just trying to scare you."

"He succeeded."

J.D.'s control slipped a notch. "The son of a bitch can be glad he's dead," he said softly, too softly.

Against her will, Courtney's mind flashed back to another time, another place—another silken threat. *Get your hands off the lady. Or I'll take them off for you.* She went very still.

Abruptly J.D. turned back to the stove.

Courtney stared at him, tried hard to stare through him. This was insane. She really was losing her mind. What other explanation could there be as to why this long-haired, brown-eyed stranger continued to rouse memories of Jack? "Can I...?" Her heart hammered and she stopped. *Can I what? Can I look under the bandage on your left arm? Can I see if just by chance there might be a certain tattoo there that would finish off what's left of my sanity?* She coughed, choked, cleared her throat. "Can I help you with any of that?"

She expected a dismissive no. Anything to maintain the illusion of distance between them. Instead, J.D. scooped up a half-dozen brown-skinned potatoes and brought them over to her. He spread a clean towel over the coverlet and offered her a peeler. "Have a ball."

Courtney accepted the utensil, her fingers brushing ever so lightly against J.D.'s. She prayed he didn't notice just how badly she was trembling. The bandage on his arm was just inches away. Ragged, bloody. It wouldn't take much effort at all to yank it free. She snatched up a potato. "You're bleeding again," she said.

"I'll live."

"You must have a first aid kit. At least let me change the bandage."

"Not necessary."

Why? she longed to ask, but the word wouldn't come.

Dammit. She slashed at the potato. *Why was she persisting in this madness?* The man had already assured her time and again that the wound wasn't serious. It was her own overactive imagination that was making too much of all this. And as for her memories of Jack . . . They were just some kind of traumatic regression brought on by the helicopter crash. If the truth be told, she wasn't all that sorry that he had been the last thing on her mind when she thought she was going to die. Their night together really had been magic.

Until . . .

"Damnation!" She jabbed the potato peeler into her thumb. Muttering more curses, she stuck the injured digit into her mouth.

"I prefer bloodless spuds," Jack said blandly.

She scowled at him, thinking diabolical thoughts about what else she might do with her trusty peeler. He chuckled, as if reading her mind. Courtney went back to mangling potatoes.

"It'll be a while for the chili," J.D. said. "If you're hungry, I can rustle you up another can of fruit or something."

"Please."

J.D.'s movements, despite his mountain man appearance, were deceptively smooth, effortless, as he strode about the cabin. Jack, too, had walked with the grace of a jungle cat. J.D.'s thighs, outlined in his well-worn jeans, were tight, well muscled, just as Jack's had been. His hands ...

Stop it! These mental gymnastics were getting her nowhere. What kind of odds was she talking about anyway? Odds that she should be kidnapped and crash-land on the exact side of the exact mountain where Jack Sullivan had conveniently taken up residence as a hermit.

Things happen for a reason.

Reasonable things, she argued inwardly. Not crazy things.

But what if it wasn't a coincidence? What if ... ?

J.D handed her a bowl of apricots and a fork. "Are you okay?" The man actually looked concerned.

"Just thinking too much."

She expected him to scurry back to his stove. Instead, he lingered at the foot of the bed. "I know all this has been rough on you. I'm sorry."

"You say that like it's your fault."

"I'm just sorry, okay," he said, gruffly this time.

"Okay. Thank you."

"And don't thank me."

Courtney blew out an exasperated breath. "You are the most infuriating man. Do you know that? First you're nice, then you're nasty, then you're nice, then you're ..." She stabbed an apricot with her fork. "Well, I'm afraid you'll just have to forgive me. I was raised to be polite. I can't help it. Unlike you, who were no doubt raised by—" She held up a hand. "No, erase that. I can't insult wolves. Which reminds me ..." Her voice softened and she smiled. "Your carvings are magnificent."

J.D.'s jaw went bowstring tight. "Made yourself right at home didn't you?"

"I looked around a bit," she acknowledged. "But only after you hadn't bothered to show that hairy face of yours for six hours. For all I knew, you weren't planning to come back at all."

"You thought I'd desert you?" Now he looked offended.

"You're the one who said you didn't like company."

She had him there. And he knew it. He scowled. "I didn't mean to scare you."

"If you don't intend to scare me, why do you insist on roaming about looking like an escapee from *A Nightmare on Elm Street?*"

His mouth quirked. "You don't care for this look?"

"It's perfect, if you're trying out for the cover of *Wolfman Quarterly.*"

He swore. "And you call me infuriating? If you aren't the mouthiest little—"

"Don't you say that! Don't you dare call me that again! Or I'll come up with a few choice names for you."

Muttering furiously, J.D. snatched up Courtney's towel full of potatoes and peelings and marched back over to the counter, where he slammed them down in a heap. "I don't know when you got that mouth, but..." He stopped. Cold.

"What did you say?"

He sucked in a deep breath. "I, uh." He stammered slightly. "I was just wondering if you've had that acid tongue all of your life, or if it's a recent acquisition."

"It's fairly recent," she admitted, frowning. Something about what he'd said the first time had almost made it seem as though he were making a comparison, as if he'd known— No! No! She'd been down that road once too often already today. "I happen to like my mouth," she went on, unwilling to dwell on any new suspicions. "So I suggest you get used to it. Especially if that storm out there is as bad as it looks. I may be stuck here longer than a blasted day or two."

J.D. glanced out the window and cursed. A sea of swirling white obscured even the closest trees. "I've seen late blizzards like this. We could get two feet or twelve this high in the mountains."

"I hope you're making plenty of chili," she grumbled.

He raked his fingers through his long dark hair. "Okay, enough," he said. "What would you say to a truce?"

"I'd say, if we divide the cabin in half, I get the fire."

"Good. Then I get the food."

She made a face. "I want a new truce. If you stop being a jerk, I'll stop being a—" she cleared her throat "—a you-know-what."

"Deal."

"One more term? For our peaceful coexistence?"

"What's that?"

"A shave and a haircut."

"That's two things."

"Please? Can't you at least tidy up that rat's nest on your head? Good grooming is next to godliness, you know."

"I think I look just fine."

"Which explains the complete absence of mirrors in this place," she muttered.

J.D. laughed, a genuine howl of amusement. "All right, Miss Hamilton. You win. A compromise it is."

Marching over to his chest of drawers, he came up with a wide-toothed comb. "I'll do the hair. The beard stays."

Courtney would take her victories where she could.

J.D. raised the comb and immediately sucked in a painful breath. "I'm afraid my make over will have to wait." He hoisted his injured arm. "Did I mention that I'm left-handed?"

Courtney's heart skipped a beat. Jack was left-handed. "Bring me the comb."

J.D. trod over to her.

Courtney got up on her knees and pointed to the edge of bed in front of her. "Sit."

He gave her a baleful look, but he sat.

For long seconds Courtney stared at his back, the wide shoulders, the tumbled waves of dark hair. Why didn't she just know one way or the other? To cover how awkward she felt, she sidled up behind him and peered at the top of his head. "If anything moves," she deadpanned, "I'm out of here."

She could've sworn he growled.

Slowly Courtney began to work the comb through his long, tangled locks, surprised to find the hair soft, almost silken to the touch. She quickly found herself warming to the task, taking an unexpected pleasure in it. There was something about the whole setting—the primitive cabin, the simmering chili, the crackling fire, and outdoors, the swirling snowstorm. It was as if she and this man were the last two people on earth. And here she was, some kind of Eve to his Adam, combing her man's hair before the hearth.

"You've got a nice touch." J.D.'s voice was low, husky.

"Thank you." Courtney gave herself a mental shake. Instead of thinking about Adam and Eve, she needed to be thinking about kidnappers and getting home. "There," she pronounced, tossing the comb on the bed beside her. Tangle-free, J.D.'s hair spilled down to his shoulders in burnished mahogany waves. "How does that feel?"

J.D. cleared his throat. "Fine."

"Good." Courtney went for the scissors she'd earlier spotted in a drawer. "Now for that godawful beard."

"No."

"Please?"

"No."

"A trim then? Just a foot or two?"

He snorted, but rolled his eyes in what she took to be acquiescence.

"You'll need to move a bit," she told him.

Shifting clumsily, J.D. managed to position himself cross-legged in front of her, while still being mindful of Courtney's injured ankle. She raised her right thumb in front of his face and eyed him critically, as though to judge the scale of the monumental job before her.

"I hope you're a realist and not an Impressionist," he drawled.

"You don't want a Picasso nose?" she said, giggling. "One here." She touched his left cheek. "And maybe one here." She indicated the perfect spot above his right eyebrow.

J.D.'s mouth twitched.

"None of that," she said. "Or I will cut something off by accident. Now hold still."

Carefully, methodically, Courtney set to work. She snipped and clipped and did her damnedest to ignore the very real feel of J.D.'s hot breath against her fingertips. Ignore his very generous lips. Ignore... Dear Lord, what was the matter with her? The man was a Neanderthal. Trim or no trim.

But J.D., too, seemed to sense a shift in their level of awareness. She had the distinct feeling that if he could come up with the right excuse, he'd end their barber school session in a heartbeat.

As if to confirm her suspicions, he asked impatiently, "Are you going to be much longer?"

"Done."

"Thank God."

"Except for one more tiny thing." Courtney scrambled out of bed and, hopping on her good leg, made her way over to her canvas tote bag. Rummaging through it, she found what she was looking for and hopped back to the bed.

"What do you intend to do with that?"

Courtney grinned impishly, then clambered up behind her. She took the black silk ribbon and gathered J.D.'s long hair into a queue. "Now you look like a true eighteenth-century rogue, sir."

"Complete with flannel shirt and jeans?"

"Okay, okay, from the neck up. In fact, if pushed, I could say you almost qualify as—dare I say it?—handsome."

"Almost?"

"Well, I wouldn't want that head to swell any more than it already is."

Their gazes locked. "Maybe you're right," she whispered. "Maybe I should drop that 'almost.'"

He wanted to kiss her. She knew it. In her vitals, she knew it. More than that, she wanted to kiss him back. Absurd, ridiculous. Some sort of isolation-induced lunacy. The kidnapping, the crash, this man, this storm.

Without thinking, she reached out to trail her fingers across a tiny, whitened scar near his left temple. "Don't tell me," she breathed, desperate to lighten the tension between them. "A mountain lion, right?"

"A fight over a woman."

The tension escalated. "What became of her?"

"I lost her. A long time ago."

"Did you love her very much?"

"I don't know. I never gave us a chance to find out."

"Why?"

"Because I was a fool, Miss Hamilton. A pride-bound son of a bitch who didn't know any better."

"And now?"

"Now I'm just a fool. A damned fool for ever letting you talk me into this." J.D. shot to his feet. "We're going to need more firewood. It's going to be a long, cold night." With that, he grabbed his coat and stalked out into the storm.

Outside, the snow continued to come down hard. Icy flakes stung Jack's sweat-dampened forehead. He welcomed them, turned his face into the wind for more. He wanted the cold, needed it to ease the heat that fired his blood.

Why in God's name had he let Courtney touch him? He was risking everything, everything he'd worked so hard for these past months. All because of his blasted hormones.

He needed to stay focused on Pete. He owed it to him, owed it to the memory of his murdered friend.

But, God, he wanted Courtney, wanted her so badly, it was driving him mad. Wanted to touch her, taste her, make fever-mad love to her in front of the hearth.

And he could have her. He knew it. Felt it.

But only as J.D.

She liked J.D. Was drawn to him, in spite of herself. Maybe spurred on by fear, her current dependence, or just plain loneliness. Maybe even because she sensed the wounded soul in him.

But if she knew for a minute that wounded soul belonged to Jack Sullivan, he'd have been wrestling her for that knife under her pillow.

Jack swore viciously. How had it come to this? He should have leveled with her from the first. Told her who he was, then fabricated some lie to explain his reappearance in her life. Now it was too late. Now, even if he could tell her the truth, she would never believe him.

Now, no matter what happened, Courtney would be hurt.

Again.

By him.

More than once tonight it had been all he could do not to spill his guts. To just tell her. And hope...

Hope what?

That she wouldn't hate him? God, he hated himself.

With a disgusted sigh Jack turned and slogged his way into the cabin.

"You forgot the firewood."

He slapped at the snow that still clung to him and tried hard to keep his eyes off of her. He failed. She was sitting up in his bed, her blond hair tumbled about her shoulders like a halo of sunshine, and he wanted to die. Wanted to die rather than do what he was about to do. Wanted to die rather than see her hate him.

Tell her. Just tell her. Get it over with. "You'd best get some sleep, Miss Hamilton. It's been a long day for both of us." He tossed his sleeping bag on the floor in front of the fire. Tell her.

He lay down, muttering a curse when he accidentally jarred his bad arm against the floor.

Courtney leaned down from the bed. "I can't sleep knowing that arm needs attention."

He got up, found her some bandages, some antiseptic. This would do it. This would do the job for him. He sat down on the bed and held out his left arm. "It's all yours, Courtney."

Her head jerked up, and he realized his mistake. Mistake or deliberate slip. Courtney. He hadn't called her that here. Not once. Always Miss Hamilton. She'd noticed.

Without a word she reached for the bandage on his arm. Her hands were trembling. He made no move to stop her.

Courtney tugged free the soiled cloth. For a long, tortured minute she stared at his arm, unmoving. Everything in him wanted to look at her face, to know what she was thinking. But he couldn't summon the will to look.

Because some part of him already knew.

Then came the agonized rasp that sealed his fate.

"Jack."

Chapter 5

"**Y**ou bastard." Courtney stared at Jack, willing him to look at her, but he did not. "You lying snake son of a bitch." She shook her head, her senses reeling, her mind for the moment at least filled more with shock than anger.

Jack Sullivan.

It couldn't be, couldn't be. But it was. The reality slammed into her even as her brain refused to accept the truth offered up by her own eyes. Juxtaposed against a five-inch gash of J.D.'s left forearm was the full body tattoo of a timber wolf.

J.D. was Jack Sullivan.

"I can explain...."

"Explain?" She gaped at him. "Explain twenty-four hours of dissembling and deceit?" Her anger nudged a notch higher. "Did you enjoy your sick little game, Jack? Did you have a good laugh at my expense?"

"That wasn't—"

"I don't want to hear it!" Anger charged ahead of shock. "How dare you? How dare you play out some sick joke with me? Do you have any idea what it was like for me this morning to wake up in this bed with the missing link bending over me?

"You knew damned well who *I* was. Your excavation into my purse told you that, even if your memory didn't. But did I hear any words at all like 'Take it easy, Courtney. It's okay. It's me, Jack Sullivan. I know I look like a serial killer, but it's just me. Not someone who might be contemplating eating your liver for breakfast!' Oh, no, not a word. In fact, what I did hear was 'You're not leaving, Miss Hamilton.' 'I've got bodies to bury, Miss Hamilton.' Dammit, how could you?"

"I'll tell you, if you just—"

"No, I won't 'just,'" she hissed. "Because then we go on to act two. The hair, the beard and the tinted contacts. I know we didn't exactly part friends, but I think I deserve better than that, don't you?" Her voice rose. "Don't you?"

Silence.

"Well?"

"You through?"

"Not by a long shot. But you go right ahead."

His lips compressed in a grim line. "I didn't tell you because I wasn't all that sure you remembered me."

Courtney let out a humorless laugh. "You can do better than that, Sullivan. For one thing, you've got me mixed-up with yourself. You're the one who doesn't remember names and faces, most especially, I'm sure, when it comes to the women who've shared your bed."

A muscle in his jaw tightened. "Another reason I didn't tell you," he said, "is that when you didn't recognize me, I figured I could probably get you down the mountain and home without your ever knowing, and maybe you'd even appreciate missing out on an encounter with a ghost from your past."

"Oh, it was all for my sake then," she said, her voice dripping sarcasm. "I'm so sorry. How could I have forgotten? My feelings were certainly your primary consideration the last time we were together."

"I never knew that night was such a watershed moment in your life."

More than you'll ever know, she thought bitterly. But said, "Don't flatter yourself. My only point is that I've been through quite enough lately, thank you. My father's heart attack, a kidnapping at gunpoint, a helicopter crash. It might have been nice if you had at least been a neutral face, rather than an enemy."

"I'm not your enemy, Courtney."

"No?" Very deliberately she retrieved the knife from under her pillow.

She watched Jack's eyes widen, though they revealed no particular emotion.

"Let me spell it out for you," she said. "I was in a helicopter with two kidnappers. In flight they announce that they're heading for a cabin. And that a mysterious boss has plans for me. The copter then crashes near a cabin, where you—a man with a link to my past and an attitude toward my father—just happen to be living. I know it's quite a leap—but you know what occurs to me, Jack? That you could be that boss. And that because we have a history—however brief and sordid it might have been—you needed a contingency plan. You know, in case my blindfold slipped. So you arranged to look like an ape.''

"I prefer Neanderthal."

"The tinted contacts, Jack. They're what make the deception premeditated, deliberate."

"Why in God's name would I kidnap you?"

"You announced the motive yourself, remember? Money. A whole galaxyload of money."

He swore and began to pace. "I did not kidnap you."

"Then why the masquerade? Oh, I know—you're on the lam from an irate husband. Or more likely an irate girlfriend. Or six. Or twelve."

"I've got reasons for the way I look. And they've got nothing to do with your kidnapping. You can believe that or not. Right now, I don't much care. I've been in this cabin for eight months. If you'd just shut the hell up and listen—"

"No! I've had quite enough of your lies. At least for today." She slapped her pillow. "I'm going to sleep. I'm exhausted."

"Tell me about it," he muttered, tromping over to the stove. He grabbed the handle of the chili pot, then released it with a savage curse, shaking his fingers.

"Hot?" she asked with feigned innocence.

He glowered at her.

She noted with a flush of guilt that the gash on his arm was still oozing blood, but she did not renew her offer to tend to the injury.

"You want some chili?" he asked grudgingly.

"No."

"Fine." He ladled out a bowlful, then set it aside and headed for his workroom. He returned with a can of beer. "Want one?"

"No." She pulled the covers up to her neck and tried to shut out the world. That's when it hit her. "Oh, God!" she cried, flinging the covers back and sitting bolt upright.

"Now what?"

She gripped both sides of her buttoned shirtfront. "I was naked. I was stark naked in this bed when I woke up." Her face burned with a humiliation so fierce, she thought she might die of it. "Spare me my modesty. Isn't that what you said, Jack?" Her voice trembled, in spite of her best efforts to control it. "Did you cop a good feel, Jack?"

He went rigidly still. "Think what you like about me, Courtney," he said. "About a lot of things. But not that. I undressed you to save your life. Period."

Some of the tension drained out of her. She believed him. "Thank you for that," she said simply. "But don't expect any thanks for anything else. I'm not the same little girl you bedded ten years ago."

"Obviously."

"You don't approve?"

"I wasn't aware my approval mattered," he drawled.

"It doesn't!" she snapped. "Did you change the sheets before the next occupant that night?"

He took a swig of his beer and shot her a deliberately lascivious look. "I find it very interesting that you keep getting back to that night, Courtney. I must have been good."

She slapped the mattress. "You're a pig!"

He grinned roguishly. "I must have been damned good."

"If your male ego inflates by so much as one more molecule, you're going to blow out the windows of this cabin."

He set the beer down. "You were good, too," he said softly.

"Stop it!"

"You know," Jack mused, "maybe you were right. Maybe I should have let on sooner who I was. We could have renewed old acquaintances."

Courtney cast a glance heavenward. "I finally figured it out. I thought I survived that helicopter crash. But it turns out I was mistaken. I died after all. I died—and went straight to hell!"

He chuckled. "With that storm keeping us cooped up, this could get real interesting. If the fire goes out, we've got whole new ways to keep each other warm."

"Don't even think about it. I've got the knife, remember?"

Now he laughed out loud. "You won't need it," he assured her. "If I come to your bed, Courtney, it will be because you want me there."

"In your dreams."

"No, in yours, Courtney," he said softly. "In yours."

"You asked if I thought you were good that night? The truth? You didn't even come close. If you were good, I'd remember. I don't."

"Liar."

He stood up and walked toward the bed, moving as ever like a jungle cat. "You remember, and so do I."

Courtney didn't move, didn't say a word. Her throat felt suddenly dry, parched. He drew closer. That's when she noticed his eyes. They were no longer brown. Sometime in the last few minutes he'd taken out the tinted contacts. Her heart skipped a beat. Heavy shadows danced about the room in the dull orange glow of the hearth. But she didn't need the flames to see, because Jack's eyes now seared her with blue fire.

He was going to kiss her. Worse, she was going to let him.

He put one knee on the bed and drew her to him, gathered her up in a bone-melting embrace.

"It's been too long, Courtney," he whispered, "too damned long." His lips came down on hers—hungry, wanton, ruthless.

Her head pounded, her pulses thrummed, everything in her screaming at her to stop him. Everything but the molten heat now coursing through her veins. She'd tried to convince herself that she'd forgotten, but it was no use. Her body remembered, her body remembered all too well. She began to kiss him back.

And just that abruptly, he stopped.

Bewildered, Courtney opened her eyes to see Jack standing beside the bed, those blue eyes for just an instant unguarded—brimming with passion and regret. And then the wall came slamming down. And she saw all too clearly that it had been just another game.

"Forget *that*," he mocked, striding over to the sleeping bag he'd laid out in front of the hearth.

Forget that. Her heart ached within her breast.

Forget she'd ever met him. Forget they'd ever made love.

Forget . . .

Courtney sat in her Jeep Cherokee in front of Jack Sullivan's house, the engine still running, her heart pounding. *You can still make a clean getaway,* she told herself. *Sullivan need never know how close you've come to making an absolute fool of yourself.*

She switched off the engine.

She couldn't leave. She owed him. Not just for what he'd done for her at the house in Elk Park last week. But for an even more compelling reason. A reason she'd only just found out about this morning.

Courtney sagged back in the driver's seat, recalling with distressing clarity her early-morning phone call from Roger. "Hi, sweetheart," Roger had enthused cheerfully when she'd first picked up the receiver. "I miss you."

"You must be psychic," Courtney said, laughing. It had been nearly a week since her birthday and she was genuinely pleased to hear from him. "The phone installer just left. You're my first call. How are things in Chicago?"

His voice changed. "Don't ask. Father was here yesterday pointing out all the mistakes I've made."

Courtney clucked sympathetically.

"But I didn't call to talk about dad. I really have missed you, Courtney. And I've been thinking. We need to set a date. What do you say?"

Courtney couldn't seem to find her voice. Two weeks ago her heart would have leapt with joy at the thought of marrying Roger. Now? Now the unsettling image that sprang to her mind had tousled dark hair, cerulean blue eyes and the tattoo of a timber wolf on his left forearm.

And yet the last thing she wanted to do was hurt Roger's feelings. She did still love him, didn't she?

"Courtney?" Roger pressed.

"I'm sorry, I..." She glanced out the window. "I was just distracted by some of the hammering going on outside."

"I hope all of those construction types are keeping their hands to themselves." His voice was teasing, but there was an edge to it, as well.

"They're just doing their jobs, Roger."

"At least I got rid of the worst of those muscle-bound jerks."

Courtney felt a sudden chill. "What?"

"That Sullivan character hasn't been around, has he?"

"How did you know that?" Courtney had been surprised and disappointed when Jack Sullivan hadn't returned to work, but a few discreet inquiries among the crew had given her the impression that he'd gotten a better job offer. Part of her had even been relieved. For a practically engaged woman, she'd found Sullivan much too intriguing for her own good. "Roger, what have you done?"

"I had him fired."

"You what?"

"He'll have to move to Alaska to find work."

"Roger, how could you—?"

An intercom buzzer on Roger's end of the line sounded. "Sorry, sweetheart, I've got to run. We'll talk later about setting that date, okay?"

"But, Roger—"

"Love you, Bye!"

Courtney stared at the receiver, disbelieving. Roger had had a man fired. Fired for what amounted to doing her a kindness. She slumped into a nearby chair. Butte's current unemployment rate was out of sight. Even with his obvious skills, it was doubtful Jack

Sullivan had found another job already. No matter what his former co-workers had been led to believe. Especially considering Roger's threat that the man would never find work again this side of Alaska.

Dammit. Roger had no right. She had to talk to him again. Get him to reconsider. She reached for the phone.

It rang. Quickly Courtney snatched it up.

"Roger, thank God you called back. Listen, about Mr. Sullivan. You've got to—"

A voice on the other end of the line interrupted. "Whoa! It isn't Roger, dear...."

"Daddy! I'm sorry. I thought—"

"Ah, young lovers. So eager to hear each other's voices."

"I was just talking to Roger," she said. "He had to get off the phone. But I need to call him back."

"This will only take a second. I wanted to let you know I'll be in Tokyo an extra week."

So what else is new? she thought peevishly, but said, "Daddy, I need your help." She could envision him with one foot already out the nearest door, his quicksilver mind teeming with details of his next multimillion-dollar deal. But one phone call from Quentin Hamilton could straighten out any "misunderstanding" Roger may have caused with Sullivan's employer.

"I guess I can spare a minute."

To Quentin Hamilton, a minute meant precisely sixty seconds. Courtney rushed her words. "There was a man at the new house last week. He was part of the construction crew. Roger had him—"

"You don't have to say another word," Quentin cut in. "Jack Sullivan. Roger told me all about him."

"Told you?" Courtney's heart sank. Roger couldn't possibly have told her father the truth, not and made Jack Sullivan come out as any kind of villain.

"Sullivan's a hothead," Quentin went on. "I've had dealings with him in the past. His father once worked for me. I hired him on the house as a favor to his mother. And the young bastard repays me by making a vulgar pass at my daughter."

"But, Daddy, that's not—"

"I've got people waiting, dear. Oh, but by the way, congratulations to you and Roger. I'm delighted. I'd have to be. I'm about to welcome the world's greatest son-in-law to the family."

The connection ended. Courtney sat there hurting, heartsick, feeling an uncharacteristic surge of outrage—both on her own behalf and on Sullivan's. She couldn't set things right about her engagement. Not right now anyway. But she could certainly do her best to set things right with Sullivan.

Grabbing up the phone book, she flipped to the *S*'s and groaned aloud to find over a hundred listings under the surname Sullivan, many with the first name John or Jack. Truth to tell, the man might not even have a listed number. Or he could be sharing a place with someone else.

A woman? She swallowed. A wife? And five kids?

Well, if the man did have a family, she reasoned virtuously, it would only serve to intensify her obligation to him. An entire household could be without an income right now because of Roger's vindictiveness.

Courtney started dialing Sullivans. Ten calls and a busy signal later, she realized she'd best come up with some kind of story, rather than just presenting herself as some anonymous woman looking for a man named Jack Sullivan. She didn't dare use her real name. Her father might miss her school plays, her birthdays, her graduation, but he could detect the slightest whiff of scandal to the Hamilton name from half a world away in three seconds flat. The wary tenor of the voices on the other end of the phone suggested they weren't interested in being party to any tale carrying, either. Thus far she'd been suspected of being either an irate bill collector or a jilted lover.

The latter made her smile. Not the jilted part. But the thought of having been Jack Sullivan's lover.

And then she blushed. From the top of her head to the bottom of her toes every square inch of her turned beet red. So much for her altruistic motives.

She punched up another number. And another. On the thirty-second call she found the Holy Grail. A cousin.

Courtney assured Cal Sullivan she was an old friend of Jack's from his high school days, praying all along that Sullivan had indeed attended Butte schools. "I kind of had a crush on him," she admitted shyly. "I know it's not my business, but I was wondering if, well, if he still lived around here, if he'd ever gotten married, that kind of thing."

"Jack?" Cal snorted. "That'd be the day some female ties that boy down."

Courtney ignored the rush of relief she felt. "Do you know where I can find him? I'd love to just say hi."

Cal chortled. "I'd sure like to find out what that boy's got, then bottle it. You ladies always did flit around him like bees on a honey pot."

The blush was back. "Please, Mr. Sullivan, if you could just—"

"I'm pretty sure Jack's up to Helena today. Lookin' for work. My wife talked to his mother earlier in the week. Said Jack had some kind of trouble on his last job."

Courtney winced.

"He should be back tonight, though. He's stayin' at his mom's place in Walkerville. Had to give up his apartment."

Dear Lord. The man was already in dire financial straits.

Courtney thanked Cal, but before she hung up she couldn't resist asking, "Has he...has Jack...changed much since high school?"

"Not so's you'd notice. He'd still give you the shirt off his back in a blizzard. And he's still got a good-size chip on his shoulder, if you know what I mean."

"Chip?"

"Someday that pride of his is going to swallow him whole. You tell him I said so."

"I'll do that," Courtney said, knowing she never would. She thanked Cal again and signed off. She needed to go to Jack's now, if she was going to go at all.

Before it got dark—was the lie she preferred.

Before she chickened out—was the truth she acknowledged.

She took time only to change her clothes, selecting a pair of khaki slacks and a deep purple silk blouse. She'd been told purple accented the green of her eyes. Not that Jack Sullivan was supposed to notice the green of her eyes.

As she drove down the rutted road toward the entrance to the Hamilton property, she heard thunder rumbling in the west. It would rain soon. The roiling clouds mirrored her mood.

Three times on the twenty-minute drive to Walkerville, Courtney almost turned around and went home. Her palms sweated on the steering wheel, and her heart thudded painfully against her ribs. Was she out of her mind? Going to the home of an all-but-complete stranger? A man now out of a job in large measure because of her. What would his reaction be to finding her on his doorstep? And what in the world was she going to say to him?

It's time you found out, she told herself, opening the door of the Jeep. She'd stalled long enough. Walking around the vehicle, Courtney studied the smallish two-story white frame house in front of her. On the mailbox was the stenciled name M. Sullivan. Jack's mother? The house was of a similar type to many other homes along the street. Built cheek by jowl at the turn of the century during Butte's biggest boom period, the houses had a strangely impermanent look to them, as though the builder had intended them only as temporary dwellings, to be replaced by more elaborate structures at a later date. A later date that had never arrived.

Patches of weeds fought for survival in the hard-packed earth that served as a yard. But she could tell that the porch had recently undergone some refurbishing. She smiled. Jack was a thoughtful son.

Marching up two wooden steps, Courtney crossed the porch and stopped in front of an aluminum screen door. She raised a hand to knock, then curled her fingers into her palm. One last chance, she thought. One last chance to back out, go home.

You owe him.

She knocked.

A minute passed, then another. She knocked again.

She heard sounds from within the house—someone tromping down a flight of stairs. The inner door opened and a shadowed figure stood on the other side of the screen, wearing a white T-shirt and faded jeans. His jeans were zipped, but unbuttoned. She yanked her gaze upward. His rumpled hair suggested she'd awakened him from a nap.

Jack pushed the screen door open a crack. Courtney swallowed nervously. Correction—not a nap. A hangover, if the bottle of beer in his hand meant anything. The smile of welcome Courtney had expected, hoped for, did not materialize. He stared at her, his blue eyes chips of ice. "Took your own sweet time, didn't you?" he growled.

"I beg your pardon?"

"To come and inspect the carcass."

"No, I mean…I only found out… I…I'm not here to inspect anything." Though the notion of inspecting that body sent a wave of unwelcome pleasure rippling through her. She dragged her thoughts back to the task at hand. "I came to explain, to apologize."

"You think an apology makes up for costing me a damned good job? Even one that involved working for Quentin Hamilton?"

"No. Of course not. That is… Please, may I come in?"

"That would be entirely against my better judgment." He pushed open the door. "But then I've never been a slave to my better judgment."

Courtney stepped across the threshold and followed Jack into a small living room. A quick glance took in a couch, coffee table, TV, an overstuffed recliner and assorted bric-a-brac. Everything was serviceable, though worn.

"Doesn't exactly compare to that little Elk Park cottage of yours, does it?"

"Please, don't."

"Ah, the typical little rich girl," Jack drawled with more than a trace of derision. "Feeling guilty about all of Daddy's money."

Courtney flinched. He'd hit a nerve with that one. She'd always had a sense of unease about her family's wealth. Especially when the gulf between the haves and have-nots in Butte often seemed so wide, it was beyond measuring. Still, she managed to straighten her shoulders. "My father worked hard for his money."

"So did mine," Jack said acidly. "He was a copper miner. Worked strip mines in the fifties. One of your daddy's. By the late sixties he was coughing up blood. He died when I was thirteen."

Courtney's hands twisted in her lap. "I'm sorry."

"So am I."

"Please, Mr. Sullivan..."

"Jack. My dad was Mr. Sullivan. To all the kids in Dublin Gulch anyway." Dublin Gulch was a designation of sorts applied by locals to differentiate one ethnic neighborhood from another. Courtney remembered hearing other such names, too, such as Corktown, Finntown and Little Italy. Most of the old neighborhoods, such as Dublin Gulch, were long gone, condemned and consumed by the mines.

"May I sit down?"

"No. You're not staying."

*The man's been drinking, and he's lost his liveli-
hood,* Courtney reminded herself. It was only natural
that he be a bit surly. "What did...what did your
employer tell you, if I may ask?"

"That I'd insulted the boss's daughter, and I could
clear out my locker."

"I promise you, I had nothing to do with it."

"I know."

She blinked, surprised. "Then why?—"

"Am I acting like an ass?" He rubbed a hand over
his face. "I'm not really sure, to tell you the truth. I
think I'm a little unnerved having a Hamilton in my
house. Especially one as pretty as you."

She managed a tentative smile, warmed by the unexpected compliment.

"I know it was your silk-suit boyfriend who got me
fired, Miss Hamilton. He didn't have the guts to face
me man-to-man, but it doesn't take guts to make a
phone call."

"I don't know what got into Roger."

"He probably saw the way I was looking at you."

Courtney swallowed. "And how was that?"

"The same way I'm looking at you right now." The
heat in that gaze sent sparks of fire dancing along her
spine. He held out the beer. "Drink?"

She shook her head. "I, uh, I came here to talk
about your job."

He took a long pull on the bottle. "Did you?"

"Yes." She tried to sound resolute, but failed.

"Okay. We talked. You apologized. I accept. Now
you'd better go."

"But what are you going to do about a job?"

"I'll manage."

"If you need money—"

It was the dead wrong thing to say.

Any trace of cordiality or sympathy vanished from those sky-blue eyes. "The day I take Hamilton *charity*," he fairly spat the word "—is the day *after* hell freezes over, Miss Hamilton." He pointed toward the door. "You know your way out."

Courtney felt deflated, irrationally rejected. She turned to leave, her gaze falling on his left arm. "I can't go. You haven't told me about your tattoo."

"I changed my mind."

"Please."

A muscle in his jaw jumped. "Tell you what... I need to change my clothes. I fell asleep in these." He gestured toward the stairs. "You come up to my room, and I'll tell you all about my tattoo."

He was issuing a challenge, daring her to follow him to his bedroom. Courtney bumped her chin up a notch. "Lead the way."

His bedroom was as simply furnished as the living room. A bed, a dresser, a night table, a small reading lamp and an electric radio were the room's only accoutrements. The radio was on and playing country music. Courtney hovered near the open door as Jack crossed to his dresser. She tried to concentrate on the darkening clouds outside his window, a flash of lightning creating brief static in the radio. But her gaze shifted back to Jack, as though drawn by a magnet. She could only stare as he peeled off his shirt, mesmerized by the play of muscle across his chest, his back, his arms. From his closet he selected a short-sleeved denim that he shrugged into, but did not button.

Needing to distract herself, Courtney asked, "How long have you been a carpenter?"

"Six years. Working my way through school. Taking night courses, correspondence. Any way I can get the credits."

"To stay in carpentry?"

"No. I've got other plans."

Thunder rumbled overhead.

"I saw you watching me, you know," he said.

"I beg your pardon?"

"At your log house in the country, I saw you watching me from the kitchen window."

Maybe the earth would just open up and swallow her. At least she could hope.

"It's okay," he drawled. "I was flattered. Why do you think it took me four days to finish that railing? Whenever you were at the window, I'd find an excuse to be in front of it."

"Why?"

"I wanted to know if you'd ever do anything but look."

"I liked to watch you work," she managed. "Is there anything wrong with that? You're very good with your hands."

"Oh, princess, you don't know the half of it." He said the words with deliberate provocation. Then seemed to catch himself. "I'm going to try real hard to be noble, okay? It's not my nature, but I'll give it a shot. I want you to turn around and go down the stairs and out the door. Between the way you look and this beer, I'm not thinking real straight. Having Courtney Hamilton in my bedroom is a fantasy that's proving a little hard to resist."

"You say that like this isn't the first time you've thought about having me here."

"It isn't, princess. Believe me, it isn't."

"Why do you call me that?"

"Because it was the way you looked the first time I saw you. Two years ago in your daddy's downtown office building. I was in the lobby, waiting for my mother. Maddie Sullivan. She's your daddy's cleaning lady."

He said the last as though he were embarrassed, but Courtney wasn't going down that pride-bound road of his again. "Maddie Sullivan is your mother?" She hadn't even made the connection. "She's a wonderful woman! I adore her!"

"Well, it seems we have one thing in common at least. We both think my mother is terrific." He walked over to the window and opened it to its widest aperture. A stray breeze teased his shirttail as easily as it did the window's Irish lace curtains. "You were dressed in some kind of Cinderella ball gown. Sequins and satin. Your hair was all done up like a crown of curls. I think you even had flowers in it."

"Baby's breath." Courtney smiled wistfully, remembering. "I won a part in community theater. I went to the office to show my father. He couldn't come to the play. He was too busy. I think he gave me twenty seconds."

Outside, the rain began to fall. The radio offered up a mournful tune of pain and heartbreak and loss.

On impulse, Courtney crossed the room and stopped just inches behind him. "If I'm a princess," she said softly, "maybe you could be my Prince Charming. Just for a minute?"

"I don't think that would be a very good idea." He did not turn around.

"Dance with me? Please?" She raised her arms. For an instant he hesitated; then, with an almost fatalistic shrug, he turned and drew her to him, as naturally as if he had done so a thousand times before. With a dreamy sigh Courtney rested her head against his shoulder, allowed one large hand to engulf her smaller one, felt his other hand settle gently, almost shyly, on the small of her back.

Thunder rattled the window, and she instinctively moved closer to him, smiling as Jack tightened his embrace.

The rain fell, the music played and they danced. On and on, they danced.

Nothing existed in the world but she and Jack. Yesterday was gone. Tomorrow was an illusion. To-day—this minute—was all either one of them had.

She turned her head.

His kiss was as natural as the rain, as sweet as summer honey. The tang of beer on his breath only added to the heady sensation of forbidden pleasure. The pressure of his lips increased. The stubble of his beard abraded her tender flesh. Courtney tilted her head and sighed his name.

And just that abruptly he released her.

"What is it?" she asked, still dazed by the tender assault of his mouth on hers.

"You need to go. Now." His eyes were twin flames of desire. He was breathing in ragged gasps. She didn't miss the telltale bulge straining behind the zipper of his jeans.

Courtney wasn't sure what she was feeling. She only knew she didn't want this time to end. Not now. Not yet. She walked over to his bed and sat down on the edge of it. "You haven't told me the story of your tattoo."

"Dammit, Courtney..."

"I like it when you say my name."

He cursed vividly. "You're playing with fire, princess."

"Would you burn me, Jack?"

"In a heartbeat."

She picked at the chenille coverlet on his bed. "I want to know about the tattoo." She was pushing him, she knew. Maybe it was the storm, maybe it was the unrelenting pressure from her father and Roger, or maybe it was simply being in Jack Sullivan's bedroom, but she was feeling things she'd never felt before. Reckless, careless . . . and a little dangerous.

Lightning flashed, casting phantoms of light and dark across Jack's rigidly still features. He seemed to be deciding something. And whatever it was, his answer was to cross the room and sit beside her on the bed. His left arm brushed against her right.

Courtney switched on the reading lamp and stared at the tattoo. "May I touch it?"

He didn't say yes; he didn't say no.

Courtney caressed the wolf. Beneath her fingers, Jack's flesh grew fire hot.

"I was fourteen," he began, his gaze locked straight ahead. "My dad had only been dead about a year. He was my whole world. To get back at God for taking him, I was busy raising hell all over town. My poor mother did her best. But I was one messed-up kid. That's when Pete Wilson came into my life."

He leaned forward, resting his arms on his knees. "Pete's a cop in Butte. We met over a Snickers bar." His mouth crooked into a self-deprecating grin. "I was vandalizing the machine it was in at the time. Pete could've arrested me. Instead, he took me fishing. Then he took me to Alaska to hunt caribou. If I didn't know there was a God, I knew it when I saw that land. And heard it. A quiet like I've never heard anywhere.''

He regarded her with a sudden intensity. ''Do you understand?''

She nodded. She understood perfectly. ''I've been up in the Sapphires. Hiking. I spent the night once. All alone. I was a little scared. But I'd do it again in a minute. Sometimes it was so quiet, I could hear my own heart beating.''

He looked away again, and Courtney was certain that it wasn't because he didn't like what he saw. But because he did. Maybe too much. Her pulses sang.

''We were with this guide, a barrel-chested Inuit named Yancy. We were out on a snow-covered plain, near dusk. Yancy got us within sixty yards of a herd of caribou. That's when we saw them. On the horizon, just coming over a hillock. A wolf pack. Maybe seven animals with this big silver male in the lead.

''We just sat back and watched. Within about ten minutes the pack had culled out an old stag. He probably wouldn't have put up much of a fight. But then all of a sudden the wolves scattered. I looked up and saw a plane, a single-engine Cessna coming in low.''

Courtney watched Jack's face change, darken with anger.

''Yancy cursed. I asked Pete what was going on. He said they were likely poachers come to shoot animals from the plane. It made me sick.

''A rifle barrel with a scope so big, a blind man could sight on it, jutted out the window of the plane. Then the spineless bastard started shooting. He hit the alpha male square in the chest.''

Courtney closed her eyes.

"His mate went wild. She was howling, screaming. Like something ripped her heart out. She wouldn't leave him. He lay at her feet, bleeding in the snow.

"The plane circled, looking for a place to land so the cowards could claim their trophy. I wanted to shoot 'em, just shoot 'em right out of the sky. I've never felt anything like that before. Not even when my dad died." He was trembling, his hands balled into fists.

"I ran to the wolves. Pete and Yancy both tried to stop me. But I was faster. I got there, went down on my knees. The other wolves hung back. Except the female. She watched me. Like she'd been expecting me.

"The male didn't even growl. It was just him and me in this frozen wilderness. I cradled his head in my lap. I felt him die. At that same instant I felt his spirit come into my body. I know that sounds crazy. But it was real. He was part of me."

Courtney's eyes burned. She longed to touch him, hold him, but knew she didn't dare.

"The plane landed. Pete showed the so-called 'sportsmen' his badge. He didn't have any authority up there, but they left in a hurry anyway. I carried the wolf into the woods and covered him with branches. Then I lit a fire. I didn't want those bastards coming back for the pelt."

He straightened. "I got the tattoo as soon as I got back to Butte."

For a long minute the only sound came from the radio and the rain. Finally Courtney found her voice. "Thank you."

Jack's face reddened. "I'm sorry. I didn't mean to get carried away. I never told that story to anyone be-

fore. My mom just got mad when she saw the tattoo.
My sister—she lives in Seattle now with her husband
and two kids—she figured it was just boy foolishness.
So I kept the story to myself. Except for Pete.''

"I'm honored. Truly."

He shot to his feet. "Okay, you heard it. Now you'd
best go."

She stood up next to him. "Thank you again. For
the dance. And for the story."

"You're welcome."

She touched his arm. "I truly am sorry about your
job, Jack. If there's anything I can do. . .''

He took a step back, forcing her hand to fall away,
then rubbed a hand across the back of his neck.
"Never say that to a drunk and horny man, Miss
Hamilton."

"Please, don't be crude. Not now."

"I'm a crude guy."

"I don't believe that."

"No?" He turned toward her, and she could actually feel the pent-up tension in him, coming off of him
in waves. She didn't move.

"Leave," he said.

"No."

"Fine," he breathed. "Just remember—you were
warned." With a tortured groan he pulled her to him,
his mouth finding hers once more. Where his earlier
kiss had been tender, this one was savage. Where he'd
been gentle, now he was ruthless. Where he'd given,
now he only took.

Outside, the storm grew fiercer.

Without a word Jack tumbled her down onto his
bed. "I want you, princess. I want you with every cell
of my body. Right here. Right now." His eyes glit-

tered, fever bright. "You want to take your angel-sweet body and leave, do it now. You stay, and I'm going to make love to you until you can't walk. Until neither of us can walk."

He rolled onto his back, his arms splayed wide. "It's your choice."

Courtney levered herself onto one elbow. Using her free hand, she brushed aside his unbuttoned shirt, trailing her fingers along the bare wall of his chest, feeling the thundering beat of his heart beneath her palm. She already couldn't walk. Her knees were weak. Her every sense, every nerve ending was tuned to this man. If the house were on fire, she wouldn't have left his bed.

She had no idea what kind of sorcery he employed, no notion of how in such a short span of time he could so thoroughly captivate her. But he had. She wouldn't be so rash as to say she loved him. But she could. And soon. Very, very soon.

She acquiesced to his superior skill and knowledge, lying in breathless anticipation as he began to undo the buttons of her blouse. Gently, gently he eased the filmy fabric off of her shoulders, his rough, callused palms skating upward to slide beneath the lacy barrier of her brassiere.

"Courtney, Courtney," he rasped. "I can't believe this. I can't believe . . ."

He worked the clasp of her bra and wisped away the last obstacle between his hands and the quivering mounds of her breasts. He teased, suckled, worshiped, seeming to know always when to touch and when to withdraw.

Courtney arched upward, seeking, aching, her body on fire with need, passion, lust. Never in her life had she felt this way. Never in her life had she known she could feel this way.

And then the last of her clothes were gone, and somehow Jack, too, was naked. Lightning blazed at the window beside them, jagged streaks that highlighted the sheer magnificence of his body.

Cool night air whispered across her overheated skin. Tiny droplets of rain misted through the screen to settle on her naked straining body.

Again and again Jack brought her to the brink of some unknown precipice, and again and again he eased her back, never quite allowing her to slip over the edge.

"Jack...Jack, please..." She twined her fingers in his hair. "I need—oh, please..."

"Patience, princess," he whispered. "Patience."

He slid his hands between her thighs, urging her to open to him. Mindlessly, she obeyed. He dipped his fingers between the curls at the apex of her legs and teased the very core of her womanhood. She hurtled back to the rim of that precipice. "Let me go," she whimpered. "Please." Again he lured her back.

Bold, desperate, she reached between them, touched his pulsing shaft, reveled in his throaty, bliss-filled gasp.

"Now," she urged. "Please, Jack. Now."

He rose above her, staked his arms on either side of her and without a single word drove himself inside her. For just an instant, the spell was broken. His face, contorted with ecstasy, stilled, as his eyes went wide with astonishment, disbelief.

"Don't stop," she pleaded.

He wanted to. She could tell. But his body, so fearfully aroused, would not be denied. He buried his length in her velvet softness, let her grow used to his hardness, his size. Then, with an animal cry that bordered on madness, he drove them both over the edge into the shimmering mists of paradise.

Slowly, slowly reality returned, intruded. Courtney fumbled for her clothes.

Jack cursed. "Why did you let me?" he demanded. "For God's sake, Courtney, you were a virgin."

"I wanted . . ."

"What? Points for a construction worker? Was this part of sorority pledge week?"

"Don't say that. Don't spoil it. Please."

"Spoil it? My God! I don't do virgins."

He was angry, furious. Hurt? She didn't know. She was too busy trying to decipher her own feelings. In the throes of passion, she'd never felt more needed, more wanted, more cherished. But now . . . now . . . Lord above, what had she done? She didn't even know this man. She'd always sworn she would be a virgin on her wedding night, keeping Roger at arm's length for over a year now. And yet here she was, in Jack Sullivan's bedroom, in Jack Sullivan's bed. A man she had known scarcely a week. She must be out of her mind.

"I'm not sure what happened," she said forlornly.

"Honey, neither am I." He sat up and tugged on his clothes. "Neither am I."

"It doesn't . . . I mean . . . we can see each other again. Can't we?"

He started to say something, then must have noticed how shaken she was, how undone by her own emotions. He pressed a kiss on her forehead. "Help me look for my mind, will you? I seem to have lost it somewhere in this room tonight."

She smiled, just a little, cupping his face in her hands. "I could love you, Jack Sullivan."

He closed his eyes. "Maybe we should just start with a movie, okay?"

She smiled shyly. "Okay."

"How about?—"

The phone rang. Jack grimaced. "I'd better get that. It could be my mother. She might need a ride home from work." He rolled out of bed and headed downstairs.

Courtney rushed to get dressed. Her emotions were still too raw, too new to explore. She sat on the bed and waited for Jack. Several minutes passed before he returned. He paused briefly in the doorway, looking shaken, grim, but it must have been a trick of the light, because when he came closer, the unease she had sensed was gone.

"Was it your mother?"

"No."

"Is something wrong?"

"It was just a buddy of mine, wanting to go out for a beer tomorrow night."

She came over to him. "When will I see you?"

"You won't. I'm leaving Butte."

Her heart dropped. "What?"

"I've got a friend in L.A. He invited me down. He thinks he can get me some work."

"When? I mean, when did you decide this?"

"Three days ago."

"But you just said . . ."

"It was a pipe dream, Courtney. It took a few minutes, but I've managed to regain my senses."

"But . . ."

"Don't get hysterical on me. I didn't ask you to come here."

She swallowed back tears. This couldn't be happening. How could everything have disintegrated so quickly? The tender, considerate lover of only moments before was gone, vanished, replaced by this man, who it seemed couldn't wait to have her gone.

Too numb to even think, she followed Jack down the stairs. She would call him later. Or he would call her. It wasn't over. It couldn't be.

But he didn't say a word as he pushed open the screen door and they stepped out onto the porch. Still bewildered, hurting, she turned back to him. "Jack, I..."

She was interrupted by a buxom woman of about twenty who came bounding up on the porch. Without preamble she brushed past Courtney and planted a big, wet kiss on Jack's mouth, a mouth that had so recently brought Courtney to ecstasy. "Am I late, Jack?" the woman asked.

"No, Christal," Jack said, curving his arm around her waist, "I'd say you're just exactly on time."

Christal giggled and tugged at Jack's belt buckle. "I got off the second shift."

Jack looked at Courtney. "Was there something else, Miss Hamilton?"

Bile rose in her throat. He intended to take this woman to his bed? To the very same bed in which... "No," she managed, summoning a wellspring of pride she hadn't even known she possessed. "No, nothing else, Mr. Sullivan." She turned to leave, then stopped, straightening her spine. "As to your earlier question, the one where you asked how many points for construction workers. The answer is none. Zero. Because that's exactly how much a man like you is worth.''

The light on the porch wasn't good, so she could never be certain, but for just an instant she could've sworn she'd cut him straight to the bone.

But her victory was a hollow one. In one night she had fallen in love with him. In one night he had broken her heart.

Two months later she married Roger Winthrop.

Courtney lay in bed in Jack Sullivan's mountain cabin, staring up at nothing. *Things happen for a reason.* Is that what she had so cavalierly announced to Jack earlier today? What amazing arrogance. It had been ten years, and she still hadn't figured out the reason for that long-ago night.

By all rights she should hate him. She *wanted* to hate him. But she didn't. Couldn't. And for the life of her, she didn't understand why.

And now he was back. And she didn't understand that, either. But if life was indeed a test, then Jack Sullivan was her doctoral thesis.

Things happen for a reason.

Her spirit, she assured herself, was up to the challenge. But God help her, if that kiss tonight was any indication, even after ten years, she couldn't be so sure about her heart.

Chapter 6

Courtney started awake, her every sense alert. This time it was no painful dream that roused her, but something else. A noise. A sound. Something not in sync with the normal night rhythms of the cabin—the crackle of logs in the hearth, the soughing of the wind, Jack Sullivan's deep, even breathing in the sleeping bag five feet from her bed.

Levering herself onto her elbows, Courtney held her breath and listened. But whatever the sound had been, it was not repeated. Sagging back onto her pillow, she closed her eyes, still shaken by an onslaught of memories, by fragments of the dream that seemed determined to stay with her, torment her.

You're playing with fire, princess,
Would you burn me, Jack?
In a heartbeat.

It was almost as if her unconscious were trying to tell her something, something vital that she had overlooked. The feeling disturbed her, because with it came a very real fear. A foreboding. Something wasn't right. But she had no idea what it was.

Her lips thinned. She was being absurd again. Her life was not some old Alfred Hitchcock movie. Every happenstance did not have to be loaded down with symbolism and significance. It had been a dream. An unpleasant, distasteful recollection of a night that for a time had been magic. Until Jack Sullivan had shown himself for what he was. A heartless, deceitful son of a—

A soft moan escaped Jack's lips. Courtney's head jerked in his direction. She watched his body shift restlessly within the confines of his sleeping bag. "Jack?" she inquired softly.

No response.

She let out a grateful sigh. Reliving the night they'd made love had stirred memories more intimate, more intense, than she would have thought possible after ten years. No way could she face him just now. She needed time to recover, regroup. Think.

No. Cancel that. She'd already done entirely too much thinking about Jack Sullivan. What she really needed was to give the subject a rest. Give her over-worked emotions a rest.

Besides, her body's physical requirements were clamoring for their own share of her attention. She needed to make another trip outdoors. A glance toward the window made her shiver even to think about it. The snow had stopped. The sky had cleared. But the crystalline brilliance of a billion stars illuminating that winter wonderland suggested that the temperature had also plunged precipitously. Perhaps an empty bladder wasn't really that much of a priority, she thought, then shifted uncomfortably.

Yes, it was.

"Get it over with," she muttered.

Tossing back her blankets, Courtney almost changed her mind when her feet hit the floor. The cabin temperature itself had dropped to meat-locker potential.

Altering her agenda, she hobbled first to the hearth and rebuilt the fire, taking care not to disturb Jack. This way, she mused, if she froze various unmentionable parts of her anatomy outside, she stood a better chance of thawing them out in a hurry. Gritting her teeth, she limped toward the door.

On her previous outdoor venture, she'd found an old parka and pulled it on. Now, since it was closer—and less disreputable looking—she shrugged into Jack's sheepskin coat, then shoved her stockinged feet into his hiking boots. A search of his pockets for mittens or a cap yielded only a folded piece of paper.

Drawing in a deep, determined breath, she opened the door. A blast of Arctic air hit her square in the face. *Take a note, Courtney,* she told herself, stepping out into the bone-chilling night. *The next time you're kidnapped, have the bastards crash next to a five-star hotel.*

Outside, she took care of business in record time, then stumbled back into the cabin and slammed the door. Hugging Jack's coat tight against her, she hurried over to the fire, allowing a quick glance in his direction. The man should have wakened to the sound of her teeth chattering alone. But he slept on.

"Good thing I'm not a hungry grizzly." She held her trembling hands in front of the fire. Minutes passed before she finally stopped shivering. She unbuttoned Jack's coat and started to slip it off when she remembered the slip of paper she'd found in the pocket. Curiosity prodding her, she looked at it in the light of the fire.

On it was a series of numbers and letters, the first of which was CD-H-4791327-WR. Courtney frowned, wondering first why she'd even felt it necessary to read something she'd found in Jack's pocket. Then wondering further why she felt cheated that the paper contained nothing significant.

Significant about what?

Annoyed, she stuffed the paper back where she'd found it. What had she been expecting? The names and addresses of her kidnappers? More likely it was a list of Jack's myriad girlfriends encrypted so that no one else could steal them.

She took off the coat and started back toward her bed. Then she stopped cold. Names and addresses of her kidnappers? Of course! Why hadn't she thought of it before?

She limped over to Jack and knelt down beside him. She needed to ask him something, and she didn't want to wait until morning. But as she reached for him, she hesitated, remembering the scorching kiss they'd shared, remembering her own dream about the night they'd made love. Maybe the middle of the night in front of a glowing fire wasn't the best time to disturb him.

She started to rise.

"No!" Jack's voice.

Courtney gasped, then realized he was still asleep. As she watched, he began to shift restively again, mumbling something she couldn't make out. His agitation increased, his unzipped sleeping bag slipping off his bare chest.

Courtney felt a niggling of irritation. Surely the man hadn't stripped before he'd bedded down. The thought of him buck naked under there made her furious. He should have had some consideration for her sensibilities!

And what sensibilities are those, Courtney? she asked herself. *The ones in your eyeballs that are currently glued to that chest?*

It was as magnificent as she remembered, stirring sensations she would have sworn no longer existed, except in memory. Her marriage to Roger had wounded her in a lot of ways. Her pride, her self-esteem, her confidence in her own instincts about other human beings. But one wound she had actually considered a blessing was her loss of interest in the opposite sex. She'd assured herself she liked it that way. She could devote more time to her career, helping other women escape the cycle of violence that trapped them in abusive relationships.

But the stirring of her blood as she watched Jack sleep was fast putting the lie to that rationale. As had that unfortunate kiss earlier. Her libido wasn't dead after all. It was merely frozen, suspended. Held in check by a crippling fear she didn't want to acknowledge even as it stared her in the face. A fear that because she couldn't trust her own judgment about men, she was doomed to repeat past mistakes over and over. Better not to take the chance was the rule she'd lived by for four years. And the one she should adhere to now with this man—this man whom those very instincts had once prompted her to trust, only to have him betray her utterly.

"No! Didn't mean . . . no . . ."

Courtney trembled, the words from Jack's dream uncannily seeming almost a denial of her thoughts. Shaken, she decided against waking him. Her questions could wait until morning.

"No! Gun! Emmett . . . no!"

He was practically shouting now, though his tone seemed more anguished than angry. "Emmett, for the love of God. This can't be happening . . . can't be . . . Gun! Gun!" His voice broke on a strangled sob.

Courtney could *feel* the suffering in him, feel the hurt. Maybe she should wake him after all, put an end to the nightmare. Or would it be better to let him ride it out? To wake him now was to risk his wrath and his embarrassment. But she couldn't bear watching this much longer. He was in agony.

She reached for him. At the same instant, his eyes flew open, though there was no immediate awareness in their blue depths. Slowly the images from his dream must have receded. She could actually see his face relax, feel the tension in him ease. And then he noticed her.

"Enjoy the show?" he asked tersely.

She bit back a nasty retort, saying instead as evenly as she could manage, "Are you all right?"

"Fine. Go back to bed. I don't need a nursemaid."

Courtney dug her fingernails into her palms. Had she actually been feeling sorry for this vile-tempered jerk? "Did the kidnappers have any IDs on them?"

"What?" He stared at her, still obviously tired and embarrassed, and now suffering just a bit of whiplash from her complete non sequitur.

"I was thinking about something tonight," she went on testily, his mood freeing her from any concerns she might have had about his feelings. "About names and addresses. And it occurred to me that the kidnappers were probably carrying wallets. You know, with driver's licenses, credit cards, video store memberships—that kind of thing. Did you check their pockets before you buried them?"

"No."

"Why not?"

"It didn't occur to me to steal from dead men."

She slapped her thigh. "It would hardly be stealing. I have every right to know who they were. Don't you see? I might even recognize their names. Maybe one or both of them were disgruntled employees of Winthrop-Hamilton."

"I'll tell the police where to dig up the bodies."

"No. I think you and I should go up there. Later today."

"In a foot and a half of new snow? I don't think so. You'd never make it on that ankle. Now could you please just go back to sleep?"

"How about in a day or two, then? When my ankle's better? Or maybe when the snow melts a little?"

"We'll see."

"Good. Thank you." She crawled over to the bed on her knees, determined now to give her ankle as much rest as possible. She was genuinely excited about at least the possibility of identifying her kidnappers. Corporate spies, money-hungry thugs—somehow putting a name or a motive to the men would help ease her mind. What she was really hoping for was a chance to allay her fears that their grudge might have been personal, not against her father, or the company, but against her.

And if it was personal?

SILHOUETTE®

AN IMPORTANT MESSAGE
FROM THE EDITORS OF
SILHOUETTE®

Dear Reader,

Because you've chosen to read one of our fine romance novels, we'd like to say "thank you"! And, as a **special** way to thank you, we've selected <u>four more</u> of the <u>books</u> you love so well, **and** a Porcelain Trinket Box to send you absolutely *__FREE!__*

Please enjoy them with our compliments...

Leslie Wainger   Senior Editor,
Silhouette Intimate Moments

P.S. And because we value our customers, we've attached something extra inside ...

EDITOR'S
FREE
GIFT
SEAL
THANK YOU

PEEL OFF SEAL AND
PLACE INSIDE

HOW TO VALIDATE
YOUR
EDITOR'S FREE GIFT
"THANK YOU"

1. Peel off gift seal from front cover. Place it in space provided at right. This automatically entitles you to receive four free books and a beautiful Porcelain Trinket Box.

2. Send back this card and you'll get brand-new Silhouette Intimate Moments® novels. These books have a cover price of $3.75 each, but they are yours to keep absolutely free.

3. There's no catch. You're under no obligation to buy anything. We charge nothing—ZERO—for your first shipment. And you don't have to make any minimum number of purchases—not even one!

4. The fact is thousands of readers enjoy receiving books by mail from the Silhouette Reader Service™ months before they're available in stores. They like the convenience of home delivery and they love our discount prices!

5. We hope that after receiving your free books you'll want to remain a subscriber. But the choice is yours—to continue or cancel, anytime at all! So why not take us up on our invitation, with no risk of any kind. You'll be glad you did!

6. Don't forget to detach your FREE BOOKMARK. And remember...just for validating your Editor's Free Gift Offer, we'll send you FIVE MORE gifts, *ABSOLUTELY FREE!*

YOURS FREE!

*This beautiful porcelain box is topped with a lovely bouquet of porcelain flowers, perfect for holding rings, pins or other precious trinkets — and is yours **absolutely free** when you accept our no risk offer!*

THE EDITOR'S "THANK YOU" FREE GIFTS INCLUDE:

▶ Four BRAND-NEW romance novels
▶ A Porcelain Trinket Box

PLACE FREE GIFT SEAL HERE

YES! I have placed my Editor's "thank you" seal in the space provided above. Please send me 4 free books and a Porcelain Trinket Box. I understand I am under no obligation to purchase any books, as explained on the back and on the opposite page.

245 CIS AWJM (U-SIL-IM-09/95)

NAME

ADDRESS   APT.

CITY   STATE   ZIP

Thank you!

DETACH AND MAIL CARD TODAY!

THE SILHOUETTE READER SERVICE™: HERE'S HOW IT WORKS

Accepting free books places you under no obligation to buy anything. You may keep the books and gift and return the shipping statement marked "cancel". If you do not cancel, about a month later we will send you 6 additional novels, and bill you just $3.12 each plus 25¢ delivery and applicable sales tax, if any.* That's the complete price, and—compared to cover prices of $3.75 each—quite a bargain! You may cancel at any time, but if you choose to continue, every month we'll send you 6 more books, which you may either purchase at the discount price…or return at our expense and cancel your subscription.

*Terms and prices subject to change without notice. Sales tax applicable in N.Y.

If offer card is missing write to: Silhouette Reader Service, 3010 Walden Ave., P.O. Box 1867, Buffalo, NY 14269-1867

SILHOUETTE READER SERVICE
3010 WALDEN AVE
PO BOX 1867
BUFFALO NY 14240-9952

BUSINESS REPLY MAIL
FIRST CLASS MAIL   PERMIT NO. 717   BUFFALO, NY

POSTAGE WILL BE PAID BY ADDRESSEE

NO POSTAGE
NECESSARY
IF MAILED
IN THE
UNITED STATES

She shuddered. She would deal with that, too. "Jack?"

"Yeah?"

"Do you think my father's still alive?" It was a ridiculous question. Jack would have no more idea about Quentin Hamilton's state of health than she did. In fact, less.

"A man as arrogant and dictatorial and rich as Quentin Hamilton would need more than a heart attack to kill him."

She managed a wan smile. "Thanks. I needed that."

"You're welcome." He started to lie back down, then suddenly sucked in his breath.

"What is it?"

"Nothing."

"It's your arm, isn't it?"

"It'll wait 'til daylight."

"If you've got a first-aid kit, I could bandage it now. I'm not tired."

He cursed. "Fine. Suddenly, neither am I."

He flung back his sleeping bag and Courtney gasped, averting her eyes, recalling her earlier all-too-vivid notion that he was sleeping in the raw.

"Don't worry, Miss Hamilton," he drawled. "Your virtue will not be assaulted. I'm wearing my jeans."

"You just never mind my virtue," she snapped. "And put on a shirt. After the way you kissed me tonight, not giving a damn about the fact that I was completely unwilling—"

He laughed out loud. "Excuse me? I don't recall any struggle. Nor, if memory serves, do I recall the word *no* being used."

She'd walked right into that one. "Just see to it that it doesn't happen again," she said as haughtily as she could manage.

"I'll get the first-aid kit."

He brought a large box over to a scarred-up table, along with a kerosene lantern, which he promptly lit. Courtney pulled up one chair. Jack spun the second one around and sat down. "I'm all yours."

Courtney refused to rise to the bait. Instead she rummaged through the kit, pulling out bandages, tape, scissors and anything else she thought she might need. "Looks like you're ready for the next invasion here."

"Pete believed in being prepared."

"Pete Wilson?"

He nodded, obviously pleased that she'd remembered.

"Your cop friend. The one who straightened you out, set you on the right path in your life." She gave a disdainful glance to their ramshackle surroundings. "Remind me to convey my congratulations. He did a spectacular job."

Jack's expression hardened; his voice went stone cold. "I wish I could. Pete's dead."

Courtney winced. Only now did she recall an earlier comment by "J.D." that the cabin had once belonged to a friend, who had died. "I know he meant a lot to you, Jack. I'm sorry."

"So am I."

"How did it happen?"

"Drop it. Please."

Chastened, Courtney returned her attention to the first-aid kit.

"The arm needs stitches," Jack said.

"I can see that."

"You up to it?"

"Of course." She said the words, even as her stomach turned over. She wasn't about to let the insufferable bastard know just how queasy she was at the prospect of sewing up human flesh.

"Maybe you're *too* up to it," he groused.

"Excuse me?"

"I'm not sure I should give you free rein on my body with a sharp object. You might enjoy yourself a little too much."

Muttering under her breath, Courtney grabbed Jack's left hand and turned his arm in such a way as to give herself the best view of the wound. Not for a second did she allow herself to dwell on how warm his flesh felt, how unsettling it was to hold his hand even for a heartbeat. "It...it looks a bit infected. You shouldn't have let it go this long."

"I dumped some antiseptic on it. It was the best I could do. I believe I was fairly busy caring for your injuries at the time."

His reminder of what he'd done for her was deliberate, she knew. She ignored him. "Here." She picked up a packet of foil-wrapped pills. "It's something called ciprofloxacin, generic." The description on the attached pharmaceutical printout called it a quinoline broad-spectrum antibiotic for skin, soft tissue and upper-respiratory infection. "Are you allergic to anything?"

He gave her a rueful look as though to say "Besides you?" then shook his head.

She gave him the pills, then took up the needle and thread. Despite her best efforts, her hand trembled.

"It's okay," he said, this time gently. "I trust you."

"I wish I could say the same."

He sighed. "I guess I deserved that."

"Let's not get into what you deserve, Sullivan."

He chuckled. "You're sure a helluva lot more feisty than I remember."

"As if either one of us can say we ever knew each other. But, yes, as a matter of fact, I have changed. A lot."

"You've certainly acquired some interesting skills for a..."

"Spoiled rich bitch?"

"For a Hamilton," he said smoothly. "Barbering, sewing up human beings."

"I'm afraid it comes with the territory. Not that I've ever actually sewn anyone up before." She took a deep breath, pinched both sides of the ragged cut together, then poked the needle through his skin.

Jack didn't move.

Courtney was certain she was going to throw up. Breathing through her mouth, she eased the needle through the wound's opposite side and drew up the thread, then repeated the process. "I've seen it done. Too many times." The image of a towheaded little boy, tight-lipped and very brave as he lay on a hospital gurney rose unbidden in her mind's eye.

Jack's brows furrowed. "Where?"

She told him about her job.

His blue eyes glinted with a new respect. "Those women have a real champion in you."

Courtney blushed, flustered by the unexpected warmth in that husky voice. Her next prick of the needle went too deep and he yelped, jerking his arm back. "I'm sorry, I'm sorry." She grabbed up a piece of gauze and dabbed at a spot of fresh blood. "Damn, I'm sorry."

"Don't worry about it."

"I didn't mean to hurt you." Her voice shook.

"Courtney, it's okay. You didn't hurt me. You just kind of surprised me a little, that's all."

Her eyes burned with unshed tears.

"Courtney, please...it's okay." He caught her hand in his much larger one, the needle and thread dangling to one side.

"I'm sorry. I don't know what got into me. I..." She let out a shaky breath. "Yes, I do. All of this just suddenly reminded me of something, someone."

"Who?"

"A little boy named Danny."

"Danny had stitches?"

She knew what Jack was doing. He was trying to take her mind off of the fact that she'd nearly skewered him with the needle, but she didn't know if she could talk about Danny. "He was five. With bright green eyes and a cherub's smile. And he loved to play with toy trains." She paused.

"Tell me more."

Courtney took a deep breath. "His mother's name was Addie. She came to the shelter the first time when Danny was three. She had a black eye and a broken heart. It was the fourth time her husband had beat her up. Each time he swore he'd never do it again."

Courtney resumed her needlework.

"Addie and Danny came three more times," she went on. "Each time we tried to counsel her, advise her, help her find a way out, but each time Derek would draw her back with his pleading and his promises. 'I'll never hit you again, Addie.' 'I'll get help this time I swear, Addie.' 'You know I love you, Addie.'

"The last time was four months ago. This time he hadn't just beaten Addie. When Danny tried to intervene, to help his mom, Derek tossed him down the basement steps. Danny had sixty-three stitches in his scalp. Sixty-three. They had to shave off his beautiful blond curls.''

"Courtney, you don't have to—"

"He told me that now he was a Mohawk Indian. And would I help him set up his trains?

"Addie got a restraining order. When Derek came to beg for another chance, she called us. We stood by her, while she had Derek arrested. The judge gave him six months. It wasn't much, but it was something. Except one day they gave him a pass to go to the dentist. A pass. Like he's in high school, instead of jail.''

Her whole body was trembling now. "No one called Addie. No one warned her. Derek went to her house. Danny was sitting in the living room playing with his trains.'' Her voice broke. She had long since stopped stitching Jack's arm. "I know he was playing with his trains, because that's where I found him. Derek had blown Addie away with a shotgun, then Danny, then himself. After—" she swallowed "—after the police were finished, I washed the blood off his trains. I made sure they buried him with the little engine. He loved that little engine.''

Jack didn't say a word. He just pulled her into his arms and held her. For a long, long time, he just held her.

At last, reluctantly, Courtney drew back. "I'm sorry. I didn't mean to burden you with all that.''

He trailed the back of his fingers down one cheek, brushing away a stray tear. "You're a helluva woman, Courtney Hamilton."

"Yes, well, I'm proving to be a rather lousy nurse. I'd best finish up this arm before I'm dealing with scar tissue." She was babbling now, but she couldn't seem to help herself. "I really don't know what got into me. I never discuss a case with anyone. It must be the trauma of being kidnapped, don't you think?"

"Yeah, that must be it." They fell silent then. For long minutes Courtney worked on his arm and neither one of them said a word. But there was an awareness between them that hadn't been there before. Courtney knew she didn't dare look at his eyes. If she did, she would be lost.

Finally it was Jack who broke the silence. "I didn't sleep with her."

She tied off the thread, then snipped away the excess. "What?"

"Christal. The woman who came to my house that night. I never slept with her."

"I really don't—"

"I want you to know."

"It was a one-night stand, Jack. It doesn't need any more postmortem than that."

"She was Pete Wilson's daughter. After I got a call that night...from the friend who wanted to go out for a beer, I called Christal, told her I needed a favor. She was a good friend, but there was never anything romantic between us. I spun her a line about how much of a pain in the butt you were. That I'd been trying to get rid of you for months. Christal came over, did her bit, then when she saw your face, she almost lost it. After you'd gone, she let me have it with both barrels. Called me every name I'm sure you wish you would've called me.''

"Why would you do such a thing?"

"Why?" He looked her square in the eye. "Because I was ashamed. Ashamed of my mother's house, of my bank balance, of being drunk, of being a Sullivan. Ashamed of everything and anything. I held myself up to the Hamiltons and lost on every count." He raked a hand through his shaggy hair.

"It was a whole lot later before I got it right. Before I was ashamed of being ashamed. But I wanted you to know about Christal."

"Thank you." She said the words, but she wasn't at all sure just how grateful she really was. She'd been having a hard enough time sorting out her feelings for this man. Even though, for ten years she had believed he'd taken another woman to his bed five minutes after she'd left it. Now... now... to find that the whole performance had apparently been put on because of his damnable pride... She honestly didn't know what to think. "It's still a few hours 'til dawn," she managed. "We'd best get some more sleep."

She needed to put whatever distance she could between them, no matter how minimal it might be. She was feeling terribly vulnerable just now. Climbing back into bed, she made certain to lie down facing away from Jack, who had remained sitting at the table.

Courtney closed her eyes. But she didn't sleep. She couldn't. Her thoughts were too filled with Jack. Something still wasn't right here. She didn't know what it was. But it was real and terrifying. Just as her feelings for Jack were real. And terrifying.

In her life she had learned that to trust any man was a gamble. But Jack Sullivan? He'd already broken her heart once. Dare she tempt fate a second time? Or were these battered instincts of hers screaming a warning because some part of her knew that this time the stakes were high enough to destroy her?

Courtney woke to the aroma of bacon and eggs frying. Her cholesterol level went up a notch just savoring the smell. She opened her eyes. Jack was hard at work at the stove. "I could get used to this," she murmured.

"Breakfast in bed? Or a personal chef?"

"Both." Or maybe the chef in bed. She started. She hadn't said that out loud, had she? Jack's lack of reaction assured her that she had not.

"The eggs are powdered. Hope you don't mind."

She didn't. Taking extra care to keep her mouth shut, Courtney pushed herself to a sitting position. She couldn't believe she'd actually fallen asleep. The way she'd tossed and turned after her stint as Florence Nightingale, she'd resigned herself to passing the remainder of the night by counting the number of times she called herself a fool for even thinking about trusting Jack Sullivan again.

At a million twenty she hesitated.

At a million twenty-one she gave in. Heaven help her, she decided to trust him.

Up to a point, she amended quickly. Then grimaced. She was not going to start counting again.

"It'll be just a few more minutes," he told her.

"Fine." Courtney studied him covertly. The man seemed almost cheerful. But she wondered if his mood wasn't at least partially defensive. A reaction to too many shared intimacies last night—his nightmare, her telling him about a boy named Danny, those long minutes she'd spent in the sheltering cocoon of his arms.

She could understand the awkwardness. In fact, she was surprised she didn't feel more of it herself. But then a lot of her feelings these past few days surprised her. It was almost as if she were waking up from a long sleep.

Still, she needed to be careful. The man was hurting. Or at least that was the spin she'd chosen to put on the shadowed edges of her newly reborn trust. He hadn't imprisoned himself on this mountain because he liked the view. No matter what he said. Perhaps her next step should be to get him to trust *her*.

As long as she kept in mind the fact that it wasn't her job to fix him. She'd learned the folly of that mind-set over six years of a progressively abusive marriage. A caring therapist and the nonjudgmental love of her best friend, Maggie Blake, at Angels' Wings, had helped Courtney accept that there was only one person in the world she could ever truly "fix"—and that was herself. With a lot of hard work, she'd come a long way toward doing just that.

But her therapist hadn't quite covered everything, Courtney mused wryly, allowing herself another quick glance at Jack, who was still vigorously attacking his panful of scrambled eggs. Like how did one handle a chance reunion with a man who'd once broken her heart, and who seemed, despite her best efforts, to be making new inroads into that carefully reconstructed organ?

What do you think, Maggie? she reflected inwardly, knowing her friend's response would be appropriately raunchy. *Do I take a chance here?*

Depends. Courtney could see actually Maggie, her hazel eyes twinkling with mischief. *How good was he in the sack?*

Courtney blushed, remembering all too well.

Grab him! Maggie chirped. *Grab him. Lock yourself in a room with him and throw away the key!*

Courtney shoved back her bedcovers. It was suddenly much too warm in the tiny cabin.

But wait, Maggie said, her voice growing suddenly serious. *There's another question, Courtney. And you know exactly what it is. Can you trust him?*

Courtney hesitated, despite her overnight debate.

Maggie's voice came back crystal clear and nonnegotiable. *Dump him. Dump him and run.*

"Are you okay?"

Courtney looked up to see Jack beside the bed with a heaping plateful of bacon and eggs, and a steaming cup of black coffee.

"I'm fine," she croaked out. *Except for a lengthy schizophrenic conversation and the fact you look entirely too sexy with those bedroom eyes, clean-shaven jaw and that blasted lopsided smile.* "Just daydreaming. How's your arm?"

"It's good. Don't quit the day job. But it's good."

Courtney settled the plate on her lap, while Jack set the coffee on the table next to the bed. "It smells heavenly," she said and meant it. "It's been a long time since I've indulged myself like this."

"He-man food," he grunted, thumping his chest. "Put hair on your chest."

"You sure you want it to do that?" She glanced at her flannel-covered bosom, then blushed at her audacity.

Their gazes met. She did not misinterpret the raw want she saw there. "Maybe not," he murmured, then seemed to shake himself. "I'll, uh, I'll let you eat. I've already had mine." Abruptly he turned and headed for the small workroom at the back of the cabin.

You're treading on dangerous ground here, Courtney. Are you sure you know what you're doing?

Of course not! But she wasn't about to let that stop her. A window had opened. Somehow, some way they had both, for the moment, let down their guard. She sensed it, felt it. She wasn't about to let such an opportunity go to waste.

Quickly she finished what she wanted of her artery-clogging breakfast, then gathered up her crutch, her coffee and her courage and headed toward the workroom. She found Jack sitting on the hip-high stool, holding the wolf carving that had so affected her yesterday, the one in which the animal had its leg caught fast by a steel-jawed trap.

"I wish you could set him free," she said quietly, taking up a position at the workbench that was at a right angle to where he sat. Resting her elbows on the tabletop, her hands were less than five inches from Jack's.

"So do I. But I don't know how." Using a tiny carving tool, he eased away a sliver of wood from the wolf's left flank. "This is just the way the piece came to me."

"It's remarkable." She took a sip of her coffee. "But then, you always were good with your hands."

He gave her a close look, apparently wondering if he should read anything salacious into that remark, as well. But she had meant it as a sincere compliment. Only now—with that look—was she reminded of another set of skills residing in those masterful hands.

In a voice both shy and bold, she whispered, "There's something happening between us, isn't there, Jack?"

"Yeah." His voice was hoarse. Their gazes locked. "Courtney, there's something I need to tell—"

Somewhere to the north, a wolf howled.

Jack closed his eyes, and Courtney could almost feel him change his mind, decide against telling her whatever he'd been about to say.

Disappointed, she glanced at his injured arm, where the bandage hid his tattoo. The wolf howled again. "A relative?"

His mouth twisted.

The tension between them eased a little. "I didn't know there were wolves in Montana."

"A pair down from Canada. I've seen 'em maybe a half-dozen times in the last eight months. A big silver male and a black female."

"I love to hear them. So wild, so free." She picked up one of his other carvings and trailed her fingers along a gamboling pup. "I was in Alaska three years ago. A half-dozen of us intrepid hikers and one grizzled old guide." She smiled. "Maybe he was Yancy's brother. Anyway, I thought a lot about your wolf story then. We got to see a pack, maybe fourteen animals strong, trailing after an elk herd. It was the most incredible thing to actually see them in the wild." She put the pup down and rubbed her arm. "You'll notice, however, that I drew the line at getting a tattoo."

He grinned. "I don't know. It might have been kind of sexy. Depending, of course, on where you put it."

They were back to that dangerous ground again. Dangerous, because Courtney had no idea where it would lead. Or even if it should lead anywhere at all.

"It won't work, you know," Jack said quietly.

She blinked, misunderstanding.

"The wolves. They'll never survive here."

"Oh." She swallowed. "Why not? Aren't they protected now?"

"It doesn't matter. They can be legally shot for attacking livestock." He set down his carving tool. "But you know as well as I do that a wolf doesn't have to be within twenty miles of a steer for some tunnel-visioned rancher to drag out that time-honored Western motto—Shoot 'em, shovel 'em and shut up."

Courtney eased around the table to where he sat. Jack twisted on the stool so that she was now standing between his legs. "How could anyone kill anything so beautiful?" she whispered.

"A man would have to be out of his mind."

"Uh-huh." She laid a hand against his bandaged arm.

"Out of his mind," he rasped.

This time his kiss was not about possession, not about a test of wills. Sweet, warm, gentle, his mouth moved over hers, and Courtney melted against him, her arms sweeping up to pull him close. Ten years fell away as nothing. They were back in his bedroom, storm raging, music playing, each of them oblivious to anything, everything, but the steadily increasing rhythm of each other's hearts.

"Courtney, Courtney..." His mouth trailed liquid fire down the slender column of her throat.

She arched her neck to give him better access, then twined her fingers in his thick, dark hair. She wanted this, ached for it, even as every logical cell still functioning in her brain sounded a warning.

With one hand, he eased open the buttons of her shirt. With the other, he brushed aside the flannel to knead the pliant flesh of her breasts, teasing her nipples until each was pebble hard beneath his touch.

And then her shirt parted, and his mouth explored where his hands had been.

Courtney's knees threatened to buckle. Her whole body burned with need, need for this man and his touch.

"No." At first she didn't even recognize that the word had come from her own lips. "Jack...please. No."

He drew back, his breathing ragged, his eyes still alight with blue fire. "What?"

She had to shut her eyes to say the word again. "No."

His hands fell away, and somehow Courtney found the strength to back up a step or two. "I'm sorry," she said weakly, fumbling with the buttons of her shirt.

"It's okay. You're right."

"Jack, I..."

"You don't owe me any explanations." His voice was tight, tense, but she had the feeling he was relieved, as well.

"But I want..." She faltered. What did she want? To tell him how frightened she was of a relationship with a man, any man? But especially with Jack Sullivan, a man she'd once dared to love. Even if it was only for one night. "I'm sorry." She picked up her coffee cup and fled back to the cabin's main room.

Jack followed. "We need more firewood. I think this is as good a time as any to get it." He crossed to the door and shrugged into his jacket.

"When will..." She felt suddenly foolish and unexpectedly bereft by the distance they were quite obviously trying to put between one another. "When do you think you'll be able to take me back to Butte?" She wanted out of here. She was embarrassed and strangely hurt by how easily he seemed able to back off from their abortive tryst.

"It'll be another day or two at least."

"But why?"

"Your ankle, for one thing."

"Then drag me on a sled or something."

"I doubt my arm would appreciate that."

"You're about to chop wood with that same arm."

He had no answer to that. Instead, he stomped out the door.

With a heavy sigh, Courtney sagged onto the bed. Damn him anyway. What was going on? She couldn't have misread him that badly. He'd wanted her. But then what man wouldn't want a willing woman? Especially when she was the only woman available for several dozen square miles.

And she'd been willing. Oh, Lord, had she. Which was one of the reasons she wanted so badly to get out of here. More days and nights under the same roof with this man and she doubted she'd have it in her to say no again.

Jack spent four hours chopping wood. He came back into the cabin, sweating, exhausted, looking for all the world as if he were ready to drop.

Courtney had been spending her time doing a little mending on the clothes she'd been wearing when the copter crashed. Jack had washed them out as promised. Her cream-colored bulky knit sweater was never going to make the cover of *Cosmo* again, but she was pleased when she could put it back on. She was tired of looking like Jack's fraternal twin.

"You hungry?" she asked.

"No."

"Angry?"

"No." He flopped down on top of his sleeping bag.

"How about tired?"

"Bingo." He closed his eyes.

"Jack?"

"Yeah?"

"If you won't take me out of here, will you at least take me to the copter crash? I want to check those guys for identification."

"I thought we went through that."

"You went through it. You said no. But I still want to do it. Maybe you're used to spending whole days in this cabin without a whole lot to do, but I'm getting a bit stir-crazy. The copter crash is less than a mile. My ankle could handle that as long as I had a crutch."

"That's not a bike path out there. It's a mountain."

"I know what it is," she snapped, her patience thinning. "Dammit, you get to work off your excess energy chopping up trees. I need to do something, too, okay?"

He sat up, one arm slung carelessly over a raised-up knee. "Give it a day or two. I'll think about it."

"No! Not one more minute!" She glared at him, all of her pent-up tension spilling free. "Maybe you've forgotten, but I didn't exactly drop in by here of my own free will. I have kidnappers to find, a sick father

to tend to and a career that's vitally important to me."
She jammed her hands on her hips. "Maybe you don't
have a life, Sullivan, but I do!"

He swore, clambering to his feet. "Is that another
Hamilton judgment? If I'm not behind some corporate desk somewhere, my life has no assigned dollar
value?"

"That's not what I meant at all! And you know it.
Dammit, Jack, I have no idea why you've decided to
turn your back on the world. And your reasons may
be perfectly valid. God knows, if I'd had a cabin to
run off to four years ago after Roger—" She stopped.
"You're getting me off the subject. I want to go to that
helicopter."

"Wait a minute. Wait just one damned minute." He
was in her face, his eyes probing, seeming to see
straight through her.

And he did.

She saw it the instant he made the connection.

"Your job," he said quietly, too quietly. "It isn't
some philanthropic pursuit, is it?"

"I don't know what—"

"He beat you. Winthrop beat you, didn't he?" His
voice rose. "Didn't he?"

"That's not your business."

His face twisted into a mask of anguish. "That low-
life sack of—" He raked a hand through his shaggy
hair. "As if I have a right to say anything. I'm the guy
who sent you running back to him."

"No." Her voice was firm, absolute. "I made my
own choices. If I've learned one thing in ten years,
Jack Sullivan, it's not to hold other people account-
able for what I do. Yes, that night with you hurt. It
hurt badly. But it wasn't the reason I married Roger.

It's a lot more complicated than that. My marriage was about feeling needed, about pleasing my father and, ultimately, about not feeling very good about me."

He didn't look convinced.

"Please, don't put this on yourself, Jack. This is about my life. My decisions. My road back. As hellish as it was, and I know this will sound strange to you, I don't regret it. I've learned a lot about myself. That I'm much stronger than I thought I was. That I can be alone and be okay. And that I have a lot to give to other women who are still caught in the same cycle of violence." She flushed. "I'm sorry. I didn't mean to get up on my soap box."

He came over to touch her face. "Maybe you don't blame me, angel. But I sure as hell do." He twisted away and paced to the window. "I should have killed the bastard. I should have just killed him."

"You could hardly murder him for grabbing me that night at the house."

"Not then," he gritted. "Later."

She stared at him. "You saw Roger again?"

"In Butte six years ago. I was back visiting my mother." He blew out a long, slow breath. "She always kept me up-to-date on Butte happenings, even in L.A. She was forever sending me clippings. The Winthrop-Hamilton wedding made the front page."

"So did the divorce," Courtney put in ruefully.

"Pete Wilson and I went to the M & M Cafe for dinner one night, and who should come waltzing in, but Roger with a redhead on his arm."

Courtney's mouth twisted in disgust, but she wasn't surprised. "Roger had a lot of women. Most of them had my sympathy."

"Pete tried his best to talk me out of it, but I walked over to Winthrop's table. He actually remembered who I was. I know, because he turned about six shades of yellow, then tried to explain away his 'date.'

"We exchanged a few words. I slugged him. He came at me with a wine bottle." Unconsciously, he touched the scar on his forehead. "Then I knocked him cold."

Courtney had the feeling she was getting a heavily censored version of what had actually gone on, but she didn't press for more details. "That must have been the time he told me he had a skiing accident. His nose was broken. He told me he ran into a tree." She was very careful not to show how shaken she was by the knowledge that Jack had been her champion yet again with Roger.

"When I get you back to Butte," Jack said, his voice tight, "I'm going to find him and finish what I started in that restaurant."

"That isn't your place, Jack. Besides, Roger's in South America. Running W-H operations there."

"I'll get a passport."

She was standing beside him, looking up into that handsome, tormented face. "Let it go, Jack," she said softly. "I have. I took what I needed to learn, and I made a better life for myself. Living in the past doesn't work."

Something flashed in those blue eyes that made her wonder if she'd cut just a little close to home with that one. "Tell me," she murmured.

"I can't." Her heart hurt at the despair in that voice.

"We're not the same people we were ten years ago, Jack. Maybe this is a second chance. A chance to do it right."

The agony in his eyes sent a chill skittering up her spine. Whatever he wasn't telling her, hovered there between them like a living thing. But he did not speak. Instead, he marched back over to his sleeping bag and lay down. Shutting his eyes, he effectively shut her out.

Two days went by. Two days in which they spoke less and less to one another. Because each time they spoke, Courtney could feel Jack edge closer and closer to telling her what he very obviously did not want her to know. The cramped confines of the cabin made their attempt to live separate lives all the more maddening.

Finally Courtney could bear it no longer. On a bright, sunny morning with the temperature inching toward forty degrees, she confronted Jack. "I can't be in this place another minute," she told him. "I'm losing my mind. I can't concentrate on reading. You won't talk to me. Hell, I can't even call out for a pizza."

When he said nothing, she continued. "My ankle is much better. This crutch you made me—" she held up the forked branch "—works really well. I've gathered up the stuff you found for me—Pete's boots, his parka, his gloves. Now—" she pointed "—I am going out that door, and I am going to find that helicopter." Quickly she yanked on Pete's things, grateful that the man had not had large feet.

"You're staying here."

"No, I'm not. Because digging up bodies is preferable to spending another day cooped up with you. And if you don't like it, you can just—" She slapped herself in the side of the head. "Call out! Jack! Of course, why didn't I think of it before?"

"What?"

"The helicopter! It had a radio. I remember the static. We could call for help!"

"The radio doesn't work. I tried it."

"We could try again. Maybe it just has a loose wire or something."

"Courtney, it doesn't work."

She tromped over to the door. "You just don't get it, do you? My father could by dying or dead. I have to get out of here. If you won't help me, I'll help myself."

Jack was at the door in two strides, his hand slamming against the rough panel. "You're not going anywhere, princess."

The word was like a bullet.

He must have realized it, too. Because his face changed, went a ghostly gray.

Princess! What her dream had been trying to tell her. What Jack had called her the night they'd made love.

And?

Courtney staggered back. *You're in enough trouble, princess.* What the pilot of the helicopter had called her!

"It was you!" she cried out, horrified, disbelieving. "You were flying the helicopter. You were the pilot! You!" Betrayal, rage and a black hate such as she'd never known roared through her in a single heartbeat. "My God, the crash was deliberate, wasn't it? To set up this whole fantasy. Your pervert friend in the back seat—"

"Is dead," Jack said tightly. "Just like you and I could've been. Do you really think I would've purposely jeopardized your life like that?"

She managed a sick laugh. "They said they would do anything to get information out of me! Anything! God in heaven, did that include sleeping with me again, Jack?"

"Courtney, please, just—"

Wild, unthinking, she swung the crutch, catching him hard on the side of the head. Jack reeled back, collapsed. She thought she saw blood, but she took no time to look.

This was what he had sunk to. This was what he had become, what he been hiding from her all this time! He was a felon. A hired gun. Without the slightest trace of morality or ethics or human decency.

He had used her. Again.

Made her all but love him. Again.

Damn him! Damn him straight to hell!

Crutch in hand, she bolted from the cabin and scrabbled painfully up the slope. The knee-deep snow weighed her down with each step she took. But she didn't stop. The helicopter was her only chance now. And it was an almighty slim one. She stumbled on, offering up a fervent prayer that Jack telling her the copter's radio didn't work was just another one of his endless lies.

Chapter 7

Courtney sagged to her knees, gasping, her lungs feeling ready to burst. She'd been slogging her way through calf-deep snow for over an hour now. In some places, windblown drifts came up to her chest. A mile to the copter, Jack had said. She felt as though she'd already gone a thousand.

Her ankle throbbed. Her cheeks burned. Despite the parka, the boots and the mittens, the effects of the thirty-plus temperature had taken its toll on her body heat. Her feet were numb. She wanted nothing more than to sink into the layering blanket of whiteness and disappear. Forever.

Jack Sullivan had kidnapped her.

Jack Sullivan had stalked her, attacked her, chloroformed her, bound and gagged her, and dragged her unconscious body on board a helicopter. And then he'd allowed his perverse confederate to put a gun to her head, allowed him to put his hands... She swallowed the bile that rose in her throat.

So much pain. So much deceit. For what? For money? For some sick revenge against her father? She'd been closer to the truth than she'd realized earlier. But somehow he'd managed to finesse his way around her suspicions. Make himself seem yet again more protector than predator.

Why? Why the charade? Why not just say, "Courtney, tell your father to give me a million dollars?" He could easily have done so, especially when she still thought of him as the anonymous J.D. Instead, he'd allowed her to discover his identity—hardly a wise move while committing a felony.

She supposed such deliberate carelessness could portend more sinister motives. That the witness wasn't intended to survive. But despite her hurt and betrayal, she could not believe Jack capable of murder.

Then why had he let her unmask him? Surely he hadn't expected a happy reunion. That she would forgive and forget.

Or had he just expected her to jump into his bed?

Courtney shivered—this time not from the cold—at how close she had come to doing just that. If he hadn't slipped up, called her princess...

Damn him.

Gritting her teeth, Courtney forced herself to her feet. This was no time for self-recrimination. She had to keep moving. One foot in front of the other; one foot in front of the other. In her mind she created a new image of Jack Sullivan—first on trial for her kidnapping, then being found guilty, then spending the rest of his life in prison paying for what he had done to her.

The image kept her going.

Another half hour passed before she again collapsed. The first nigglings of fear began to surface. A mile. How long should it have taken her to travel a mile, even in deep snow? Jack had said the wreck was north of the cabin. The sun's position told her she was heading north. But had he meant due north? Or had he been speaking in generalities?

Maybe she should have forgotten the copter. Tried to go down the mountain toward the nearest trailhead instead. But Jack had told her the nearest speck of civilization—a crude parking area—was at least two days hike from the cabin. She could hardly survive two days of this.

She shivered. Would she even survive one?

Enough. She would think about it later. Right now, she had plenty of daylight left and she intended to find that helicopter. How hard could it be? A hundred square miles of wilderness. One smashed helicopter buried under a new snowfall. Piece of cake.

A piece of white cake on a white plate on a white tablecloth in a white room with white walls in a . . .

It's too soon to crack up, Courtney. When the sun goes down and you still haven't found the copter, then you can go quietly nuts.

She glanced back down the slope at her trail and winced. A blind man could follow her tracks.

But then, it was no secret where she was headed. Again she glanced behind her. No sign of Jack.

Her heart turned over. Had she killed him?

No. *You hit him in the head, remember?* she thought acidly. More likely she'd damaged her crutch.

No matter, she should've checked on him. If he'd been unconscious, she could've tied him up, spared herself this whole ordeal. At the very least she could've taken a few precious minutes to gather some supplies. Instead, she'd panicked. Flat-out panicked and run. Now she was paying the price.

Behind her, a twig snapped. Courtney whirled, ready to fight, make a stand. There was nothing there.

But he was coming. She knew it, felt it.

He was coming.

Another hour passed, maybe more. Cloud cover moved in, obscuring the movement of the sun. With every step she took, the muscles in her legs screamed for her to stop. Her ankle was so swollen inside her boot, she feared the blood supply had been cut off. One of these times she was going to fall and not be able to get back up again. She thought of her father, and how they would never resolve the pain between them. She thought of her dear friend Maggie and knew that at least the women and children of Angels' Wings were in good hands. Then she thought of Jack, felt a surge of pure fury, and took another stumbling step forward.

And another.

And another.

She stumbled smack into the helicopter. Hidden beneath dozens of snow-covered branches, she might have passed it by. But she'd tripped over a protruding landing skid.

Here amongst the trees and rocks, the pilot had managed to guide the wildly spinning copter into a small clearing. Blind luck? Skill? Divine intervention? With Jack Sullivan as the pilot she would vote for A or B. She refused to consider C. The Almighty could not possibly have had a hand in this madness.

But at least she'd found the copter. Still, she didn't crawl inside it. Not yet. She was so tired, she feared that if she did, she would simply curl into a fetal ball and go to sleep. She spent the next several minutes tromping about in the snow, trying to restore some circulation to her numbed feet. As she walked, she slapped her arms against her sides.

Finally she headed back toward the copter. She hadn't gone six steps, when she tripped over an unnatural swell in the snow-covered earth and went sprawling. Spitting out a mouthful of snow, she cursed vividly, holding her right knee. Perfect. Just perfect. What the hell was—?

She gasped, scrabbling off the mound of stones. Heaven save her, she'd tripped over a grave! A grave with two wind-tilted markers at one end. Her back seat tormentor, she presumed. And?—

Sickened, but resolved, she fell to her knees and pawed at the stones. When she uncovered a booted foot, she gagged. But she didn't stop. Long, torturous minutes later, she confirmed her worst nightmare. The shallow grave held only one body, a body she could not identify.

The last tiny ray of hope she had held out that she had made a terrible mistake about Jack was gone.

With waning strength and less interest, she shoved some of the stones back over the remains of her kidnapper. It was better than he deserved. Her previous scruples about even kidnappers having mothers who loved them vanished in a haze of anger and despair. If Jack were here, she'd toss him in right next to his perverted friend. And she *knew* Jack had had a mother who loved him.

You're losing it, Courtney.

Pushing to her feet, she staggered over to the helicopter. Dragging aside a couple of branches, she practically fell into the cockpit. That's when she saw the radio. Or rather, what was left of it. It hung in a tangled heap of exposed wires, the kind of damage that couldn't possibly have occurred in a crash. No wonder Jack knew the radio didn't work. He had personally destroyed it!

The tears came then. She couldn't stop them. Tears of frustration, rage and hopelessness. It was suddenly all just too much. She was in the middle of nowhere without food or supplies, the temperature hovering near freezing. She had been a fool to come up here. She should've just bolted down the mountain and hoped for the best. Any chance of rescue she might have had felt as shattered as that radio. Nor was the irony of the situation lost on her. After all she'd been through, she was going to die in this helicopter anyway.

At least Jack wouldn't get his blood money. Fletcher Winthrop would never authorize any ransom payment unless he could speak to her personally, assure himself that she was unharmed. Of that much she was certain.

But it was hardly consolation.

If only she had some matches. She could get by without food, even shelter—as long as the weather held—if she could just build a fire.

Desperate, she shook off her mittens and groped around in the pockets of her parka. Maybe Pete Wilson had been a smoker. She would give her family fortune for a lighter. In the right side pocket, she found a small notebook. She was about to shove it back in her pocket in disgust when she noticed a phone number scrawled on the first page. She stared at that number, her heart skipping a beat. The number was to her father's private line in his Butte office. Only a handful of people in the world knew that number. Why would Pete Wilson be one of them? She closed her eyes. No, not Pete. Jack. The parka had been in Jack's possession. The call about her father's "relapse" had come in on Quentin Hamilton's private line. Somehow Jack had gotten the number. *One more nail in that coffin full of lies, Sullivan.*

She shoved the notebook back where she'd found it, then unzipped the parka's inner pocket. Her last chance. She said a quick prayer. After all this, it was time she had a little *good* luck for a change.

Snugged up against a bottom corner of the pocket she felt something. With a whoop of pure joy, she pulled free a dilapidated book of matches. The advertising read M & M Cafe, Butte, Montana. Inside were seven precious matches.

Matches—and a very real chance to stay alive. She felt ecstatic, rejuvenated. She would build a fire, get warm, then find a way to get herself home. But first she needed to get as far away from the crash site as she could before sunset. Because Jack was still out there somewhere. And this would be the first place he'd look.

With a new sense of purpose Courtney headed toward a stand of lodgepole. Quickly she manufactured what she hoped was a convincing false trail into the woods. Then, taking special care to obscure her tracks, she took off in the opposite direction.

Some two miles into the trees, she stopped. Above her, an opening in the canopy of branches reached all the way to the sky. Here, melting snow from the heat of her fire wouldn't drop onto the flames. Using her bare hands, Courtney scooped out a two-foot-wide fire pit, then scavenged the forest floor for dead branches. Her forest-ranger-wannabe days were coming in quite handy. In fifteen minutes she had herself a fine camp fire and had only used one match.

Next, she began the agonizing process of pulling off her boots. Her right boot offered only minor problems. But her left, the ankle swollen to nearly twice its normal size, was a much more grim task. She almost didn't take the footwear off, fearing that if she did, she'd never get it back on. But it was a chance she had to take. She needed to inspect her chilled flesh.

Finally the boot pulled free. Peeling off her sock, she was pleased to see that while the flesh was indeed swollen, there was no sign of frostbite. Pete Wilson had had good taste in high-country bootwear.

For the next half hour, Courtney massaged her feet, then endured the arduous task of putting her boots back on. She couldn't risk being caught barefooted by some prowling forest creature—or some two-legged counterpart with tousled dark hair and Montana-sky eyes.

She let out a soul-weary sigh. The last thought was the true agony of being stuck here for the night. Worse than any physical discomfort was the unwelcome opportunity to think. Think about Jack. About his warmth and compassion when she'd told him about Danny. About his outrage at the knowledge that Roger had abused her. About how aroused he had been when he'd caught her up in his arms and kissed her. Was it really all lies? Just role-playing in some sick, twisted game?

"I hate you, Jack Sullivan. I'll hate you until my last breath."

"Can't say as I blame you," came his quiet voice.

Her head jerked up and she gasped. He was standing between two pine trees not fifteen feet away from her. She noticed two things: he had a nasty bruise on the left side of his face near his eye, and he was carrying an oversize backpack, which he began to ease off of his shoulders.

It would be her only chance. As he struggled with his pack, Courtney scrambled to her feet and ran, just ran, not caring which direction she took, only knowing that she had to get away.

But her ankle betrayed her. It buckled, just as Jack launched himself at her from behind. He caught her just below the knees. Courtney pitched forward into the snow, just barely getting her arms out in time to catch herself. With a cry of pure rage, she twisted onto her back. She kicked, fought, cursed, pummeling him with her fists. But he was too strong, and she was too exhausted. He caught first one wrist, then the other, pinning her arms down on either side of her head as he straddled her middle.

"You're going to listen to me," he said.

"Never!" She bucked upward, and he pressed down harder, so hard, she could scarcely breathe.

"So typical!" she hissed.

He eased back a little. "What's that?"

"The tried-and-true male method to get a woman to do what he wants—brute force."

Jack's eyes glinted like blue steel. "Don't put that on me, Courtney. I've never raised a hand to a woman in my life."

"No? What do you call kidnapping me at gun-point? Letting that partner of yours paw at me."

"That was never supposed to happen. If I'd known what he was doing, I would've broken his arms."

"Liar!"

Abruptly he rolled off her and climbed to his feet.

Courtney, too, scrambled to stand, all the while keeping a wary eye on him. At the slightest hint he meant to harm her, she would run again.

"I can see we're not going to get anywhere trying to talk this out," he said. "So I'll just say it—you're stuck with me 'til I say otherwise. If you run, I'll find you. And next time I'll tie you to the nearest tree."

"Right. God forbid you lose your big payoff."

He rubbed a hand across the back of his neck. "Let's get one thing straight, shall we? I did not kidnap you."

"And I'm not standing in the middle of a pine forest, talking to the world's biggest son of a—" She turned her back on him, shaking with fury.

"I'm not trying to scare you, Courtney. I'm trying to save your life."

"You were the pilot of that helicopter, Jack. Every single thing you say to me goes straight back to that single incontrovertible fact."

"I want to show you something," he said quietly, walking around in front of her and reaching into the inside pocket of his sheepskin jacket. He pulled out what looked like a leather billfold. "I was in on your kidnapping, yes. But not for the reasons you think."

"Flying lessons?"

He ignored her sarcasm and continued, his voice calm, almost gentle. She wanted to hit him. "I got wind of the plot to kidnap you ten minutes before it was supposed to happen. I had just enough time to arrange for the original pilot to have a little accident. Luckily, he was the bigmouth who told me about the plot."

"So let me get this straight. You knew I was going to be kidnapped, but it didn't occur to you to stop it. You just said, 'Hey, great idea,' and joined in?"

She got him that time. A muscle in his jaw jumped, but his voice remained remarkably even. "I was there to protect you. But the kidnapping had to proceed as planned."

"Why?"

"I can't tell you that, except to say it was the only way to get certain evidence."

"You're talking in riddles. In fact, you almost sound like a—" She shook off the thought. Now he really was making her crazy.

And then he opened his billfold and held it out to her. "I'm a cop, Courtney."

She stared at him, stunned, speechless. He didn't blink, didn't move. She snatched the billfold from him, scrutinizing the official-looking credentials. A gold shield with the engraved insignia of the Los Angeles Police on one side, a photo ID on the other. She stared at the picture for long seconds, trying to reconcile its crew-cut, spit-and-polish image of Jack D. Sullivan with the beard-stubbled, long-haired mountain man standing in front of her.

The man in the photo also had a title. Lieutenant Detective, Homicide.

"Nice forgery," she said.

"It's real."

"Right. And if I don't buy this one, what's in the other pocket? You're the CIA? The Pope? Elvis?"

"Stop it!"

"No! You stop it," she cried, tossing the ID back at him. "How stupid do you think I am? An L.A. cop can't work undercover in Montana."

"I didn't say it was an authorized assignment. I resigned from the LAPD eight months ago. You might say I'm conducting my own investigation."

"For eight months? From a cabin in the middle of nowhere?"

"For two months." He shoved a hand through his dark hair. "The first six I was just... living here."

"So what happened two months ago?"

His voice tightened. "Pete Wilson was murdered."

Courtney staggered back a step.

"And I intend to find out who did it."

"But the Butte police—"

"Say it was an accident. He drowned ice fishing. Period."

"So how do you know he didn't?"

"I just know."

Courtney began to pace, but quickly stopped when her ankle objected. "Let me get this straight. Are you saying there's some tie-in between Pete Wilson's murder and my kidnapping?"

"I'm not saying anything of the kind. In fact, I've already said too much."

"You've said nothing! Dammit, Jack, this is my life we're talking about. That is, if I decide to believe a word you're saying. For all I know, this could just be another pile of lies to keep me in line until...until you get your money. I mean, that jerk in the back of the helicopter said you were taking me to a cabin. And that's exactly where I've been for a week. How do you explain that?"

"The cabin is—was—Pete's, Courtney. My hand to God. That piece of scum in the back seat was expecting another cabin, one up near the Canadian border. I had the coordinates for it, but I flew around in circles. Frank couldn't tell one rock from another. But I knew exactly where I was going."

"I hate you."

"We've established that."

She was wavering again, wanting so much to believe.... "I can't do this anymore, Jack. There've been too many lies."

He reached into his left-hand pocket. This time he pulled out a gun. One she hadn't seen before. He gripped it by the barrel, offering it to her, butt first. "It's a Beretta 9 mm. Holds fifteen rounds in the clip. I put a new one in before I left the cabin." He showed her how to release the safety. "Take it."

She held back, not wanting to touch the gun. "How do I even know it's loaded?"

He clicked off the safety, pointed the gun in the air and fired, the echo resounding through the trees like cannonfire. "Fourteen bullets should be plenty, don't you think?" He put the safety back on and tossed the gun at her feet.

Courtney did not pick it up.

He turned and walked back over to the gear and supplies he'd brought along. "You've got a good fire going. It's going to be dark in a couple of hours. I suggest we get bedded down." He hefted the pack over one shoulder. "We can talk more in the morning."

"Excuse me?"

"You didn't think we were going back to the cabin, did you? It's too risky in the dark."

"I was referring to the bedding-down part."
Courtney's gaze skated past him to the pack on his
back. "I only see one sleeping bag."

His blue eyes were unreadable, his voice madden-
ingly matter-of-fact. "I could hardly bring the whole
cabin with me. It's a big bag. We can share."

"Like hell!"

He shrugged. "Suit yourself. You're going to get
awfully cold, though."

"Me?"

"It's my sleeping bag."

Her lips thinned. "Fine, we'll share. But remember—" she glanced toward the Beretta "—I've got the
gun."

He laughed, amused and, she thought, just a little
impressed. Then he sobered, those blue eyes suddenly
deadly serious. He stepped close, so close she could see
all too well the ugly, purplish bruise that tracked from
his hairline to just above his left cheek.

"I'm sorry I hit you," she said.

"You thought I kidnapped you." She could tell the
thought pained him, maybe more than the bruise.
"The last thing I ever wanted to do was hurt you
again, Courtney. I swear." He reached a hand toward
her face, then seemed to change his mind. He curled
his fingers into his palm and dropped his hand back to
his side. "I've got no right on God's earth to ask you
this—but I'm going to ask anyway. I'm going to ask
you to trust me, Courtney. To trust me with—"

Behind them they heard a snuffling sound. They
both turned.

A bear cub, likely a yearling by its size, gamboled
through the trees, heading straight toward them. Jack

gripped Courtney's arm, his voice low, urgent. "The sow won't be far behind. We need to get the hell—"

The mother bear lumbered into view some eighty yards from where they stood. Her head went up, testing the air, assessing the safety of her offspring. The bear was a black bear. A tiny consolation at least. Black bears were rarely as aggressive as their grizzly cousins.

"Don't move," Jack whispered. "Don't even breathe."

Courtney had no trouble obeying. She stood, transfixed, terrified.

"Good bears," Jack said, his voice steady, firm. "Nice bears."

"What are you doing?" Courtney hissed.

"Letting mama know we're human. I'm hoping she has an aversion to the species." Very slowly, Jack stepped in front of her, putting himself between her and the bears. Courtney's throat tightened. Her eyes stung. She had the all but ridiculous urge to throw her arms around him. But she didn't move.

The she-bear seemed wary now, her dark eyes watchful. Jack continued talking, his attention on the bears, his words meant for Courtney.

"Listen to me," he said. "There's a ridge fifty yards behind you. I want you to back up—real slow. Get down those rocks any way you can."

"What about you?"

"Just do as I say." Jack spread his arms, making himself as formidable looking as possible to the four hundred pound bear, and doing his best to block the animal's view of Courtney's retreat.

She limped backward, her every instinct screaming at her to turn, to run. She did neither. The cub was rolling in the snow now some forty yards to her left, but the mother bear remained still as a statue, her eyes fixed on Jack.

"Keep moving," he said.

"Come with me," she pleaded.

"Go."

She reached the lip of the ridge. She started to call out to Jack, then everything seemed to happen at once.

The bear let out a hideous roar and charged. For her size, the animal moved at an astonishing speed, covering the eighty yard distance in seconds. With no chance for escape, Jack dropped and rolled. Courtney screamed again, certain he was going to be devoured before her very eyes. But even as she screamed, she was stumbling forward, grabbing up the Beretta from where Jack had tossed it earlier. Releasing the safety, she fired the gun skyward once, twice. The bear didn't slow, trampling over Jack with bone-shattering force. His head snapped back, colliding with a sickening thud against the icy ground.

Courtney fired again. Rearing up on her hind legs, the bear let out a blood-chilling roar. Then just that swiftly, she dropped to all fours, swatted her cub on the rump and disappeared into the trees.

Allowing herself no time to think, Courtney rushed to Jack's side and dropped to her knees beside him. He was still as death. She whispered his name.

Nothing.

She put her hand on his chest, a shudder of relief coursing through her as she felt the pulsing beat of his heart.

Quickly, she checked him for injuries. The sleeping bag furled on his back had been shredded straight down the middle by the she-bear's claws, but the only injury she could find was a bloody gash on the side of Jack's head. A gash just inches from the ugly bruise she herself had given him back at the cabin.

Again she tried to rouse him. Again he did not respond.

Swiftly, she unfurled the sleeping bag. Using it as a travois, she dragged Jack over to the fire, then swiftly bundled him up inside the bag. He showed not the slightest hint of consciousness. Her mind leaped to skull fractures and hemorrhage.

Stifling a sob, Courtney tended the fire, then snuggled into the bag beside him. Under any other circumstances, such proximity to Jack Sullivan would have had her emotions on overload—confusion, desire, anxiety, excitement, suspicion, awe. Now there was only one—fear. Fear that he was going to die.

Darkness settled over the forest. Overhead, the trees hid the stars from her view. The only light was the bright orange glow of the fire. The only sound, the only sound that mattered, was the deep, labored breathing of the man in her arms. She held him close, eyes burning, praying to God she would still hear that sound come morning.

Chapter 8

Jack was dreaming. He knew it was a dream, because he was back in L.A. Back in L.A. on a hot and ugly August night eight months ago. But knowing it was a dream didn't give him the power to stop it. Knowing it was a dream didn't give him the power to change what happened that cursed night.

It had been a rare night off for he and Emmett Washington, his partner of five years. Normally they worked second shift out of homicide, special services division, often undercover. Their specialty—gang activity. Four nights a month they opted to spend their free time at a junior high in east L.A., where a local minister kept the gym open all night. Kids from the neighborhood could come by and shoot hoops instead of shooting dope or getting into other kinds of trouble. The program had gotten high marks from various civic groups. The crime rate in the surrounding area had shown a small, but real drop. Gang recruitment had been cut nearly in half.

He and Emmett called it quits just past 3:00 a.m. "I've decided," Jack said, staggering off the court and wiping at his sweat-soaked face with the sleeve of his faded rock star T-shirt, "that three hours of nonstop basketball is my limit." The kids, a mix of white, Hispanic, black and Asian, were still going like Energizer bunnies up and down the court.

"Except we've been playin' six hours," Emmett gasped, hunching over beside Jack, and sucking wind big-time, as the kids would say. A tall, lean nononsense African-American, Emmett dabbed at the perspiration on his brow with the kerchief he'd pulled out of the pocket of his gym shorts.

"Which explains why I've been a dead man for the past three hours," Jack said.

Emmett chuckled. "It's hell to get old, isn't it?"

"You're as young as you feel." Jack groaned, straightening his aching body. "Which means Willard Scott should be wishing me happy birthday any day now."

"Hey, you guys ain't quittin', are ya?" The question came from a tall, rangy black kid who dribbled the basketball he was handling right up to the out-of-bounds line. He didn't cross the line; he just stood there, bouncing the ball and waiting for an answer.

"We're out of here, Jason," Emmett said.

"But it's early."

When howls of protests went up from Jason's teammates for him holding up the game, Jason passed off the ball and signaled for another kid to take his place on the court. Jason stepped between Emmett and Jack on the sidelines. "You're comin' again soon, ain't ya, Jack, Emmett?"

Jack nodded. Jason was one of his favorites. One of eight kids, he was third oldest in a family where the father had walked out when Jason was seven. His mom worked two jobs to keep food on the table. His two older brothers had already made wrongheaded choices and were doing hard time in prison. Jason was determined not to join them. Jack and Emmett were determined to do everything they could to see to it that he didn't. "Next week," Jack told him. "Not sure which night yet."

Jason grinned. "Good. You guys are better than most of the old—I mean, the older guys who come in here. You shoot a fair hoop, you know, for cops."

Emmett chuckled. "Thanks."

Jason stepped closer to Jack, his brown eyes suddenly serious, his voice low. "I want to thank you for gettin' me that job, Jack. Even if it is flipping burgers."

"Hey, everybody's gotta start somewhere. My first job was filling vending machines." His voice was wry. "A cop I know figured I'd have a real talent for it, since I was trying to knock one over the night he and I met."

Jason's eyes widened. "You got arrested?"

"Nope. I was damned lucky."

"I'm glad for the job, Jack. Really. Even if every time I see a pickle now, I wanna puke. It's good spendin' money. And I don't have to watch my back, if you know what I mean. Thanks."

"I got you the interview. You got yourself the job, Jason. It was all up to you once you walked through the door."

Jason beamed and headed back to his teammates. Emmett gave Jack a "well-done" clap on the shoulder, then the two of them started toward the locker room.

"You boys look a little done in." The observation came from a diminutive, gray-haired gentleman rising off his seat in the front row of the bleachers. He ambled toward them, grinning.

"Reverend Mike, how come we never see you with a basketball in your hands?" Emmett asked.

"Somebody's got to be able to call 911 for the two of you." His intelligent gray blue eyes sparkled with humor and genuine affection.

Jack and Emmett scowled good-naturedly.

Mike Hawkins sobered. "I've told you before, but I'll tell you again. You two make a helluva difference here with these kids. They get to see for themselves that cops are people with real lives and families. Which reminds me—" he glanced at Emmett "—how's that pretty little wife of yours doing? That baby's due any day now, isn't it?"

"Don't say that!" Emmett protested. "It's still three weeks. But I've got my pager—" he patted the tiny black box on his hip "—just in case."

"Thanks a lot, Mike," Jack grumbled. "Now I'm going to have to run through that whole Lamaze thing with him again. He's so afraid he's going to forget something. Like Loretta."

"I just want to be prepared. Is there anything wrong with that?"

"Yeah," Jack said. "You're going to make her obstetrician look bad." To the preacher, he said, "We'll be by your office after we shower, okay?"

"Fine. I'll be there."

They trusted everything to the locker room except their weapons. The guns were in a safe in Mike's office.

Ten minutes later they were standing outside the gym. "My abused muscles notwithstanding, I think we put in a good night's work, bro," Jack said.

Emmett nodded. "The best."

Jack smiled. They were a good team, he and Emmett. He couldn't have asked for a better partner, a better friend. He stood on the steps, his gaze shifting casually up and down the two-lane street that ran in front of the school. No traffic. The only car for two blocks was Jack's own Chevy Blazer parked across the street under the light. He knew Emmett was making the same offhanded survey. It wasn't that they were expecting trouble. It was just second nature for a cop to be watchful, alert.

Jack fiddled with the lapel of his navy sport coat, wishing he could shed the blasted thing in favor of the white T-shirt beneath it. It was too hot for the jacket. But that would make his shoulder holster a little too conspicuous. A cop was a cop twenty-four hours a day. They headed across the street.

"You gonna teach that kid of yours to be as lousy at basketball as you are?" Jack asked, as he unlocked the Blazer and tossed his gym bag into the back seat.

"Hey, it's you white guys that can't jump, remember?" Emmett climbed in on the passenger side.

"Except that I out rebounded you six to one tonight, chump."

"I believe that was the Shaquille body double you had on your team."

Jack chuckled. "Fourteen years old and six foot ten. If he ever gets coordinated, he's going to make both of us look like we're sittin' on our a—'' Jack's eyes narrowed. "What do you make of that?" He pointed across the street toward a darkened cul de sac.

A man was weaving drunkenly toward the dead-end alley.

"Just some wino with a snootful," Emmett said.

"Best sit here and watch him a minute," Jack said. Emmett nodded.

Jack reached over and punched open the glove compartment, retrieving a package of Ding Dongs. He offered one to Emmett.

"I have more respect for my body, bro."

"Coward."

Emmett snorted. "Loretta's right. You need to get married, Jack. Have a home-cooked meal once in a while."

"I been married." Jack pitched the cellophane wrapper into the back seat and munched the chocolate snack cake. "She couldn't cook."

"I mean to the right woman. Wendy wasn't cut out to be a cop's wife."

Jack's jaw clenched. "Drop it, okay?" The night had been pleasant. He didn't want to spoil it.

"Sorry, man. It's just that I'm so happy with Loretta. I can't imagine my life without her. You need a woman like that."

Jack's mind flashed on sun-gold hair and emerald-green eyes. "I had my chance. I blew it."

"The one you told me about? The one with the Fortune 500 spoon in her mouth."

"I was a world-class jerk."

"That was then, this is now. She available?"

"She's divorced. Other than that, I have no idea."

"So give her a call."

"Look, Emmett," Jack said, trying to keep his voice even, "I didn't just burn the bridge with this lady. I used C-4 on the pilings. If she were in a particularly magnanimous frame of mind, Courtney might rank me right above the plague. If not, the plague wins."

Emmett twisted in the seat. "I'm not trying to tell you how to run your life, Jack." He shook his head. "Not too much anyway. It's just that sometimes I think about that tattoo on your arm."

"What about it?"

"The lone wolf. Don't you see? It ain't natural. Wolves are sociable animals. You need a mate, Jack. The kind of woman to build a life with. Loretta worries about you. She's always raggin' me to make sure you eat right, get enough sleep. I'm tired of baby-sittin', man."

Jack rolled his eyes. "How about a compromise? A one-night stand—maybe two."

"That would be a good start."

They both laughed.

Jack glanced toward the alley. The wino had not reemerged. "Looks like our friend has bedded down for the night." He turned the key in the ignition. "Let's hit it. I—"

The man staggered out of the darkness, his drunken movements exaggerated. He was reaching out a beseeching hand, though there was no one in front of him. "Help me!"

Jack muttered an expletive. "So much for some quality sleep." He switched off the engine.

"Duty calls, bro."

Jack was out the door.

"Should I call for backup?" Emmett hollered after him.

"For what? To collar a wino?"

Emmett followed Jack. Instinctively they checked their guns as they approached the darkened alley. The glow from the streetlight did not extend beyond the first few yards of the cul de sac. Jack felt the hairs on the nape of his neck prickle. "Something's not right here. Keep an eye out." They reached the alley.

"Damn, I should've called for that backup," Emmett muttered. "The captain's been on our backs enough lately about hot doggin'."

Jack got down on one knee beside the groggy transient. "You okay, guy?" Jack breathed through his mouth. The man reeked of urine and vomit.

"He beat me up." The man's words slurred together. "The little jerk beat me up. Stole my money."

"You don't look beat-up, pops. You look drunk."

"I'm tellin' ya, the punk took over a hundred dollars cash money."

"And where'd you get that kind of change?"

"Got it workin' for a grocer. Korean fella."

"Uh-huh." He looked at Emmett. "The last time this guy had a hundred dollars, it was in a crap game. And he probably lost it on the next roll." To the transient, he said, "What did the guy look like? The one that took your money."

"Wasn't no guy. Ain't you listenin'? Was a kid. A little kid. Looked to be maybe ten years old. He's still in the alley. Was lying in wait like some jungle cat. Jumped me, I tell ya."

Jack and Emmett exchanged dubious glances.

From out of the darkness, a garbage can lid clanged. Jack and Emmett drew their guns in one motion. "Freeze! Police!" Emmett shouted.

Jack took the right side of the alley, Emmett the left. Beneath his sneakers, broken glass crunched. Jack continued to breathe through his mouth, repulsed by the stench of overturned garbage rotting in the summer heat. "Come out of there," Jack ordered. "Hands where I can see 'em. And they'd better be empty."

Jack pulled a penlight from his pocket and shone it toward the alley's end. No doors. No windows. No way out.

"Give it up!" Jack said. "You've got nowhere to go."

"Jack!" Emmett signaled toward the corner nearest him, where three huge crates were stacked. A rat skittered out. Jack started to relax, then reacted to Emmett's shout. "Freeze. Now!"

From out of the shadows came a tiny waif of a boy. Sandy hair, wide-eyed, scared to death. "I didn't mean no harm," he whimpered. "Honest. Please don't tell my mom."

"Get out here. Now."

The boy hung back in the shadows. "That man tried to grab me. Pull me back here. Do things to me." The boy began to sob. Jack doubted he was more than twelve.

"He's lyin'!" The wino cursed. "The brat tried to—"

"Shut up and get back! We'll get both sides of this later." To the boy he said, "What are you doing out here?" Jack had never seen him before. He was not one of the kids that came to the gym.

"My mom works nights. I got scared. I started to go down to where she works. It's a liquor store. Fredo's."

Jack had heard of it.

"I go there sometimes and she lets me sleep in the back room. And we walk home together in the morning."

"We've got to take you downtown. Get this mess sorted out. We'll send a car for your mom, okay?"

"Please, she'll skin me if I get in trouble." Tears streamed down his face.

Jack uncocked his gun. Emmett reholstered his.

A hundred pounds. Cherub-faced. Wide-eyed, scared to death.

"I should have known better than to tell Loretta I'd be back before dawn." Emmett took a step toward the boy.

Everything happened in slow motion. From nowhere, the boy had a gun in his hand, both arms extended. No! No! Jack's mind screamed the words, as he brought his own weapon to bear. But he hesitated. One second. One eternal second. How could he shoot a child?

The child fired his gun.

Emmett cried out, doubled over. No! He collapsed, falling on his left side, his face contorted in agony.

Real time again. Jack tackled the boy, wrestled him to the ground. In a blind rage he handcuffed him. All the while, the kid screamed obscenities—against cops, against the wino, against the world. Then, when he was cuffed and subdued, he was just a kid again. Sobbing, sobbing for his mommy.

Jack crawled to Emmett's side. "Oh, God. Oh, no. No. I'm sorry, Emmett. I'm so damned sorry."

Emmett's eyes were open wide. He was trying to say something, but no words came.

Jack pressed his hand to his partner's chest, felt Emmett's blood surging over his hand, felt Emmett's life draining out through his fingers.

"Dammit, Emmett!" Jack was screaming. Screaming for help in the hot night air, in a garbage-strewn alley, next to a handcuffed twelve-year-old murderer.

Dead. Dead. Dead.

Emmett was dead. Jack felt his own life's blood flow out of him that night. No taste for being a cop anymore. Quit. Run. They could call it whatever they wanted. But he was gone.

He went home. Back to Montana.

Pete was there. Pete understood. Pete offered his cabin. "Stay as long as you want, boy. As long as you need."

Pete. Emmett.

Blood. Blood on his hands. Blood everywhere. Jack wondered if he would ever feel clean again.

Courtney lay perfectly still beside Jack. Any movement at all, she feared, would rouse him from his nightmare. As difficult as it was to listen to him hurt, she consoled herself with the fact that he was oblivious to it. The nightmare had eased her fears that he'd been seriously injured by the bear. He seemed no more or less consumed by this bout of dreaming than he'd been the other night at the cabin. But the other night she had had the freedom to move about. Tonight the temperature and the circumstances obliged her to share a sleeping bag with the man. Nothing short of the bear's return could persuade her to wake him.

He cried out again, shifting fitfully within the limited confines of their state-of-the-art cocoon. Despite her resolve to ignore him, she reached between them and squeezed his hand. The tension in him eased, just a little.

"Damn you, Jack," she whispered. "I don't know what to do about you. I don't know what to *feel* about you."

The man had her on an emotional roller coaster. Each time she felt herself daring to care, something would happen to warn her away. Adding to her own curious jumble of feelings was her sense that Jack was just as confused as she was. Given a choice, she was certain neither one of them would have opted for this reunion. And yet here they were.

Things happen for a reason.

This is some kind of test, isn't it, God? But a test of what?

The answer that occurred to her was the one she least welcomed—and most feared.

The last thing Jack had asked of her just before the bear attacked was that she trust him. Trust him despite what had happened ten years ago. Trust him despite his current backlog of dissembling and deceit. Trust him despite her own abysmal track record with the men in her life.

Jack. Her father. Roger.

Trust.

A small word. A simple concept. And yet time and again the men in her life had abused the trust she'd placed in them.

"Get over it," one of her friends had told her once, as though it were a cold.

If only it were that simple.

It had been four years since her divorce, and she hadn't had so much as a date. It wasn't a question of trusting Jack. It was a question of trusting herself, her own instincts. Instincts about men. Time and again she had counseled other women at Angels' Wings on how to get back into the mainstream of life, how even to dare falling in love again. But when it came to her own relationships with the opposite sex, the door was not only closed, it was nailed shut. She couldn't take the risk.

Not when her emotions were involved.

And they were involved in spades with Jack Sullivan.

A breeze wafted over her and she shivered. Grateful for the distraction, Courtney snuggled deeper into the sleeping bag. The bag's optimal comfort range to twenty below zero had been compromised by the bear's teeth and claws. Though she guessed the temperature to be near thirty, she still felt cold. There was a way around it, of course. To maximize the benefits from their combined body heat, she and Jack could shed their coats. In fact, she thought with a suffusion of embarrassment, they would probably be warmest if they were both stark naked.

Courtney decided she could handle a few goose bumps.

She could handle them even better, she thought grimly, if she could fall asleep. But between the chill and Jack's restiveness, sleep eluded her. Or, more honestly, it was driven off by her continuing debate about trust. There wasn't a doubt in her mind that

Jack would bring up the subject again this morning. What was she going to say? *I can't trust you, Jack, because I'm falling in love with you?*

She'd rather die.

In the end, she opted for the coward's way out. She would simply have him take her home. She would get back to her life; he would get back to his. The question of trust would become blessedly moot. Her heart might be foolish enough to make the same mistake twice about this man, but her head, she assured herself, would not. Once Jack was out of her life again, common sense would prevail. She was certain he would be just as grateful to have her gone.

That decided, she finally fell asleep.

She woke to Jack's eyes on her. Her flesh warmed. "How long have you been awake?" she asked.

"Not long. Maybe five minutes."

"Sleep well?" It was a stupid question. She knew precisely how he'd slept. And the curious regard in those blue eyes told her he knew that she knew.

"You saved my life," he said quietly. "That bear would've torn me apart."

"I did what I had to do. I couldn't watch you die."

He gave her that lopsided grin she liked too well. Then he sighed and stretched a little, stopping abruptly when his every move forced him into contact with another part of her body. "A bit cozy in here, isn't it?" His voice was light, but the strain in him was evident.

"I'll get up," she said quickly, too quickly.

"No. It's okay. I didn't mean..." His mouth twisted ruefully. "Life takes some peculiar turns, doesn't it?"

"What do you mean?"

"I mean, there've been a few nights these past ten years that I've thought about what it would be like to sleep with you again. And not once did I ever think that that's exactly what I would do."

"Excuse me?"

"Sleep."

"Oh." Courtney felt her cheeks heat; more than that, she felt an almost overwhelming urge to turn toward him, touch him, let him touch her. Common sense had no chance in such close quarters. Swiftly she grabbed for the zipper and began to extricate herself from the sleeping bag.

"Sorry," he said gruffly. "I shouldn't have said that."

"Forget it." She pushed to her feet, crying out when she leaned too heavily on her left ankle.

"Still pretty sore?"

"It didn't appreciate my cross-country hike yesterday." She hobbled over to her crutch, determined to put what distance she could between them. At least he hadn't yet tossed out the trust question. "I'm hungry. How about you?"

"I've got some dehydrated soup in my backpack." He started to get up, but his face paled, and he slumped back.

"Stay still," she ordered. "I'll handle the food." In Jack's backpack she found the soup packets, some instant coffee, a tin pan and four cups. By melting snow, she soon had a cup of vegetable soup and a cup of coffee for each of them.

"You're pretty good at this Daniel Boone stuff," Jack said, pushing up on one elbow and sipping his coffee.

"My forest-ranger dreams finally come true."

"You would've been good at it."

She flushed. "I doubt my father would agree."

"Quentin wanted you to follow in his footsteps at Winthrop-Hamilton?"

She grimaced. "Hardly. Women don't exactly dominate the company's upper echelons. In fact, I think they have just enough to keep affirmative action off their backs. Which makes it all the more astonishing that I found myself with my father's power of attorney when I got back to Butte. Fletcher was surprised, too. He wanted me to sign all sorts of papers. That's the only reason I was even at my father's office the day I was kidnapped. I was trying to make heads or tails of some corporate documents on his computer."

"Your father's been unconscious since his heart attack?"

She nodded. "That's been the hardest. Not being able to talk to him." She closed her eyes, fighting back a sudden wave of emotion. "Do you realize that I don't even know if he's still alive? Do you have any idea what that's like?"

He didn't answer.

"I need you to take me home, Jack." Almost against her will, she added, "Please."

He seemed to wince, then said, "There's more to your kidnapping than you know, Courtney. More than it's safe for you to know. I can't take you back. Not yet."

"Why?"

"I can't tell you that. You'll just have to trust me."

There it was. Just like that. "And if I can't?" She expected him to be disappointed. What she saw in those sky-blue eyes was hurt.

He picked up a dried pine needle, twisting it between his fingers. "I can't take you home, Courtney. I'm sorry."

Her fingers curled into her palms. She was at his mercy and she knew it. "Then at least take me back to the cabin. I find the accommodations here are a bit...cramped." She glanced meaningfully at the sleeping bag.

"I couldn't agree more." Again he tried pushing to his feet. Again he failed.

Courtney had to rein in her frustration. The man had been attacked by a bear. "You'd best sleep awhile longer."

"I'll be fine." The only color in his face was the bruise over his left eye.

"I can't carry you, Jack," she snapped. "Just sleep, okay?"

He shot her a penetrating look. "If I do, will you still be here when I wake up?"

She started, surprised. It hadn't occurred to her that he thought she would run off again. "I'm still here, aren't I?"

"That's not exactly a yes."

"It's the best I can do."

He muttered a curse, but lay back. Five minutes later, he again tried to get up. He took two steps and sagged to his knees. Courtney rushed to his side, easing him back onto the sleeping bag. "I told you to sleep," she said tightly. "Not try to prove you're superhuman."

"Such a tender bedside manner."

"You're lucky I don't hit you in the head with a rock."

His eyes grew serious. "I'm sorry about all this, Courtney. More than you know."

"Right." She was entirely too close to him. Her position, leaning over his supine body, entirely too compromising.

He reached up and trailed the backs of his fingers along her cheek. "Anybody ever tell you you're one beautiful lady?"

"You're delirious."

"Nope. Stone sober."

Courtney did not resist as he pulled her toward him. His kiss was hot, hungry. Courtney's pulse leapt. She could feel the fire in him, the need. For her. She wanted so much to believe—in his passion, in Jack himself. She could feel her defenses crumbling, feel her heart clamoring for her to give in, surrender.

Trust.

Don't do it. He'll break your heart.

No, not this time.

Trust.

The kiss went on and on. Dreamily, Courtney wondered at the feasibility of making love to a man in forty-degree temperatures. The sleeping bag might merit five stars yet. But then Jack's fervor began to ease. Courtney drew back, puzzled, hurt. Until she saw how ashen he looked. The man's spirit might be willing, but his flesh was committing treason. He was practically unconscious.

Her mouth tipped upward. "Sleep," she said.

"Trust me," he murmured.

She stilled. Is that what his kiss had been all about?

"No," he gasped, seeming to read her mind. "Not what you think." He tried to raise a hand toward her, but it fell back. "Not what you—" His eyes closed. He was out cold.

Courtney stared at him, her senses reeling. Stay calm, she urged herself. Think. Jack Sullivan was no fool. If he'd been trying to seduce her into trusting him, he would've been a bit more subtle. Still, his timing shook her to the core. She'd been close, so close to making that leap of faith.

She pushed to her feet, still trembling. When he came to, she would renew her efforts to get him to take her home. For now, she would busy herself tending the camp. The fire needed more wood. She hobbled off in search of some.

She was gone too long. By the time she returned, the fire was completely out. Guiltily she checked on Jack. He seemed to be sleeping peacefully. Hunkering down beside the fire pit, she reached into her parka for her matches, then changed her mind. She would save her miracle matches. Just in case.

Crossing to Jack's sheepskin coat, she felt around hoping he'd brought along matches or a lighter; frowning when she encountered a solid, rectangular object.

She pulled it free, staring at it in stunned disbelief. Trust him? Is that what he'd asked of her?

I can't take you down the mountain, Courtney.

I can't notify your dying father that you're all right, Courtney.

She gripped the cellular phone so hard, her knuckles went white. He'd had the means to put her mind at ease all along. He'd had the means to martial any forces he wanted to rescue her, guard her, get her off this damned mountain. And he'd done none of those things.

She stared at him, his features relaxed, almost boy-ish in sleep. *Enjoy your rest, Jack,* she thought sav-agely. *The next nap you take will be in jail.* She yanked out the cell phone's antenna. It was time to make a few calls.

Three hours later, Jack stirred and opened his eyes.

"You never stopped lying, did you?" she snapped.

He blinked, disconcerted, then he saw what she was holding. "Tell me you waited for me to wake up," he said, his voice oddly strained. "Tell me you didn't call anyone."

"I'll admit it was hard to get through in this ter-rain. But I managed to raise a few people. A ranger station not far from here for starters, then a 911 op-erator."

Jack looked sick. "What did you say to them?"

"What do you think? I asked them to relay a mes-sage. To tell my father's people that I'm all right. Mostly, I told them to contact Fletcher Winthrop. Get a rescue team headed up here. And the police. The real police."

Jack pushed himself to his feet, staggering slightly. His face paled, but he forced himself to remain stand-ing. All the while he cursed viciously. "We've got to get out of here."

Courtney stood her ground, hands on her hips. "I'm not going anywhere with you. Not anymore. I'm waiting right here for my ride home."

"Dammit, Courtney." He raked a hand through his disheveled hair. "Why couldn't you—?" He stopped, his whole manner suddenly bone weary, lost. "No. Why would you? This is my fault. All of it."

"Finally," she murmured, "the truth."

"Yes, Courtney, the truth." Those blue eyes bored straight through her. "You just signed your own death warrant. Fletcher Winthrop is the man who ordered your kidnapping."

Chapter 9

Jack stood splaylegged across the camp fire from Courtney, waiting for his words to sink in. He hadn't wanted to be the one to tell her about Fletcher Winthrop's complicity in her kidnapping, but she'd left him no choice. His reluctance didn't stem from any particular sensibility about Winthrop's place in Courtney's life, but from the battle he knew such an accusation would bring. Courtney did not disappoint him.

"I knew you were a world-class liar, Sullivan," she said through clenched teeth, "but I didn't think you were stupid. If you think for one minute that I believe—"

"I don't give a damn what you believe, Courtney." His head throbbed, and his whole body was one big ache. "All I can tell you is the truth. Fletcher Winthrop arranged, everything—the pilot, the man in the back seat, the chloroform, the gun. All of it." His words were cold, calculated—necessary. He needed to break her considerable bonds of loyalty toward Winthrop—and fast. He had no way of knowing precisely when the 911 operator Courtney had talked to might have gotten through to the man. To be safe, Jack had to assume the worst—that Winthrop was now fully aware that Courtney was alive and well, and that something had gone terribly wrong with his plan. "Help me break camp. We've got to get out of here."

"Maybe that head injury affected your hearing," she gritted. "I'm not going anywhere. Not with you. I'm waiting for Fletcher. By now he's got help on the way."

Jack cursed low under his breath. "The only thing Fletcher Winthrop has on the way is a hired assassin."

Fury sparked in those green eyes. "That's it. Now I know you're crazy. First you link my kidnapping to a man who's been like a second father to me all of my life. Then you up the ante to murder." She shook her head. "You must really be desperate."

"Bingo," Jack said. "I am desperate. Desperate to get you the hell out of here. If it means destroying the image of a man you care about, so be it." Ruthlessly he went on. "As for Winthrop and murder, it isn't as much of a reach as you might think. It isn't as though it would be his first."

She stared at him.

"He already has at least one homicide to his credit."

"What are you—?"

"Pete Wilson."

Courtney sank to her knees, her lovely face shrouded with hurt, confusion. "I don't believe you."

She said the words, but her voice no longer carried the same conviction it had had before.

With everything in him, Jack resisted the urge to go to her, to pull her into his arms, tell her everything was going to be all right. He was the last person from whom Courtney Hamilton would seek comfort. Time and again he'd asked her to trust him. Time and again she'd turned him down flat.

Not that he blamed her. Given the same circumstances, he wouldn't trust Jack Sullivan, either. The ashes of that bridge he had burned years ago still lay smoldering between them.

"If I could make this easier for you, Courtney," he said, "I would. But there's no way to make something like this go down easy."

She kept shaking her head. "I'm not buying into this, Jack. I don't know what you're up to, but I'm not buying in. I won't."

"Fine," he said. "Don't believe me. But come with me. Now." He squatted down and scooped handfuls of snow onto their camp fire, then started rolling up the sleeping bag. Several times he had to pause, as things swam out of focus. He cursed the weakness of his own body. If he hadn't passed out again, Courtney wouldn't have found the phone, wouldn't have made that call.

He glanced at her, still settled on her knees in the soggy turf. She looked so bewildered, so lost—and yet so incredibly beautiful. He wanted so much to make love to her, make all the hurts go away for a little while at least. But he couldn't summon the arrogance for such an act. So much of her pain was his fault.

"Courtney, please," he said. "We need to go."

A tear slipped down her cheek. "Do you know what Fletcher Winthrop did when I divorced his son? He put his arms around me, told me everything was going to be all right, that Roger would never hurt me again. My own father—" her voice broke "—my own father asked me what I'd done to provoke him."

Jack closed his eyes.

"I don't think any words have ever hurt me more," she said. "I was at the lowest point of my life, and the one person I thought I could count on to be there for me ripped out what was left of my heart."

"I'm so sorry, princess."

She raised her gaze toward his. "Do you see why I can't believe you?"

"I see why you don't want to. But it doesn't change what is. I'm sorry."

She stiffened her spine. "You don't quit, do you?"

"Not when your life's at stake."

She pushed to her feet and began to pace, pace insofar as her crutch and her injured ankle would permit on the uneven ground. "All right," she allowed, "for the sake of argument, let's say I never met Fletcher Winthrop. That still leaves you with the rather monumental task of convincing me the co-owner of a multibillion-dollar international conglomerate would involve himself in kidnapping and murder. Tell me it was Roger, and I'll believe you in a heartbeat. But Fletcher. It can't be."

"It's a long, ugly story, princess. But I swear I'll tell you every sordid detail just as soon as I get you somewhere safe."

She sent him an almost-pleading look, and Jack could sense that she was indeed beginning to waver, to doubt. But he could sense, too, that the notion that

Winthrop meant her physical harm was almost too much for her to bear. He made the decision to back off. For the moment anyway. Deliberately he changed the subject. ''Tell me what you told the person on the phone. About where you were, who you were with.''

''I told him I was in the Sapphires. I tried to describe where I thought the cabin might be.''

''He believed you? He didn't think you were a crank call?''

''He believed me.'' She managed a wan smile. ''Maybe I sounded kidnapped, I don't know. Anyway, he'd heard about it. Heard the Hamilton name. He said tabloid reporters are crawling all over the state. There's quite a massive search going on for me, I guess.'' She met his eyes. ''Up near the Canadian border.''

Score one for my side, Jack thought. He'd told her that was where the intended cabin was.

''But the kidnappers could have leaked out phony clues,'' she said. ''They'd want the search to be in the wrong place, wouldn't they?''

Stalemate. He frowned. ''So I take it the police have heard from another contingent of your kidnappers?''

''According to the 911 operator, they're demanding a ten-million-dollar ransom. Payable two days from now. Or—'' she swallowed ''—I'm to be killed.''

''Winthrop must be pulling out all the stops. Obviously he let the story leak to the media. The FBI is probably fit to be tied.''

''Have you actually talked to Fletcher, Jack? Is that why you know he's the person in charge of all this?''

''No,'' he admitted. ''I came into the kidnapping too late to make any contact with anyone before the copter took off. All I had was a phone number the original pilot had on him.

"The number turned out to be a go-between, a buffer between the helicopter crew and the boss. After all, he doesn't want to advertise his identify to any more people than absolutely necessary. I told the guy the chopper had gotten off course, that my best guess was that we went down somewhere in the Bitterroots. I told him Frank was dead, and that you and I weren't doing much better. That I didn't know if either one of us was going to make it. Then I broke the connection.

"Winthrop must have proceeded on the assumption that we both froze to death. He's playing out his hand however he pleases. But now there's a fly in the ointment. You." He pressed a hand to his temple.

"Are you all right?"

"Just dizzy. It'll pass." He straightened. "What else did you say to the operator?"

Very deliberately, Courtney pulled the Beretta from her pocket. "I told him one of the kidnappers was dead, and that I'd managed to get a gun away from the other one."

Jack eyed the weapon ruefully. "Good. That'll jive with what I told Winthrop's middleman."

"Isn't that convenient for you?" she said tightly.

"Meaning what? You still believe I'm one of them?"

She let the gun fall to her side. "I don't know what I believe, Jack. Not about anyone. Or anything."

"Then believe this." Fear prodded him now, fear that he wouldn't be able to convince her to go with him after all. "Yesterday when I asked you to trust me, you could consider it an intellectual exercise. Now your life depends on it. My hand to God, Courtney, I'm on your side."

"Why couldn't you just have told me the truth, Jack? Why in heaven's name didn't you at least tell me about the phone? My father could be dead. Do you understand that? Dead."

"No," he told her quietly. "Quentin Hamilton's alive. In fact, he's even made some progress. They've taken him off the ventilator, but he's still unconscious."

Betrayal sparked in those green eyes. "You *knew* that and you didn't tell me?" she shrilled.

"I wanted to tell you." The words sounded hollow even to his own ears. "But I thought it was best not to."

"You thought it was best that I not know if my father was alive or dead?"

"If you knew about the phone, you'd would've wanted me to send for help."

"Damned straight."

"And you would've wound up in the same danger you're in now. Hate me all you like, Courtney. But hate me someplace else. Stay here, and you're dead. I promise you, they will kill you." His gaze tracked skyward. "The weather's clear. They could already have a plane in the air. One more time, Courtney. Will you trust me?"

Her voice was anguished. "You don't know what you're asking."

"Yes, I do."

He could almost see the war going on inside her. A minute passed. The longest minute of his life. But at last her shoulders slumped and she murmured, "All right. All right, Jack, I'll trust you." She thrust the Beretta in her pocket. "But I'll keep the gun."

"Deal."

They headed out, Jack taking the lead.

Scarcely five minutes passed before Courtney stopped. "This isn't the way to the cabin."

"We don't dare go there. You told them about it, remember?"

"But we're not pointed toward the trailhead, either."

"They'll look there, too. I know a cave about five miles from here. We can rest there for a day or two, even longer if we have to."

"A cave? Days? In that torn-up sleeping bag?" She looked incredulous. "I can do Daniel Boone, Jack. But I'm not a bleeping polar bear!"

His mouth ticked upward, and he traced the line of her jaw with his fingertips. "Maybe not, but you're the gutsiest woman I've ever known."

For just an instant those defenses of hers crumbled and he could almost believe that she didn't hate him. Not completely anyway. But then the walls were back. She settled her crutch beneath her armpit, glowered at him and limped on.

Hours passed. Hours in which they seemed to take turns stumbling to their knees. Jack's head felt ready to explode. Though she never once complained, he guessed Courtney's ankle felt much the same.

Near midafternoon, as they crossed a clearing, she fell and did not get up.

"Are you all right?" Jack asked, gasping. The thin mountain air coupled with his head injury had been steadily wearing him down all day.

She managed a weak nod, but did not rise.

"We can't stay here," he said. "It's too exposed. Come on. The cave isn't much farther." He caught her arm.

"You said it wasn't much farther two hours ago."

"Just get up. I'll carry you."

"No. I need to rest. Just give me a minute. Please."

He heard it then. Somewhere in the distance. The steady thrum of a helicopter engine.

Courtney must have heard it, too, because she turned her head, scanning the eastern sky.

"We've got to hide!" Jack shouted. "Hurry!"

"No." He could see the sudden indecision in her, all of her mistrust resurfacing. To her, the copter meant dry clothes, a clean bed, a warm meal. Most of all, safety. From him.

Briefly, he considered dragging her toward a nest of boulders some twenty yards away. But in his weakened state, if she resisted, he could never force her. He made himself wait. She needed to make up her own mind. Besides, she could be right. Maybe the copter belonged to the forest service. Maybe Winthrop hadn't been able to get his hired gun on board under false pretenses. Maybe...

Courtney was on her feet. Her face a mask of irony, she said, "I've got to be the biggest fool on the planet to trust you again. But I do." Then she slogged toward the boulders.

Relief washing through him, Jack followed. It had occurred to him that Winthrop money might even be able to buy off a ranger.

Several minutes later the copter passed overhead. A private hire, Jack noted, as it continued south to disappear beyond a stand of trees. He blew out a long, slow breath. They had not been spotted.

"Do you think it was Fletcher?" Courtney asked.

"Not in the flesh. But I wouldn't care to wager on the allegiance of the crew. Until I can get you to my contact in Butte, I'd rather play it safe."

"Your contact?"

"If I fall off another cliff, put in a call to Mark Segura. He's a D.E.A. agent and a good friend of mine and Pete's." Jack scribbled down a phone number and handed it to her. "I've been keeping Mark up to date on things. He'll take good care of you."

It took them another three hours to reach a small opening at the base of a massive granite bluff. "Wait here," Jack told her, though both of them were so exhausted they could barely stand. "I want to go in first, make sure no four-legged residents have staked a prior claim." He ducked low—the cave's ceiling topping out at barely five feet six. Flicking on his lighter, he held it out in front of him like a miniature torch. A hundred feet into the mountainside the cave ended. "Come on in," Jack called back. "It's all ours. Home sweet home."

Shivering, Courtney staggered into the cave and promptly collapsed. Jack hurried to her side, helping her to her feet, then helping her over to the near wall of the cave. Gratefully, she leaned her full weight against it, sinking slowly, slowly to the cold, muddy floor. "Fire," she murmured. "Please. A fire."

"No. We can't take the risk. It could be seen."

She sent him a look of abject misery.

Swiftly Jack unfurled the sleeping bag. Catching her up, he eased her into it.

She continued to shiver. "What about you?" she asked. "Aren't you going to join me?"

His brows furrowed, and he felt her forehead.

"I'm not sick," she grumbled. "I'm freezing. Freezing enough not to mind the idea of subletting half of these luxurious accommodations to you."

He chuckled, pleased that she'd recovered enough spunk to be crabby. She'd said little on their long trek, her thoughts absorbed, he was certain, by Winthrop's treachery. "I don't know how I could refuse such a gracious offer," he drawled. "But I'm going to have to. For the moment at least. I've got a few things to take care of."

He headed back out of the cave. Conducting a quick foraging expedition, he returned minutes later with an armload of pine boughs, which he spread out as a cushion for the sleeping bag. "Are you warm enough yet?" he asked.

She didn't answer. He leaned close, a tender smile creasing his lips. She was fast asleep.

Very carefully, he settled down beside her, though he did not take her up on her offer to share the sleeping bag. The temperature in the cave was holding at around forty. Tolerable with his jacket, clothes and long underwear. And considering the direction of his thoughts, a much more prudent choice than spooning his body next to hers in that damnable bag.

He'd been spending entirely too much time lately thinking about another night when he and Courtney Hamilton had slept together. A fantasy come to life in his bedroom. He'd even pinched himself to make certain he wasn't dreaming. Rejoicing in the pain, because it meant the golden-haired woman in his bed was wonderfully, magically real.

And then it all came crashing down. The woman of his dreams. He'd had her and lost her in a single night.

And now here she was again. With her flip remarks about fate and destiny and karma. Very tenderly Jack reached out and eased a stray tendril of hair away from her face. Surely those Fates couldn't be so cruel as to take her away from him a second time.

Then he cursed himself for a fool. She wasn't his to be taken. She was an independent woman—strong, courageous, rebuilding her life in the aftermath of Roger Winthrop's abuse. What could he offer such a woman? A ramshackle cabin in the middle of nowhere?

He closed his eyes. Enough. He wasn't in this for himself. He was in this for Courtney. Here to get her down off this mountain safe and alive. Toward that end, he realized he needed to regain his strength. Shutting out his troublesome thoughts, Jack closed his eyes and slept.

It was full dark when he woke, Courtney still sleeping beside him. Outside, the moon illuminated the shadowy sentinels of the lodgepole, standing guard in stark relief against the bright white of the snow-laden hills.

He shifted, rubbing his arm. He'd fallen asleep using it as a pillow. Now the blasted limb was asleep.

"Are you all right?" came Courtney's sleepy voice.

"Fine," he whispered. "I'm sorry. I didn't mean to disturb you."

"It's okay." She stretched and sat up. "I wasn't having very pleasant dreams anyway." Her tone sounded almost defeated. "Are we going to live through this, Jack?"

"Guaranteed," he said, hoping he sounded more convinced than he felt.

"I can't believe Fletcher would do this. What possible motive could he have?"

"It can wait 'til morning."

"No. I'm awake. I want to know now."

Jack gave an inward shrug. Now or later. What was the difference? "His motive's the same one we've been talking about all along. Money."

"You're kidding, right?"

"Not a bit."

"You may find this hard to believe, but ten million dollars isn't all that much to Winthrop-Hamilton."

"Maybe, but I doubt you'd say the same if the prize was a *billion*."

"A billion? That's half the company."

"Exactly. The Hamilton half."

"But that doesn't make any sense. My father's been a friend and partner to Fletcher for forty years. Why would he suddenly want the whole company to himself?"

Jack pushed to a sitting position beside her. Despite his physical complaints and the less-than-pleasant subject matter, he was taking a genuine pleasure in the simple act of being in this woman's company, sharing thoughts and feelings in the darkness.

"Maybe I'd better start at the beginning," he said. "Tell you what I've been able to piece together so far. For me, it started eight months ago. Though I didn't know it then. I'd just resigned from the LAPD, and I was having a pretty rocky time of it. Pete offered me his place here in the mountains. He came up most weekends. We hunted, fished, talked. It took a while, but I started feeling alive again.

"About that time—maybe four months ago—Pete started filling me in on a case he was working on. A kind of private investigation. I kept telling him I wasn't interested, that I wasn't a cop anymore. But Pete could be pretty persistent. I think he saw the case as a way to bring me back. To reconnect me with the real world."

"Did it work?"

"I don't know yet," he said honestly. "Anyway, Pete was really excited. He said the trail had led him to bigger fish then he'd ever dreamed of. He was going to stand Butte on its ear. Maybe he was going to stand the whole country on its ear.

"I figured he was blowing smoke. Exaggerating to try to get me jazzed about it. So I called him on it. He brought me a whole boxful of faxes, computer printouts, canceled checks. He told me he got them from a snitch working on the inside."

"The inside of what?"

He hesitated, but there was no help for it. If he didn't tell her, she'd only guess. "Winthrop-Hamilton."

Though he couldn't see clearly in the heavily shadowed interior of the cave, he could feel the blood drain from her face. "I can stop if you want me to," he offered gently.

"No. No, I want to hear it. All of it."

"It seems some of the dealings Fletcher got himself into over the past few years haven't been all that legitimate."

"But why would he take such a stupid risk? He's one of the wealthiest men in the world."

"You were in Butte when the last of the mines went under, weren't you? When the Berkeley Pit and the others shut down?"

The Pit had been a massive strip mining operation begun in the fifties. A last gasp to try and recover a glimmer of Butte's late-nineteenth-century glory, when the mines worked twenty-four hours a day and the streets were so dark with pollution that the gas lamps were never permitted to go out. Cost overruns and foreign competition soon doomed the resumption of above-ground mining at both the Pit and Winthrop-Hamilton sites.

"The mines didn't matter, Jack. Not to the overall health of the company. Winthrop-Hamilton diversified years ago. Granted, I don't know much about the business, but I do know Father and Fletcher own everything from minimalls to multiplex movie theaters. A lot more than boarded-up mines."

"But they couldn't diversify the mines out of existence. They own those sites. In Butte and other places. Three years ago, the kind of slipshod operations that cost my father his health finally came to the attention of the EPA. The piper wanted to be paid. Three dozen lawsuits in six states were slapped against W-H—with clean up costs projected to run into the billions. Winthrop and your father were facing bankruptcy, and they both knew it. They hired a raft of lawyers to try to bail them out."

Courtney thought about her father, of how sadly detached she had become from his life. She'd had no idea the company was in such serious trouble. She hadn't even picked up on it in the three weeks she'd been home. But then, she thought, maybe Fletcher hadn't wanted her to.

"Roger Winthrop was in South America when the lawsuits were filed," Jack went on. "He started making inquiries. It wasn't long before he had himself a drug connection. That's when the serious money laundering got started.

"I don't have all the particulars. But I know they're desperate to find a certain computer disk." He withdrew a small floppy from his inside jacket pocket. "This is the one you had in your purse."

"I remember it," Courtney said. "The files were encrypted. I couldn't get into any of them. I'd just ejected the disk from the computer, when the phone rang telling me about my father's supposed relapse. I must've tucked the disk in my purse without thinking."

"Somehow Pete got the code, a few letters and a series of numbers. He passed it on to me, but he never found the disk. If Pete was right, the information on this thing could be worth a cool billion."

"Which might," Courtney conceded, "give Fletcher and Roger a motive. But that doesn't explain your motive, Jack. Why couldn't you tell me about all this from the beginning?"

He didn't answer.

"My God," she whispered. "I was a suspect, too, wasn't I?"

"Not a suspect," he said slowly. "But I thought you might know things you didn't know you knew. Like having your father's power of attorney. I was investigating his company, Courtney. I still am. I guess I figured you'd be more forthcoming to a mountain man you'd never seen before, than to a cop named Jack Sullivan."

"My father." Courtney's voice shook. "Is he part of this, too?"

"Kidnapping you? Absolutely not. As to the rest of it, I'll be honest, I'm not sure. I do know Winthrop recently transferred some debt-heavy properties solely into your father's name. Fletcher and Roger are setting themselves up to skate free with their laundered blood money. Pete got too close. And he died for it."

"This is all so incredible. Fletcher must have been desperate. That's the only explanation. But Roger? I'm surprised it took him so long. He was always boasting about how he'd show his father up one day, bring the company ten times the success Fletcher and my father ever had. It was an obsession. And with Roger, success was only measured one way—in dollar signs."

"I guess he didn't care if those dollar signs came from videotapes or cocaine." In the darkness Jack found her hand and brought it to his lips. "I'm just grateful you got away from that bastard. When I think of him hurting you—" His gut clenched.

She laid her head against his shoulder. "I want to thank you."

"For what?"

"For being the man who kidnapped me."

Until now, his impaired body had been a boon to his determination to keep his hands off of her. But the lilting warmth in that voice was almost his undoing. "I think we'd better get some sleep," he said, praying she would acquiesce and he could then somehow calm his surging hormones.

Instead, she sidled closer and asked softly, "What was it like being a cop in L.A.?"

He wasn't going to sleep. He was going to make love to her. He knew it, wanted it, ached for it. "It was hell. And it was heaven. I worked my butt off to make detective. I wanted Pete to be proud of me."

"I'm sure he was."

"Yeah." Desire beat in every cell of his body.

"So why did you turn your back on it? Why did you stop being a cop and shut yourself off from the world?"

Several minutes ticked by, and Courtney thought he wasn't going to answer. Then slowly, haltingly, the story came out. A story filled with guilt and rage and despair. And when he was finished, she knew why Jack Sullivan had nightmares.

"For a split second I hesitated, and my partner paid with his life."

She laid a hand inside his coat, felt the powerful beat of his heart. "If the situation were reversed, do you think Emmett would have shot the boy?"

"It doesn't matter."

"I think it does. You held your fire against a child."

"I let my partner die."

Not even talking about Emmett was taking the edge off of his desire to make love to this woman. Here. Now. In this cold, damp, godforsaken hole in the very walls of the earth.

"Were you found at fault?" he heard her ask.

"Not even a write-up in my file."

"But you wish there had been. Some concrete evidence of your guilt."

"Maybe." Why did she have to understand? Why did she have to care? He didn't want to hurt her. Not again.

"I know it's just words, Jack, but you've got to forgive yourself. Let it go. I tore myself down for years for allowing Roger to hit me. For not walking out the first time he so much as called me names. But we can only do the best we can in this life. It's all any of us can do."

"You've done a helluva lot better than I have, Courtney. You made something of your life. You work in a battered women's shelter. You face your demons every day. Me? I ran. Hid out in a cabin in the woods."

"There's nothing wrong with taking time to heal, Jack. More people should do it. It just so happens that working with other battered women has helped me heal."

A wolf howled. Close. They looked up to see a pair silhouetted against the snow about a hundred yards from the mouth of the cave. Courtney touched the talisman at her throat, resting her other hand on Jack's bandaged arm. "They mate for life, you know."

"Don't . . . Courtney . . ."

"Don't what?" She leaned close.

"I want you too much."

"What if I want you back?"

He groaned deep in his throat. That was it. The end. He had no more resistance. None. He wanted this, wanted it so badly. More than that, he wanted to believe again. In something. In someone. Maybe even in himself.

Later, neither one of them would be able to say exactly how they accomplished it. But Jack rolled out of the sleeping bag and built a tiny, smokeless fire inside the cave. Then they both stripped, stark naked. Eager, wanton, they came together in the darkness, oblivious to anything, everything, but their need to touch and be touched.

"Ten years," he rasped. "Ten years I've dreamed of being with you again."

She kissed him, hard, deep, then brought his mouth to her breasts. "Then, on some of those nights," she told him softly, so very softly, "you and I were having the exact, same dream, Jack Sullivan."

He worshiped her—with his hands, with his mouth, with his words. He memorized every part of her, reveling in what pleased her, what tickled her, what made her tremble with need.

And then she was doing the same for him. If they'd been in the middle of a snowbank, neither one of them would have noticed, so hot did their passion blaze.

With a cry of surrender Courtney lay back, opening her legs to receive what she'd ached for for so very long. Union with the man she loved. Had always loved. Would always love.

And then he was inside her, moving, thrusting, loving her in return. And she wept from the sheer wonder of it, the magic, and then she gloried in the salty sweetness of Jack's own tears. Together they swept past the edge of madness, a place of such exquisite pleasure that for as long as Jack was there with her, Courtney would never wish to come back.

Courtney came awake slowly, not wanting to disturb the man sleeping so peacefully beside her. She smiled. He looked ten years younger. An hour before dawn, sated, exhausted, they had managed to crawl into their tattered cocoon, drawing it up around them before they collapsed into sleep. Now, from the shadows on the ground outside the cave, Courtney guessed it to be around ten in the morning. Their tiny camp fire had long since gone out. As to that other fire, the one they seemed to have ignited in each other, Courtney still felt hers burning deep inside her.

She sighed, wondering what Jack's reaction would be to the night they'd just shared. Joy? Regret? A marriage proposal? She smiled inwardly. Somehow she doubted the latter. But, strangely, she had no more doubts about his feelings for her. The man loved her, just as she loved him.

Of course he didn't know it yet. Or if he did, he wasn't prepared to admit it. But that was okay. Now that *she* knew it, she had faith that things would work themselves out.

Especially if she helped them along here and there.

Ten years ago Jack Sullivan had held his life up to hers and found himself wanting. False pride hadn't let him believe he could be part of her life. But he was well past such foolishness now.

Now he was a man in every sense of the word. Strong, compassionate, brave, kind, sexy, stubborn, scared.

Scared for her.

She leaned over and kissed him lightly on the mouth.

"What was that for?" he mumbled groggily.

"Felt like it."

His mouth ticked upward. "Feel like it again."

She did.

"A man could get used to this."

"So could a woman." She grazed her fingertips across the bruise on his forehead. "How do you feel?"

"Like I died and went to heaven." He wiggled his brows suggestively.

"I'd check your directions, Mr. Sullivan," she said primly. "You look positively devilish to me. Be-sides—" she cast an unamused look at their accommodations "—I would hope heaven had classier rooms."

"Oh, you want classy. Why didn't you say so?" He pushed up on one elbow, then snugged down the zipper of the sleeping bag far enough so that he could lean out and grab for his backpack. While Jack rummaged through the pack, Courtney admired the ebony dusting of hair on the flat plane of his chest. He'd shrugged back into his flannel shirt and his jeans after they'd made love, but he hadn't bothered to fasten either one.

"Eureka!" he pronounced, holding up two pieces of beef jerky. "How much classier can you get?" He proffered her a piece. "Breakfast in bed."

Courtney made a face, but accepted the jerky. Her heart was singing. Lovemaking certainly seemed to have agreed with Jack. But then, why not? It had agreed with her, as well. Kidnapping, murder, drug trafficking—all seemed a million miles away. As wretched as this cave was, she suddenly found herself reluctant to leave it. Outside of its dank walls, the real world waited. The real world that could get them both killed.

She made a swipe at her disheveled hair, determined to distract herself from such morbid thoughts. "So help me," she said, "when I get home, I'm spending three days in a Jacuzzi."

"Want some company?"

"Love some."

He kissed her then, hard. And Courtney wondered if a Jacuzzi could be installed in a cave.

"I hate to break this up," Jack said, pulling back. "But we've got to get going."

"Do we have to? A little work—some curtains, paint, a couple of plants—and I can do wonders with this place."

"We've got to go, Courtney. I'm sorry."

"I know." She stood up and helped him break camp. "Just where are we headed anyway?"

"Somewhere where the cell phone will get me through to Mark Segura. I want him up here. I want to get you someplace safe."

"I'm safe with you, remember?"

"I want you under police guard, princess. Twenty-four hours a day."

"Only if I get to pick the policeman." She eyed him playfully, but he did not smile.

"I'm sorry, angel, but it won't be me. I have to go after Winthrop."

"But I could help you. Wear a wire, a tape recorder, whatever they call it. I could get Fletcher to talk."

He stared at her, astonished and, she saw, furious. "You think I've been through all this, doing everything I know how to keep you alive, so that you can just waltz into the lion's den?"

"You'd be nearby. So would Segura, I'm sure. And half the Butte police force. I'd be fine."

"Absolutely not. You can consider that a direct police order."

Her lips thinned. "For one thing," she stated, "Montana is not a police state. For another, you're not really the police. You resigned. You're a private citizen, just like me."

He raked a hand through his dark locks. "Maybe not exactly like you."

"Excuse me?"

He cleared his throat. "Maybe I forgot to mention that Pete took care of a little paperwork for me."

"What kind of paperwork?"

"Three months ago I was reinstated on the L.A. force, then reassigned—temporarily—as a special agent—" he flushed guiltily "—with the FBI."

"The FBI!" Courtney stamped her good foot on the cave floor. "And you just forgot to tell me that?"

"It didn't seem important."

She stared at him. "Not important. Jack, I've been scared to death that when this was all over you'd be back up in your cabin still brooding over Emmett."

"I'll always feel guilty about that. But I came to realize just exactly what you said yesterday. Life goes on. And my feeling sorry for myself in that cabin did no honor to Emmett's memory."

She circled her arms around his neck. "I'm glad for you."

"You're not angry?"

"I'm furious. But I'm still glad for you."

He kissed her, and she kissed him back.

"We'd better go."

She hesitated. "I need to ask you something first."

"What?"

"You're FBI, so your investigation is official, legal."

"Right."

"I need to know, if your going after the Winthrops is strictly about justice for Pete."

"What else would it . . . ? Oh." His gaze hardened. "You think I wouldn't mind getting another fish caught in my net. Say Quentin Hamilton."

"It occurred to me," she said, lifting her chin.

His cheeks reddened. "To be honest, it occurred to me, too. But I'd never use the law as a personal weapon, Courtney. Never."

"I'm sorry. I had to ask."

"It's okay. I'm glad you did. Come on. It's time for another invigorating hike in the woods."

The day's temperature was tolerable at least. Some of the snow was beginning to melt. Here and there, sprigs of grass were even beginning to poke through. She and Jack spoke little, concentrating on the terrain. Courtney knew that he was also keeping a wary eye out for company.

Toward midday they found a place where the cell phone would work static-free. Jack punched up Mark Segura's number and the two men talked for maybe five minutes. "It's all set," Jack said, tucking the phone back into his pocket. "We'll meet him on an old logging road about two hours from here. You should be in Butte by sunset."

"You're not planning to hand me over to this Segura guy, are you?"

He didn't answer.

Courtney fumed, but decided against arguing. From the look on Jack's face, it would get her nothing but strained vocal cords. They continued their hike, coming to rest some two hours later. Jack pointed toward the deeply rutted tracks of an old, muddy road. "We wait here."

"Then what?"

"Then Mark takes us to Butte."

"No," she said slowly. "I mean, then what for us?"

He stepped closer. "You know what I want to say? I want to say you and I get married and we make fantastic love and we have three kids and we live a terrific life. And when we hit our fiftieth anniversary, we don't show up for the party because we're in bed somewhere, still making love."

"But?"

"But I've got a murderer to bring to justice. And I've got to make sure you're safe. I can't think of anything but those two things right now. I can't."

She let out a long sigh. "Okay."

"Oh, and by the way, I love you."

Her head jerked up. "What?"

"I love you, Courtney Hamilton. I just wanted you to know that."

She threw her arms around his neck. "I love you, too."

"I know." His eyes were overbright. "I know."

He kissed her until she thought her bones would melt. And then he kissed her again.

He loved her.

She loved him.

All was right with the world.

Now all they had to do was get through the next few days without being murdered.

They turned toward the sound of a heavily strained motor. "There he is." Jack pointed. Mark Segura was coming up the road in a mud-encrusted all-terrain vehicle. He hopped out of the ATV before it had come to a complete stop. He and Jack exchanged a hearty handshake.

"Good to see you breathing amigo," Segura said, slapping Jack on the arm.

"Good to be breathing." He turned toward Courtney. "Mark Segura, Courtney Hamilton."

Segura tipped the Chicago Cubs baseball cap he was wearing. "My pleasure, Miss Hamilton. My same congratulations on your breathing abilities."

She laughed, liking this man at once. "Thank you. And call me Courtney."

Segura was of obvious Hispanic descent with deep ebony hair and a swarthy complexion. His grin was infectious, his eyes dark and penetrating. Courtney would hate to see this man angry. Segura excused himself, and he and Jack walked off a ways to share a lengthy discussion. She tried eavesdropping, but it was clear the two were talking in some kind of annoying cop code. She was less certain than ever what their plans for her might be. But if Jack Sullivan thought for one minute he was going to pass her off to anyone else, he was going to find himself sorely mistaken.

The men returned to the vehicle. Courtney found herself frustrated by the inscrutable looks on both of their faces. Couldn't at least one of them be an open book?

"Mark's going to put us up for the time being."

"Why?"

"It seems Fletcher Winthrop has no permanent address in Butte these days," Segura said. "I'm afraid he's helped himself to your father's place in Elk Park."

Courtney gasped, outraged. "Then I'll throw him out."

"You'll do no such thing," Jack gritted. "Winthrop isn't to know that you're even in town. Do you understand?"

She didn't answer.

"Do you understand?" he repeated tightly.

"Yes."

"Good."

She looked at Mark Segura. "Why not a hotel?"

"You'll prefer my place, believe me. The hotels are swarming with media types. The quasinews, my-mother-slept-with-Bigfoot people."

"Oh. But I really don't want to inconvenience you." Actually, she was thinking more along the lines of three's a crowd.

Segura sent Jack a wink. "Don't worry. I won't be there. I got a girl over on Granite. She'll be overjoyed to put me up for the night."

The three of them then climbed into the ATV and began the bone-jarring ride back toward civilization. Segura drove, Jack sat in the back, Courtney in the passenger seat.

"How long have you known Jack?" she asked, raising her voice to compete with the ATV's vociferous engine.

"Jack and I go back a ways. You might say Pete Wilson brought us together. As I recall, Pete caught Jack knocking over a vending machine. Along about that same time I was trying my hand at stealing a radio out of a car."

"Pete took you under his wing, too?"

"Pete Wilson had pretty big wings and a bigger heart. That's why Jack and I are in this so deep."

"You decided to be a cop, too, because of Pete?"

He laughed. "No, I'm afraid that was in spite of Pete. He figured Jack for cop material. Me? He suggested I think about being a doctor." He grinned. "I joined the rodeo instead. Made him madder than hell, let me tell you. But he came around."

"You ride?"

"Used to. 'Til a bull stepped on my head. Figured life would be simpler if people just pointed guns at me."

Jack leaned over and passed the computer disk to Mark. "Get your best people on this one."

"Will do, amigo. Thanks."

"Do you have enough evidence to arrest Fletcher?" Courtney asked.

"Not yet. But if that son of his is ever stupid enough to leave South America, he'll do some hard time. He's sloppy. Real sloppy. I think he's taken to using some of his product, if you get my meaning."

Courtney winced.

"I'm sorry, miss. I forgot you'd been married to him."

"A mistake in another lifetime, Mr. Segura."

"Mark."

"It's just that I don't like to think of anyone wasting their life on drugs. Not even Roger."

An hour later Segura drove onto the two-lane highway that snaked through the rugged back country toward Butte. He only stayed on the road a few hundred feet, turning off into a copse of trees near a gigantic boulder. Several hundred yards into the brush, they came to a halt beside a rusty beater of a van that Mark had likely used to haul the ATV. He yanked open the rear door and gestured for Courtney to climb in. "I know it's not much, but it's safe. No one can see inside."

Courtney stared into that gaping cargo area, her mind catapulting her back to the day she'd been kidnapped. "I can't get in there."

"It's okay," Jack said. "I'll ride with you."

Only then did she climb inside. Together they huddled on the floor, Jack holding her close. The van started to move.

"It was hell for me that day," he said softly.

"Were you the one who chloroformed me?"

"Yes."

She could hear the pain in his voice. Still, she shuddered.

"I tried my damnedest not to hurt you. I tried to make Frank ride up front with me so he couldn't...try anything. When he put his hands on you in the chopper..." He didn't finish. "I'm just so damned sorry, Courtney."

"I love you, Jack." It seemed an appropriate moment to remind him.

He sighed heavily and hugged her tight. "I'm going to get you through this. My hand to God, I am."

"I know."

A half hour later the van stopped. The rear door opened, and Courtney and Jack climbed down onto the macadam behind a four-plex apartment house of fairly recent vintage. Mark handed Jack a set of keys. *"Mi casa, su casa."*

"Thanks. I'll get my backpack." He headed toward the front of the van.

Courtney turned to Mark. "I want to thank you for all your help."

"My pleasure." He touched the brim of his Cubs cap. "Oh, and I raised my contact at the hospital on my car phone. Your father's still improving. The coma's much lighter, but he's likely another day or two from waking up."

She blinked back tears. "Thank you."

Mark brushed her cheek with a kiss. "Jack was right. You're one helluva lady."

She blushed.

"And Jack's a helluva guy. He saved my butt one summer down in Tijuana when we were both a lot younger and a lot stupider. You take good care of him."

"I love him."

Mark snorted. "And the sky's blue."

"Pretty obvious, huh?"

"What's obvious?" Jack asked, striding back up to them.

"The fact that I need a shower," Courtney said, pushing a hand through her disheveled hair.

"Sorry," Mark said. "Don't have one."

Courtney couldn't suppress a groan.

"You'll have to settle for my Jacuzzi."

Courtney and Jack exchanged glances. They both grinned. "Remind me to leave a mint on the man's pillow," Courtney said.

Jack took Mark aside. "I appreciate the place to crash, amigo. But . . ."

"It's a little too exposed for your taste?"

"Exactly."

"I know. I'm going to go reconnoiter a couple of places. Find something with better security. You should be fine here for a few hours, though." He gave Jack a sly grin. "I thought you might appreciate the privacy." He paused. "And the Jacuzzi."

"You're a wise man," Jack said. "A very wise man."

"I like him," Courtney said, coming back over to Jack's side as Mark drove off.

"Me, too." He kissed her forehead. "Come on, let's get you out of sight."

To Courtney's weary eyes, Mark's modest apartment rivaled the finest European château. While Jack walked around, closing miniblinds and checking behind doors, Courtney simply stood in the middle of the living room and drank in the trappings of civilization. "Did you see this stuff, Jack?"

He paused in his inspection and gave her a puzzled look. "See what?"

"All of these exotic things. Look. Carpeting, curtains, a TV, a couch." She walked over and peeked into the kitchen. "My God—a microwave."

"You hated the cabin that much, did you?"

"Not at all," she said, astonished to realize that she was telling the truth. "But what can I say? It could use a little sprucing up."

"Like maybe a hot tub?"

She pretended to have to think it over, then said. "Yes, I think a Jacuzzi would work for me." She began to undo the buttons of her shirt. "What about you, Jack? Does it work for you?"

He went for his own buttons. "I think it's you who works for me, woman."

She spied the telltale bulge in his jeans. "Last one in scrubs my back."

Jack's pace slowed considerably.

"Okay, first one in!"

They spent nearly two hours in the hot tub. They cuddled, frolicked and made some pretty wild love. Afterward, they collapsed on the bed in Mark's guest room and slept like the dead.

Courtney woke to find Jack regarding her intently. She rolled onto her back, making no attempt to shield her naked body from his fascinated perusal. "Penny for your thoughts," she murmured, then added, "a nickel if they're sexy."

"I was just thinking I'm the luckiest man on the planet."

She reached over to trace lazy circles across his flat belly. "That's only fair," she said. "I'm the luckiest woman." She laid her head where her hand had been. "I love you, Jack Sullivan. So much. But I'm getting pretty tired of being scared all the time."

He stroked her hair. "It'll be over soon. I promise. If Mark's people can decode that disk, it could be the evidence they need to tip the balance, to get an indictment."

"Do you think Fletcher knows the authorities are onto him?"

"It's beginning to look that way. Mark's had him tailed day and night. Fletcher's getting pretty hinky. In fact, they're worried he might try and leave the country. Head for Roger in South America."

"I can't say as I would mind having them *both* out of the country."

"You won't be safe until they're both behind bars."

Courtney sighed. "I know." Sometimes this madness was all so hard to believe. "I wish you'd reconsider about my talking to Fletcher."

"Not in this lifetime."

"But I really think I could—"

The phone rang. Jack let the machine answer, only catching up the receiver when he heard Mark's voice.

Courtney watched Jack's face as he listened, his expression shifting from fretful to buoyant. He signed off, then grabbed Courtney and let out a whoop of joy. "It's done," he pronounced. "It's done."

"What is?"

"Fletcher's in jail. An arrest warrant was issued two hours ago."

A flood of emotions washed over her. She didn't know whether to laugh or cry. Part of her was overwhelmed, overjoyed, but another part, the part of her that had loved and trusted Fletcher Winthrop felt her heart break. Obviously, there had been enough evidence to issue that warrant.

Jack must have sensed her turmoil. His embrace tightened. "I'm here, princess. I'm here."

She fell asleep in his arms.

The sound of an insistent doorbell woke them. Courtney raised her head sleepily.

"It must be Mark," Jack said. "I've got his keys."

"Is that my cue to get dressed?"

"It might be a good idea."

"I don't know. Mark's pretty cute."

Jack growled.

Courtney rose and donned the khaki slacks and forest-green sweater she'd found lying out for her earlier. Whether Mark had made a special procurement with her in mind, or they were souvenirs from an old girlfriend, Courtney had no idea. Jack yanked on a pair of Mark's jeans and a sweatshirt, then gestured that she stay back as he headed for the front door.

"But why? You said Fletcher's in jail."

"Just humor me, okay?" He reached the door. "Who is it?" he called.

"It's Mark, amigo."

Jack checked the peephole. Only then did his shoulders relax. He turned the deadbolt and eased open the door. "You need a spare set of—"

The door exploded inward, Mark's body hurtling through the opening, slamming into Jack and sending both men crashing to the floor. Jack cursed savagely, trying desperately to shove his unconscious friend to one side. "Courtney, run!"

But it was too late. Far too late.

Two men, dressed in black, stepped into Mark's apartment. Both of them with guns drawn.

Courtney stood, frozen with shock. Shock that deepened to terror an instant later, when through that same door stepped her worst nightmare.

"It's been a long time, hasn't it, darling?" he purred, his voice silky smooth and cold as ice. "A very long time. But good things do come to those who wait."

Roger.

Chapter 10

Mark Segura lay unmoving on the floor of his apartment, the whole right side of his head drenched with blood. Courtney couldn't tell if he was unconscious or dead. But her real attention focused on the man beside him. Jack lay flat on his back, arms raised, his face a mask of impotent fury. The barrels of two guns pointed squarely at his head.

"Careful, gentlemen," Roger warned. "We don't want to damage him too much." He laughed unpleasantly. "Yet." He crooked a finger toward one of his gunsels. "Julio?"

"Yes, Mr. Winthrop."

"I need you to take out the trash." He pointed toward Segura.

"Yes, sir, Mr. Winthrop." The taller of the two gunmen, Julio, was a well-muscled Hispanic Courtney guessed to be in her early twenties. As she watched, he pulled two lengths of rope from his jacket pocket.

Hunkering down, he bound up Mark's ankles and wrists, as though trussing up a steer. Then he jammed a gag into his mouth. At least the gag allowed Courtney to believe that Mark was still alive.

Julio then yanked a quilt from the couch, spread it out on the floor and rolled Mark into it. With barely a grunt of exertion, he slung the inert agent over his right shoulder and carried him out the front door.

"What's he going to do to him?" Courtney demanded.

Roger's eyes glittered dangerously. "I don't recall giving you permission to ask questions. However, I'll indulge you this once, for old times' sake. He's going to deposit him into the trunk of my Mercedes. From there he'll be disposed of at my convenience. His role in our little drama is finished now. I only needed him to get to you. He thought he was being so clever. But I've had his movements monitored for weeks."

Roger gestured toward his other hired gun. "William, please be so kind as to accord our other guest the same treatment Julio gave to Mr. Segura."

An ugly grin spread across William's acne-scarred features. He pulled out his own lengths of rope and started to tie Jack's hands.

Jack's jaw clenched. Courtney knew it was killing him not to fight back. But for now the odds were weighted so heavily against him that he didn't dare risk it. He would bide his time, wait for an opening. For her part, Courtney would do whatever she could to provide him with that opening.

"Hold up, William," Roger said. "I have a better idea." He reached into the pocket of his coat and pulled out a pair of handcuffs. "Try these. Compliments of Mr. Segura."

William removed the rope, then squeezed the handcuffs onto Jack's wrists so tightly, they nearly cut off the blood supply to his hands.

"Roger, please," Courtney said. "This isn't going to work. You'll never get away with it."

"On the contrary, my dear, I've been getting away with it for years. Until you came stumbling back into my life. And stole all my money. Not a wise decision on your part."

"I don't have your money."

"Oh, but you do. That computer disk, remember?"

"I don't have that, either." Mark had taken it. The fact that Roger still didn't have it meant Mark had at least managed to secure the disk before being waylaid by Roger and his thugs.

"Another mistake on your part," Roger tsked. "A potentially fatal one, I'm afraid. But let's not spoil the mood. For the moment, believe it or not, I have more important things on my mind. Like saying hello to an old and dear friend."

Roger ambled over to where Jack lay, his wrists secured. William gripped the chain that connected his handcuffs and gave it a savage yank. Jack was forced to climb awkwardly to his feet. "Christmas comes early this year, Sullivan," Roger said silkily. "Imagine my surprise at crossing paths with you again. I must have been a very good boy."

"You're a sack of—"

Roger drove his fist into Jack's stomach. Jack doubled over, gasping, then very deliberately, insolently, he straightened. "I'm impressed. I didn't think you knew how to use those hands for anything except dialing a phone."

Courtney remembered Roger's long-ago call to have Jack fired.

Roger rubbed the back of his abused knuckles with his other hand. "We'll see how smart you are by the time this night is over. For now, I strongly suggest you keep your mouth shut. Otherwise—and this I promise you—Courtney will pay the price for any more of your... transgressions."

"Touch her, and I'll kill you."

For an instant Roger's bravado vanished. Courtney saw fear in those pale green eyes. Then he looked at William and nodded his head ever so slightly.

William attacked Jack with savage ferocity, beating him unmercifully about the head and upper body. Jack went to his knees, blood dripping from his nose, his mouth.

"Roger, please!" Courtney caught at his sleeve. "Make him stop! Please! I beg you!"

Like some perverse despot, Roger held up his right hand. As quickly as it had begun, the beating stopped.

"Thank you." She said the words, though they almost made her vomit.

"You're welcome." He touched her cheek with the back of his hand, and Courtney willed herself not to recoil. For the briefest heartbeat the old Roger stood there, the young man who had wooed her, courted her and for a tiny space of time, genuinely loved her.

And then he seemed to shake himself, his voice deadly soft, lethal. "Don't ever ask me for anything again."

Courtney backed away, trying desperately not to be sick. That voice, that voice. So many times he'd used that voice just before he'd started to beat her. *Jack. Think of Jack. He needs you. He needs you to stay strong*. She looked at him, his face battered and bloody, and yet she could feel the defiance in him, the rage.

Roger was opening a briefcase. From it he removed a small vial and a hypodermic syringe. To William, he said, "Hold him steady."

Jack tried to jerk away, but it was hopeless. Roger jabbed the needle into Jack's arm and pushed down the tiny plunger. "Don't worry, it's nothing. A little sedative to make you more...docile, shall we say. We've got a bit of a ride ahead of us, and I wouldn't want you getting too rambunctious."

Jack tried to look at her, but his eyes rolled back in his head. He slumped forward, unconscious.

Courtney felt suddenly, chillingly alone. And responsible. Responsible not just for her own life. But for Jack's. He was helpless now. Until he regained consciousness she had to do whatever she could to keep them both alive.

Julio returned to the apartment, his task evidently accomplished. Mark was nowhere to be seen.

"More trash," Roger pronounced.

At once Julio and William took up positions on either side of Jack's unconscious body. Together they held him erect. Then Roger gripped Courtney's arm and stuck a gun in her ribs. "Any sound, any warning, anything I construe as an attempt to get away, and I will put the first bullet into Sullivan's brain. Do you understand?"

She nodded. "Just don't hurt him anymore, please."

Roger looked amused. "My God, you're in love with him, aren't you?" He clucked his tongue. "Such

low-brow taste. No wonder I came to loathe you so."
He shoved her toward the door.

Outside, the parking lot was pitch-dark. All four
security lights were out. No doubt, compliments of
Roger's personal vanguard of vandals. Julio and William
went first, keeping Jack on his feet as best they
could. A jacket had been draped over his manacled
wrists. Courtney and Roger followed. As they crossed
the macadam toward the Mercedes, a man appeared
out of the inky darkness walking his dog.

"Evenin'," the man said, though Courtney could
see that he was eyeing their peculiar entourage with
more than a little nervous curiosity. His dog, a black
Lab, growled and whined, tugging on its leash, anxious
to be somewhere else.

"Do pardon us," Roger said. "My friend here is an
alcoholic. Tonight we've done what's called an intervention.
We've forced him to see himself as he really
is." Roger shook his head. "Which as you can see is
blind drunk. But, praise heaven, he's agreed to check
himself into a clinic. To get the help he needs." He
turned toward Courtney. "Jack certainly does need
help, doesn't he, darling?"

"Yes," she whispered, "yes, he does."

"Good luck to you," the man said, then acceded to
his dog's wishes and moved on.

Courtney's heart sank. She hadn't wanted to involve
an innocent bystander, but at the same time she
had hoped the man had sensed something amiss. That
he would hurry off to phone the police. But that was
the sort of thing that happened before the I-don't-want-to-get-involved
era had strangled so much humanity
out of the world.

They reached the Mercedes, and Courtney couldn't help looking at the trunk. Was Mark in there? The gag had been so brutal. He could be suffocating. Or, she thought, her gaze flicking to a large nearby Dumpster, he might not be in the trunk at all.

She had no time to worry further about Mark. Roger ordered her into the passenger seat, then got behind the wheel. Julio and William played bookends to Jack in the back seat.

"Where are we going?" she asked.

"You'll know soon enough."

And she did. They were headed for the Hamilton estate in Elk Park.

"My father's so looking forward to your return," Roger said.

"I thought Fletcher had been arrested."

"Oh, that." He laughed. "I'm afraid I convinced Mr. Segura to tell your boyfriend a little white lie. Mr. Segura complied when I mentioned that I knew where each of his six siblings lived. And his mother. And his grandmother."

"You're despicable."

Roger's arm snaked out, and he grasped her by the back of the neck. "When I want your opinion, I'll ask for it." His fingers tightened cruelly, but she did not cry out. She clenched her teeth so hard, her jaw ached.

"Ask me to stop and I will."

Involuntary tears sprang to her eyes, but she kept her mouth shut.

"Ask me," he repeated tightly.

"Go to hell."

He slammed her away from him so hard her head rebounded against the passenger side window. But she did not reach up to rub the injured spot, nor did she knead the aching flesh at the back of her neck.

"How's our friend in the back seat?" Roger snarled.

"Still breathing, boss."

"See that he stays that way. I have a special treat in store for him at the house. The house where he first dared humiliate me."

Roger stopped the Mercedes at the security gate on the Hamilton grounds. Her father had had the property fenced in, over her objections, years ago. Only a quarter mile now separated them from the house. A thin-faced man, obviously posted as some sort of lookout, leaned into the car's interior with a flashlight. He didn't so much as blink at the bloodied passenger in the back seat.

"Good to see you again, Mr. Winthrop," the man said, as though he saw half-dead men every day of the week.

"You, too, Vern. Has my father called out for anything tonight?"

"No, sir. He's workin' real hard in the office up at the house." Vern scratched his chin. "I thought you told me he didn't want to be disturbed. Otherwise, I would've—"

"No, Vern, you're exactly right. In fact, make a note. I don't want anyone coming near the house the rest of the night. Understood?"

"Yes, sir."

Roger eased the car forward.

"Where do you find these vermin?" Courtney asked.

"Money buys a great variety of parasites, my dear. All shapes and colors and creeds."

Roger pulled up to the house and switched off the car. "My earlier threat still applies," he said smoothly. "You're too familiar with the grounds. I wouldn't want you trying anything foolhardy. If you do, Sullivan won't be alive to thank you."

"I'm not going anywhere, Roger."

"So compliant. If you'd managed to do a little more of that during our marriage, perhaps I wouldn't have had to get so angry."

She didn't dignify his pathetic excuse with a reply.

Inside the house she kept pace with Roger as he headed toward her father's study. Behind them, William and Julio dragged the near-motionless form of the man she loved. She hadn't heard Jack so much as moan on the thirty-minute drive out here. What if he'd suffered some kind of reaction to Roger's illicit drug? He could be dying.

Her fears were hardly eased when they stepped into the study. Fletcher Winthrop was there all right. Tied to a chair behind her father's antique, mahogany desk. The big man's head drooped onto his chest. He was mumbling something she couldn't understand, oblivious to the fact that he now had a roomful of company.

"My God, Roger, you drugged your own father?"

"It seemed the thing to do," he said. "Father never did appreciate me, or my ideas to take Winthrop-Hamilton into the twenty-first century. Never so much as a word of credit for the millions of extra dollars I brought in. Not one word."

"Maybe he didn't appreciate those extra profits coming from cocaine."

"He didn't give a damn how the money came in. As long as it came in."

"Then why is he tied to a chair?"

"Because of you, my darling. My father could look the other way when it came to a minor bit of moral turpitude like drug trafficking. But he was much more intractable about kidnapping you. He finally agreed to having you removed from the scene. 'Kept out of harm's way,' I believe was the way he put it."

Courtney took some comfort in that at least. Fletcher had not wanted her killed.

"I countermanded his orders, of course. I couldn't see any purpose in having you return and cause me all sorts of legal hassles."

"Excuse us, Mr. Winthrop."

Roger turned toward Julio and William. They had continued to hang on to Jack.

"What do you want us to do with him?" Julio asked.

"Let him go."

They did exactly that. Unsupported, Jack still handcuffed and groggy collapsed like a rag doll. Courtney winced as his head hit the polished wood floor with a decided thud. These bastards were killing him an inch at a time. She didn't know how much more of this she could take. If they continued to hurt him, she would have to do something, no matter how reckless, how hopeless.

"You want us to take care of that other matter?" Julio went on.

"Yes, I think now would be a good time. The shovels are behind the house. You'll find a nice grove of aspen about two hundred yards south. Three holes, very deep. Correction, make that four. I forgot about our friend in the trunk."

The two gunmen started out of the room, but Julio paused. "You sure you'll be okay, boss?"

"Please, I can handle a half-dead father, a doped-up cop and a woman who is afraid of her own shadow. Besides, I've got a little insurance." He held up his 9 mm. To Courtney, he said, "I find guns terribly vulgar, don't you? But they can be very... efficient."

Julio and William left the room. A couple of minutes later Courtney heard the back door open and close. She thanked God for Roger's unrelenting arrogance. By sending his hired guns off to dig graves, he just might have given her and Jack the chance they needed.

"Now we're going to get to the heart of it, darling," Roger said. "The reason I've gone to all the trouble and expense of coming back to the States." He opened his briefcase and spread out a sheaf of papers on the desk. "I need your signature here and there. You can blame your father. If he hadn't stipulated that ridiculous mandate that you have his power of attorney, you could have stayed in Philadelphia. And if Quentin didn't have the constitution of an ox, I could even have gotten around that somehow." He shook his head in what seemed amazement. "I still can't believe he survived the drug I gave him."

Courtney's stomach dropped to her toes. "What do you mean?"

"Did you know that there's a perfectly exquisite little flower that grows in the Brazilian rain forest that can precisely mimic the symptoms of a heart attack?"

"My God, my father loved you."

"Even love is expendable when a billion dollars is at stake, Courtney. Besides, the past couple of years he began to argue with some of my business decisions. I wasn't going to stand for that. I'd already endured thirty years of that nonsense from my own father.''

"What can these papers do?"

"They'll give me complete control of Winthrop-Hamilton. My father's already been kind enough to sign his share over to me. I'll liquidate as much of the company as I can for cash, before the government gets wise."

As Roger rattled on, Courtney dared a glance at Jack. He was beginning to stir. With seeming nonchalance she moved around the desk toward Fletcher. Roger did as she had hoped. He mirrored her movements, shifting the gun and his body so that he continued to face her. Jack was now out of Roger's line of sight.

"My signature would never stand up in court. The lawyers will know what you did."

"How naive you are, Courtney. Still. When you have a platinum-plated phalanx of lawyers on retainer, one has his own personal bought-and-paid-for set of rules. No one will suspect anything amiss about this little transaction. For one thing, they'll be too caught up in the sordid details of the passion play you and your lover are about to play out. A quarrel, a tragic murder-suicide. The kind of thing those tabloid reporters eat for breakfast."

"Fletcher won't let you get away with it."

"Ah, yes . . . my dear father." Roger retrieved a second hypodermic from his briefcase, this one with a protective plastic sleeve on the needle. "In three days Father will suffer an untimely passing. It seems he will have come down with a dreadful disease that will baffle the finest doctors money can buy. They'll search valiantly, but they won't be able to discover the cause. And even if they did, there's no antidote. One by one his vital organs will deteriorate, shut down. The pain will be exquisite.

"Throughout it all, I will play the grief-stricken son, holding vigil at his bedside."

"He'll tell them you did it, that you killed him."

"Ah, that's the beauty of it. The drug incapacitates the vocal cords. Muscle spasms make it impossible to communicate in any way."

"How can you do such a thing to your own father?"

"It's easy. Maybe the easiest thing I'll ever do. For all the pain he's inflicted. Every slight. Every belittlement."

"What about all the pain you've inflicted, Roger? What do you pay? You're a grown man. You can't keep blaming Daddy for your failures."

"Shut up! Just shut up!" He yanked off the plastic sleeve that protected the needle.

"You're sick, Roger. You need help."

"Maybe you need a little taste of how it used to be." He curled his hand into a fist.

Though inwardly she trembled, she let no fear show on her face. "You can beat me. You can kill me. But you can't touch my soul, Roger. Not anymore. You can't ever make me feel less about myself again."

"Can't touch your soul? Is that a fact?" He stomped over to where Jack lay and held the hypodermic just inches from his belly. Jack didn't so much as flinch. Even if he had the strength, Courtney knew he didn't dare jump Roger with that needle exposed.

"Would it touch your soul to watch your lover die in agony, darling?"

"Don't. Roger, please."

"Ah, now I get a little respect. It's going to be such a pleasure to kill the two of you."

"You'll be back in South America. The government won't be able to touch you. Why do you have to kill us?"

"I don't have to, my pet. I want to. But who should I kill first, that's the question? Do I kill him, and let you watch? Or do I kill you, and let him watch? Decisions, decisions."

Roger nudged Jack with his shoe. "Wake up Sullivan. I want to kill you. But I want you to know it's coming."

In front of her, Fletcher moaned softly. He was coming to. She touched his shoulder. "It's all right, Fletcher. It's me. Courtney."

Roger gripped the syringe like a dagger. "Get away from him."

Fletcher's eyes fluttered open. "Courtney," he rasped, seeming to have trouble focusing. "My God, forgive me. Forgive me."

"Shut up, Father," Roger snarled. "I don't want to hear the hoodwinked saint routine."

"Give it up, Roger," Fletcher said. "This is madness. They're closing in. They know what we've done. The dummy corporations. The drugs. They know it all."

"Shut up! You wanted it as much as I did. The company. Always the company. At any cost."

"Not murder. Damn you. Not murder! How can you do this? How can you be this way? I never raised a hand to you a day in my life."

"There are other kinds of fists, Father."

Behind them all, Jack had gained his feet. Hands cuffed, he swayed drunkenly, but there was a cold fury in his cerulean eyes. Roger must have heard him, because he started to turn.

"Here's what I think of your papers, Roger!" Courtney cried, grabbing up a fistful and flinging them to his left.

Roger flinched. Jack slammed himself bodylong against him. Both men tumbled to the floor. The syringe went flying.

Between the drugs and the beating he'd taken, Jack knew his strength was dangerously depleted. He needed this fight over with in a hurry. But more than that, he needed Roger Winthrop to pay. For Courtney. For Pete. For Mark. For himself. With a cry of undiluted rage he wrapped the chain of his handcuffs around Roger's neck and pulled. With everything in him, he pulled. In seconds, Roger's eyes bulged out. His face turned a ghastly shade of purple. Still, Jack did not let go.

"Jack!" Courtney rushed over to him. "Jack, he's not worth it. Let him go!" She tried in vain to pry Jack's hands loose. "Jack! You're not a murderer. Let him go!" She touched his bruised and bloodied face. "For me," she whispered. "Please. Let him go."

The blaze of fury subsided. He relaxed his hold. Roger fell forward, gasping, his hand going to his throat. "I'll sue you," he croaked out. "I'll sue you for every last dime."

Jack jerked him to his feet and flung him onto the divan. "Move, and I'll kill you."

Courtney untied Fletcher.

"Is he okay?" Jack asked, barely able to stand.

"I think so."

"I'm sorry," Fletcher mumbled. "So sorry."

Courtney went to Jack, locking her arms around his waist. "It's over. It's really over."

"Not quite." Still cuffed, he leaned over and grabbed Roger's gun. "Keep an eye out for Frick and Frack."

She'd forgotten about Roger's grave-digging gunmen.

Awkwardly, Jack picked up the desk phone and managed to dial out.

"I'll look for the keys," she said.

He nodded gratefully. "The FBI has this phone bugged. Before I finish talking, we should be swarming with law enforcement. Then we need to see to Mark." A minute later he hung up the phone, looking puzzled, but pleased. "It seems help is already here. The place is surrounded. Julio and William are on their way to jail. Mark's on his way to the hospital."

"How did they—?"

"A concerned citizen. How about that? Some guy walking a dog called the cops. Gave 'em the number of a suspicious Mercedes. It seems that Roger—arrogant guy that he is—rented the thing in his own name."

A half-dozen officers in flak jackets burst in. Two hurried over to Fletcher. The rest started toward Roger. "No." Jack held up a staying hand. "I want this one all to myself."

"Yes, sir."

Courtney was trembling so badly, she could hardly stand. "Now that it's over I'm realizing how terrified I was."

"You did great."

''He could've killed you.''

His blue eyes clouded, but he said nothing, only hugged her tight.

Roger cursed them both. ''You think this is over,'' he raged. ''I've got the best lawyers and judges money can buy. I'll be out in twenty-four hours. I'll disappear. But I'll be back. In a month, a year, ten years, I'll be back. You'll never know where or when.''

A shiver skittered up Courtney's spine at the thought of looking over her shoulder the rest of her life.

Roger pushed to his feet. ''I'll kill you both. I'll—'' His face changed. At first, he looked puzzled, then a kind of dawning realization set in, and his face twisted with pure horror. He looked down. Courtney saw it the same time Roger did.

The hypodermic.

It was jammed into his left thigh.

The vial was empty.

Courtney made Jack take her out of the house. The walls themselves echoed with the sounds of Roger Winthrop's screams.

It took Roger three days to die. He was right on every other count, too. The doctors were baffled. There was no antidote. And the pain was straight out of hell.

As for Mark Segura, he emerged from the ordeal—with the exception of a nasty concussion—with relatively minor physical injuries. It was his psyche she and Jack worried about. Day after day they stopped by his room at the hospital. And day after day he spent their entire visit apologizing. Just as he was doing this morning.

"I led the bastard straight to you," he said, his voice choked with emotion. "Straight to you. You could both be dead because of me."

"He threatened your family," Courtney reminded him for the umpteenth time. "You had no choice."

"I'm turning in my badge."

"Pete's cabin's taken, amigo," Jack said.

Mark blinked, confused. Very quietly, Jack told him about Emmett. Only then did Mark let go of some of his guilt. Only then did he seem willing to acknowledge that he'd done the best he could.

Outside Mark's room, Courtney gave Jack a fierce hug.

"What was that for?"

"For being you."

"I'd best get down to the courthouse. I've still got a mountain of paperwork to fill out."

Courtney tried to assure herself that she was just imagining Jack's withdrawal these past few days. That he was preoccupied with official reports, TV interviews and his concern about Mark. "Will I see you for dinner?" she asked.

"I doubt I can get away."

"Jack..."

"It's hectic, princess. Things will calm down soon. Are you going to stop in to see your father?"

Quentin Hamilton had regained consciousness two days ago, the same day Roger died. He was still too weak to talk much. "Are you coming with me?" Jack had yet to do so.

"I've got—"

"I know. You're busy."

He gave her a swift hug, then left her there, feeling bereft. She hadn't the slightest idea what was troubling him. Worse, the stubborn jackass wouldn't offer up a single clue. He just kept telling her it was something he had to work out. In his own time, his own way.

Didn't he understand how much she needed him right now? How much she just needed him to hold her, touch her, make love to her, reassure her that her world wouldn't spin out of control again—for a little while at least.

But he hadn't spent more than a few minutes with her at any one time since that hellish day out at the log house. She liked to tell herself it was because if he did, whatever problem he was having would shift to the back burner while they made wild, passionate love. But the more days that passed, the more she began to wonder. To doubt.

Courtney paused outside the door to her father's room. As usual, she had to gear herself up to go inside. There were a lot of painful memories on the other side of that door.

Over her vigorous objections the FBI had brought Fletcher Winthrop by yesterday. Fletcher himself had looked like a broken man in every way. His reputation was in ruins, his son was dead, his company in a shambles.

Courtney took a deep breath and opened the door. Her father was sitting up a little straighter today. But he still looked frail and old. He seemed to have aged twenty years in the four years it had been since she'd seen him. Today his eyes looked more defeated than she had ever seen them.

"Damn the cops anyway," Courtney muttered.

"I needed to be told."

"Not this soon."

"What difference does it make?"

"Did you have any part of it, Daddy?

"I must've been some kind of father to have my own daughter have to ask me a question like that."

She made no apology.

"I swear to you on your mother's grave, I knew nothing. I found an odd entry in a computer file a few weeks back, something I know I'd never entered myself. Yet the account was for my eyes only. I confronted Roger about it. He handed me a bourbon and offered some excuse that made no sense. I told him I was going to bring in outside people to look over the books. He had the oddest look in his eyes when he said that that wasn't going to happen. And then just that suddenly I felt the most crushing pain in my chest.

"If my secretary hadn't walked in, Roger would have let me die right then and there. I don't remember anything else until I woke up here."

The door opened to a soft knock. Courtney was surprised to see Jack.

"I thought you were on your way to the courthouse," she said.

"I was." He didn't meet her gaze. "I got a phone call."

"About what?"

He didn't answer.

"I can guess," Quentin Hamilton said.

Courtney looked from Jack to her father. "What's going on? You don't seem surprised to see each other."

"Mr. Sullivan and I have had more than one conversation these past couple of days."

Courtney's eyes narrowed on Jack. "You've been to see my father? But I thought—"

"I'm sorry, princess. It wasn't my idea. Believe me."

She experienced a sudden flare of fear. "What's this all about, Jack?"

He pulled an official looking piece of paper from his inside jacket pocket. "Quentin Hamilton, it's my duty to inform you that you are under arrest. You have the right to remain silent..."

Courtney stared at him, stunned, disbelieving. No wonder he'd kept his distance. No wonder he could barely look her in the eye. He finished reading Quentin Hamilton his rights. "So you finally got your wish," she said, her voice shaking. "Your revenge against my father."

He winced, but said nothing.

"How could you?" she demanded.

"It's all right," her father said quietly. "This isn't Sullivan's doing. It's Roger's. He made certain, if any of this ever came out, that I would look as guilty as he was."

"It's not all right!" Courtney cried. "It's not all right at all!" She turned on Jack. "How could you do this to me? To us?"

"This has nothing to do with us."

She wondered who he was trying harder to convince—her or himself.

"It isn't what you're doing," she said, "nearly as much as it is your not telling me."

"I didn't tell you, because I was hoping it wouldn't happen. I've been fighting like hell with my superiors, trying to convince them—"

"Spare me any more lies, Jack. Please."

He reached a hand toward her, but let it fall back to his side. "You're tired. You've been through hell. You don't know what you're saying."

"I know exactly what I'm saying."

He stiffened, but his eyes regarded her with such an aching sadness that she had to look away.

Jack sighed. "Mr. Hamilton, there'll be a guard posted outside your door. For what it's worth, I'm sorry." He paused, then added, "More than you can ever know."

"Get out," Courtney said. "Just get out."

He started to say something, then decided against it. Without another word, he left the room.

"He's only doing his job, you know," Quentin said quietly.

"His job?" Courtney whirled on him. "Arresting a man two days out of a coma? And for what? You're innocent. I know it. And, dammit, so does he."

"I have good lawyers, Courtney. I'll be all right. It's you I'm worried about."

"Jack hates you. He's always hated you."

"With good reason I'm afraid."

She blinked. "What are you saying?"

"I'm saying I'm never going to be a big fan of Jack Sullivan's. We're too much alike, he and I. Two stubborn, hotheaded fools, who never knew how to tell a certain young lady how much we loved her."

"He's not going to get away with—" She stopped. "What did you say?"

"I said I love you." He trailed the back of one frail hand across her cheek. "When your mother died, I was lost without her. I didn't know anything about raising children, especially a little girl. I made so many mistakes, Courtney. I don't expect you to forgive me.

One of the biggest mistakes I ever made just walked out that door."

"What are you talking about?"

He gestured weakly toward a chair. "Sit down, sweetheart. Please. While a foolish old man tries to figure out a way to pay off a ten-year-old debt without having my daughter hate my guts."

Her heart thudding, Courtney sat.

Quentin Hamilton took a deep breath. "Jack Sullivan has every right in the world to hate me. It's time you knew that. It's time I told you the kind of man Jack Sullivan really is."

Courtney reined in the roan gelding beneath her and let the horse crop a sprig of newly sprouted grass from the sun-drenched hillside. Here and there snow still huddled in the deeper shadows, but nearly everywhere else spring was edging out the receding winter. By her calculations she and Jack were a half hour away from Pete's old cabin in the Sapphires. It was getting on toward late afternoon. Jack rode astride a bay several yards ahead of her.

It had taken some doing, but she'd convinced him she needed to revisit the cabin, work out some of her fears about her kidnapping and its aftermath. What she really needed to do was get him to sit down and work out what was going on between them. It had been three days since she'd lashed out at him in her father's hospital room. She had yet to tell him anything about what her father had said to her. In fact, except for their exchange about returning to the cabin, they'd spoken hardly at all.

When they reached the cabin, Courtney felt an odd sense of coming home. While Jack saw to the horses, Courtney went inside and started a fire.

"What are you doing?" Jack asked when he came inside.

"It's a bit chilly."

"It doesn't matter, we're not staying that long."

"We can't go back down the mountain in the dark. The horses could break a leg."

He scowled. "You had this planned all along, didn't you?"

She feigned an innocent look, but said, "Of course. Tell me you don't want to spend the night here."

"I want to. You know that. But..."

"But what?"

"Nothing."

She studied him in the dim light—her dark haired, blue eyed guardian angel. He was suddenly as tense and nervous as she was. They both knew what was at stake here. She arranged another log on the fire. "I heard Mark flew back to D.C. yesterday."

"Yeah. I hope he's going to be okay."

He wasn't talking about Mark's physical injuries. "I do too." But it wasn't really Mark who concerned her right now. It was Jack Sullivan. This man she had loved for ten years now. "Do you know why I really wanted to come here, Jack?" she asked.

"To make peace with what happened."

"No," she said softly. "I wanted to make peace with you. Make love with you."

He swallowed hard. "You can't know how much I want that too."

"I'm sorry about what I said the other day. I should have known you'd never use your job to avenge yourself on anyone, not even Quentin Hamilton."

"I'm not going to lie to you, Courtney. There was a time in my life arresting your father would have given me a great deal of pleasure. But now..." He shook his head. "I'd never do anything to hurt you. Not even to get back at your father."

"God knows, you have plenty to get back at him for."

He blinked, disconcerted. "What do you mean?"

She walked over to him, put her hand on his chest, reveled in the strong, measured beating of his heart. "You know exactly what I mean."

"I don't think—"

"You don't need to protect him anymore. That is, protect me, by not telling me what he did."

Jack sighed. "It was a long time ago."

"Ten years." She took his hand and together they sat down in front of the hearth. "That night we made love in your bedroom—it wasn't some old drinking buddy who phoned—it was my father."

"It doesn't matter."

"It matters a helluva lot," she said fiercely. "Roger called him in Japan, told him his daughter had her eye on a certain carpenter. Well, the great and powerful Quentin Hamilton couldn't have that. So he called you, told you that if you so much as looked my way, you'd never work again in the state of Montana." She kissed the backs of his fingers. "And when that threat had no effect, he took it a step further, didn't he?"

Jack said nothing.

"He'd done his homework. He knew that you had a pregnant sister in Seattle. A pregnant sister whose husband worked for a logging company, which just happened to be a wholly owned subsidiary of Winthrop-Hamilton. How did he put it? Your sister and her husband would be living in a tent inside of twenty-four hours if he ever caught you near me." Her whole body trembled. "I've never been so angry. If he hadn't been in that hospital bed, I don't know what I would've said."

Jack cupped her face in his hands. "He's your father. He was doing what he thought was best for you. A bit high-handedly, sure, but that doesn't change the bottom line. He was right."

"What?"

"It never would have worked between us back then, princess. I was too much of a pride-bound jerk."

She could've argued, but decided against it. The ten years were gone. There was no going back. "I guess I had a little growing up to do myself," she conceded. "Maybe ten years was just about right."

He kissed her, hot, hungry in front of the fire. And then they made love—fierce, tender, gentle, wild.

Afterward, they slept. Then Jack cooked supper. Toward midnight, they were again snuggled in front of the fire.

"Life can be pretty amazing, can't it?" Courtney murmured, planting teasing kisses along Jack's beard-stubbled neck.

"I'll say." He caressed her breast.

She giggled, then again grew serious. "I want you to know something, Jack Sullivan. As painful as some parts of my life have been, I wouldn't trade it in on anyone else's. Because the road I've been on with all of its twists and turns led me right back here...to you. I love you. I always have. I always will."

His eyes were overbright. "I love you, Courtney. More than my life."

She kissed him hard, then reached down and picked up the wood carving she'd retrieved from his workroom during supper. Her own eyes brimmed with tears as she trailed her fingers over the trapped wolf. "I wish there was a way to set him free."

"Maybe there is." Jack got up and padded to the workroom. A minute later he returned with a tiny carving tool.

Courtney handed him the wolf, then watched with fascination as the trap disappeared under Jack's masterful touch, transformed into tufts of grass. With delicate precision he then altered the animal's expression. When he'd finished, he handed the wolf back to her. Tears slid down her cheeks.

"He's free," she whispered.

Jack nodded. "We both are," he said hoarsely. "Thanks to you."

They made love again in front of the fire, sealing their trust, their love, forever.

Outside, high in the mountains snow began to fall. Somewhere a wolf howled to its mate.

* * * * *

COMING NEXT MONTH

Take 4 bestselling love stories FREE

Plus get a FREE surprise gift!

Special Limited-time Offer

Mail to Silhouette Reader Service™

3010 Walden Avenue
P.O. Box 1867
Buffalo, N.Y. 14269-1867

YES! Please send me 4 free Silhouette Intimate Moments® novels and my free surprise gift. Then send me 6 brand-new novels every month, which I will receive months before they appear in bookstores. Bill me at the low price of $2.89 each plus 25¢ delivery and applicable sales tax, if any.* That's the complete price and a savings of over 10% off the cover prices—quite a bargain! I understand that accepting the books and gift places me under no obligation ever to buy any books. I can always return a shipment and cancel at any time. Even if I never buy another book from Silhouette, the 4 free books and the surprise gift are mine to keep forever.

245 BPA ANRR

Name	(PLEASE PRINT)	
Address	Apt. No.	
City	State	Zip

This offer is limited to one order per household and not valid to present Silhouette Intimate Moments® subscribers. *Terms and prices are subject to change without notice.
Sales tax applicable in N.Y.

UMOM-295

©1990 Harlequin Enterprises Limited

Become a Privileged Woman,

You'll be entitled to all these Free Benefits. And Free Gifts, too.

To thank you for buying our books, we've designed an exclusive FREE program called *PAGES & PRIVILEGES*™. You can enroll with just one Proof of Purchase, and get the kind of luxuries that, until now, you could only read about.

BIG HOTEL DISCOUNTS

A privileged woman stays in the finest hotels. And so can you—at up to 60% off! Imagine standing in a hotel check-in line and watching as the guest in front of you pays $150 for the same room that's only costing you $60. Your *Pages & Privileges* discounts are good at Sheraton, Marriott, Best Western, Hyatt and thousands of other fine hotels all over the U.S., Canada and Europe.

FREE DISCOUNT TRAVEL SERVICE

A privileged woman is always jetting to romantic places. When <u>you</u> fly, just make one phone call for the lowest published airfare at time of booking—<u>or double the difference back!</u>

PLUS—you'll get a $25 voucher to use the first time you book a flight AND <u>5% cash back on every ticket you buy thereafter</u> through the travel service!

PROOF OF PURCHASE

Offer expires October 31, 1996

SIM-PP52